TORCH SONG

TORCH SONG
ANNE ROIPHE

Farrar, Straus and Giroux

NEW YORK

Copyright © 1977 by Anne Roiphe
All rights reserved
Published simultaneously in Canada by
McGraw-Hill Ryerson Ltd., Toronto
Printed in the United States of America
Designed by Karen Watt
First edition, 1977

Library of Congress Cataloging in Publication Data
Roiphe, Anne Richardson.
Torch song.
I. Title.
PZ4.R738To [PS3568.O53] 813'.5'4 76-42209

To Herman

TORCH SONG

A THICK FOG has rolled in off the ocean. The horn on the ferry bellows like a creature in chronic pain. The buoys clang far out in the unseen channel beyond the jetty's last stone. The gulls are nestled close to the dunes, their backs to the coming fog and wind. I fold up the beach towels. It's the kind of afternoon that makes it hard to stay in the present, hard to smile while taking out the paints and Monopoly game for the children. The little sandpipers, gray and beige, skim the foam at the shore's edge as if they were daring the waves to swamp them. I wonder if they ever get caught. Chronological time is moving at such an indecent speed that yesterday has already become odd, extinct, needing an explanation. The fog carries difficult memories, distant, almost unbelievable facts of my past that never fade entirely away but float back again and again at such uncomfortable moments.

INTO THE WHITE HORSE TAVERN on Hudson Street came the veterans of the recent Korean War who were studying at New York University. They had learned Southern talk, black and white both, in the army, and their language was in a code it took a while to decipher. There were blacks—Negroes then—in the bar too. There were Barnard students with copies of T. S. Eliot clutched to their breasts and other girls in tight leotards or blue jeans looking for beauty and truth and action. We identified with Edna St. Vincent Millay, Gertrude Stein, and Isadora Duncan. None of our heroines was living. We were nostalgic for an era we knew only by rumor and secondhand report. Others of our contemporaries were wearing plaid Bermuda shorts and gold circle pins, planning to slide into gray flannel ranch houses with *Life* magazine on the coffee table and golf clubs in the closet. Active politics and open sex were still in the closet. W. H. Auden had described the end of the civilized world from the point of view of a man on a bar stool. Here at the little tables the students of Trilling and Barzun, critics and skeptics, the ambitious and the abandoned, mixed with the romantics from Sarah Lawrence, Barnard girls who were followers of Martin Buber or Albert Camus, girls whose allegiance went to Bertrand Russell and André Gide, others who admired Rilke and Nietzsche but planned anyway to marry the Mutual of Omaha man and plant rose of Sharon in the garden each spring. We also admired the dropouts, the poets and the painters, and the would-be cartoonists who had found the university irrelevant for the life of the mind, which could better be realized in the half dark of the bar where no one would admit to believing that the bomb might not fall, the system not destroy itself, leaving nothing for the angels of the Lord (should they come searching for survivors) to admire but a handful of works of art that testified to the fact that man had indeed made some mark, some small scratches on the black wall of immense unfeeling space.

Wilson Harris, whose divorced mother worked for the telephone company in Yonkers, told us one night that in the big K (Korea) he and some buddies had made it with a local pig. "What was it like?" I asked. "No complaints," he said. "Sooey, sooey," he shouted, a word he had not learned at the Bronx High School of Science, where he had been educated till Uncle Sam called. "I did it for you, baby," he said, "so you could be safe." "Wilson," I said, "should I buy you another drink?" He never had any money because he drank all night till the White Horse closed at 4 a.m. and then slept all day in his stinky hole of a hotel room right beside the steel pillars of the West Side Highway, across from the broken-down wooden piers where stray cats walked carefully. He had chosen to live in the West Village in order to be near the classes he never attended. "All I need is a drink to survive." They all said that, but some of them meant it.

We Barnard girls skittered down Broadway each night from the safe uptown campus. There were nice girls who planned to do volunteer work in their local hospitals. My friends, however, were the other ones, the misfits, modern dancers, abstract painters, harpists, and loonies who filled the Barnard classrooms with a covey of frantic minds, scrounging like so many chickens in the dirt for what was then fashionably called identity and falsely, arrogantly, ridiculously presumed to be part of the birthright. In the White Horse under the 60-watt bulbs we drank beer and boilermakers, rye and bourbon, and shouted the credo of existentialism in ragged unison: "Thou shalt not be fooled into believing in any reasonable position—absurdity is all." And sometimes on the subway back to upper Broadway in the early hours of the dawn I would feel an urge to scream for help, a childish terror of spending the rest of my life in the White Horse. Try as I might, I could imagine myself nowhere else—only there did I seem to belong and "there" was a place for transients, dander and spores, where the conversation was about the imperatives for suicide or the achievements of great artists who at a similar age had already dwarfed my contemporaries, leaving them to prattle on, walking the plank of failure. "Swim, swim," I would cry, certain that all my friends, my mirror images, were committed to drowning. Anything less would have been bourgeois compromise.

Henry Revere was a wide, large Negro man who had been on the docks in Korea and was now studying Greek mythology at the New School. He liked my green sweater

with the hole in the front. I liked it too—even more so
after he called it a people sweater. In the mid-fifties no one
of us was yet marching in Southern cities, and we, like
prehistoric figures at the dawn's edge, groped with primitive tools. "How I see it, Marjorie," he said to me one
sweet night just before the bar closed, "is like people walking up mountains. You walk up your white mountain and
I walk up my black mountain and we don't see each other
and we don't talk to each other and we go walking on and
on; years go by, day and night, and one time we catch
each other's eye and we get together in a valley between
our mountains and you put your hand on me and we lie
down in the cool grass and we have the most beautiful
gray babies the world has ever seen. Come," he said hyp-
notically, "back to my room in the Grand Crusaders and
tonight we can begin the graying of the world—the color
of clouds, fog, silver mink—gray babies for the future."
Adrenalin—fight and flight adrenalin—flowed through my
system, mixing with the alcohol, making me slightly nauseous. How could I refuse—to refuse would be an act of
bigotry, of cowardice, of shame, of bourgeois inhibition. I
clutched the bar rail—a world of gray babies, like model-
ing clay, like New England shingles on salt-sprayed rooftops. It was a moment of choice. Did he want me for my
white genes, which were really Semitic and Tartar, or was
he merely settling for what was available in the White
Horse at 3:30 a.m.? A blonde I knew would have been
ideal. Did he really desire me or was I mere symbol, and
did I, at the edge, the frontier of race relations, have the
right even to ask the question, and beyond that, did my
action, yes or no, make any difference? Wasn't everything
random, accidental, absurd? What a reactionary view, to
question fate, when I knew that it was all equally senseless, that the winds just rose and fell, destroying at whim.

I thought of my mother sleeping in her Park Avenue apartment, secure in the knowledge that the dorms on 118th Street were locked at 1 a.m., not knowing that I had scaled the fence and climbed through an open bathroom window without being detected for two and a half years. I had gotten my dormitory room by pretending our country house in Larchmont was my only residence. Henry Revere was not the future she had in mind for me when she would say, "When are you going to realize that college isn't the real world?" She planned a businessman whose stocks and bonds and corporate know-how would enable me to sleep the rest of my life till ten or eleven in the morning, till the maid brought breakfast in on a tray, napkin securely rolled up in a china napkin ring.

"Henry Revere, I think I love you," I said flirtatiously, hollowly, like a character in a grade-"B" movie. We had then only the language (empty of real feeling) of old-fashioned courtship—the new honest words were waiting.

Off we went into the early hours among the Greenwich Avenue derelicts. Wilson Harris was passed out on the hood of a nearby car. No friend took him home that night, meaning one less person to share the floor's toilet, which didn't work anyway. Henry Revere didn't love *me*, I knew, but love, I thought, was just another of the popular myths like the virgin birth and the sanctity of motherhood. Love was transitory, illusory, and only the social-worker types believed in it. Artists and philosophers referred instead to psychological conditions or altered states of mind and knew or tried to know that everything was illusion, a means of getting through. Man created order out of boredom and called his design divine. While my sexual voice was still a mere squeak, a little baby gurgle indicating that one day language would flow, my moral scruples were in full bloom, a wild garden of thorns and roses. Henry Revere was not to suspect that I was scared of him because he was male and Negro, two conditions I found alien but I knew were neither his fault nor subject to his control.

In his room at the dingy Grand Crusaders Hotel were pin-ups of Marilyn Monroe and unknown others, books, papers, butt-filled ashtrays, beer cans, dirty underwear, socks, the musty strange smell of male odors. "Does the window open?" Outside on the narrow street a girl was running, chased by a blond boy. "I didn't mean it, I didn't mean it," he shouted as she turned the corner. Then he stopped at the curb and a stream of urine, his rainbow of accomplishment, splashed the wheels of a parked car. The street was quiet. The view from his window was like pictures I'd seen of the rooftops of Paris. I wished it were Paris. "Come now," Henry Revere said, "the meeting of souls on heights nearer the Lord, wants, waits for you to lie down, naked before His searching eye." The voice of a storefront preacher. "Sure, sure, sure," he was cajoling me, "come to my bed and let your innocence shine on my poor sheets." Like the babies we would have, the sheets and the walls were gray, and as I pulled off my leotard, smelling still of the morning's dance class where I had been a caterpillar stretching along a bed of tulips, I felt my tongue gray, my mouth ashen. I lay naked on the bed wondering if my identity was, like Peter Pan's shadow, lost somewhere in the room. As he undressed, I watched him. I wanted to lust for the union to come, but the more of his skin I saw, the more frightened I became. The ultimate weapon, the mysterious organ appeared through the fly of his undershorts. I could still count the number of times I had done it on fewer than my ten fingers. I closed my eyes. I believed, I believed in the idea of gray babies for the future of mankind. My nipples stood straight up, like nervous nannies. At any moment something violent, an accident, could occur. Henry Revere's eyes were bloodshot, and his hands, far larger than my pubic mound, stroked me soothingly. I should have relaxed gradually, breathing the deep oxygen of contentment, but I was stiff as a frozen twig in January's frost. I knew I was being prepped for the major act of penetration. A stranger was in bed with me. I wanted to scream, remembering all the times my mother, allowing me to go to a friend's house by taxi, insisted the doorman ostentatiously write down the cabbie's license number to prevent abduction, rape, and murder in a Harlem alley. "Relax, honey baby, pretty sugar," he said. "It'll be nice, smooth, easy, good feelings. I'll take care of you." "I know," I said, hoping to sound confident, but I didn't know at all. Was he diseased? I thought, and grew more rigid, as if death from madness had begun to creep up my legs and paralyze my pelvic region. Suddenly he spread my legs and the smooth top of his penis pushed at me. For a moment I felt like a wildcat. I could rip him apart for attacking me. "What's the matter," he said, "is this the first time?" "Of course not," I said coolly. I had a reputation as a woman to maintain. Then shame and regret made me release the spasm that closed the gate and he came in and I felt some pleasure, some pain, and an enormous pride in my freedom and bravery.

On the way back to Barnard in the pre-dawn hours, I realized he had just scored, made out with me, but I had scored with him too and I wouldn't be ashamed of my act of integration. The game of scoring (would he tell the others in the White Horse? He would, but I didn't care much) I always imagined as a game of archery. I knew where the bull's-eye was. Later, safe in bed in my dormitory cubicle, my thighs shaking in some suddenly remembered anxiety, I wanted to go back to that time of my life when I was the best jacks player in school and could flip them all on one hand and never make an error. When I was third-best speller in my class and could jump rope 112 non-stop times. It was a rotten shame that I would have to take care of myself—Jane in a Tarzanless jungle. Eve with no Adam, Juno with no Jupiter, Raggedy Ann with no Andy, and a candy heart that someone else had eaten. Why was I in bed with strangers when I still needed a mother? Later, after a long sleep, having missed several classes, I felt the waves of self-pity recede, revealing on shore the pure solid nugget of fright.

THE COLDER THE WINTER BECAME, the closer we huddled together under the plastic Christmas decorations. We scoffed and sneered at the primitive symbols. Every boy at the White Horse seemed to have a manuscript he wanted some girl to read—a poem, an essay on romantic illusion, a philosophical attack on reason and logic, a short story always with a moment of epiphany when the hero discovers he is an artist. Reincarnations of Stephen Dedalus appeared in the White Horse all the time, dazed and sloppy drunk. Ghosts of Dylan Thomas staggered from table to table. In the dim light, shutting out the noise, I read stories about suicide, rape, death, impotence, and rage, many of them good enough to stir me to say, "Thank you, thank you for letting me read this," to the author staring at his drink, feigning diffidence to my response. More holes appeared in my people sweater. I was reading the poems of a next year's Rhodes scholar, painful poems of homosexual search, each one like a china cup, glazed, shaped, made perfect from raw flesh, when I saw Jim Morrison again.

Taller, thinner, but with his hands still fluttering about his face, the dark glasses hiding those alligator eyes, which always looked through you to something beyond. I put down the poems-of-homosexual-suffering. "Later," I said to the Rhodes scholar, "I'll finish them later."

He now had a fake English accent; elegant and almost perfect, it slithered about the bar, drawing a crowd. He was horribly pale, something gothic and ill in the slope of his shoulders, in the long bony fingers that twirled a black cigarette holder. I had never seen an English lord, of course, nor had I seen any contemporary versions of Byron or Shelley or Rimbaud, but there was something in Jim Morrison that evoked all those images—candies the compulsive romantic couldn't resist. I eased my way through the circle around him till I was right beside him. "Can I buy you a drink?" I said. "Of course." He smiled at me, a curl of the lip, somewhat wry, ironic, intelligent, regretting so much that had already happened. "We met at a dance," I said, "years ago." "That was in another country," he said, "and besides, the wench is dead." I smiled to show I recognized his pseudo-Hemingway. "Where have you been," I said, "since our last meeting?" "In the army." He looked away. "But why, why didn't you go to college?" The maternal in me rose. He should've gone to college—even in a world that has no meaning, college is better than the army. "Oh," he said, leaning languidly on the bar, "I was so roaring, totally smashed the day of the college boards I fell on the floor and the proctors had to carry me out." "Was your mother angry?" I couldn't help asking. "She died," he said, "six months before—a heart attack in a French restaurant, dining with one of her boy friends. Don't look sad," he said to me. "Why don't you buy us both another drink instead." I did, but as it arrived he turned away from me back to the group, telling stories of his army days in Washington working on technical manuals because some aptitude test had saved him from battle, just when he was ready, prepared, to come to an early, violent end. Now he was in the philosophy department at N.Y.U. at government expense. Still living in Bay Ridge, an hour's ride by subway into Brooklyn, with his grandmother.

Like a ballet dancer, he gracefully controlled the stage, even while drunk, after many glasses of Scotch-and-water. It seemed as if the devil himself were entertaining, seducing and weaving among us with sulphur, smoke, and powers. He belonged, I knew, only to the Prince of Darkness.

When I had met him four years before he had been charming and clever, but now his talk was brilliant, filled with references to the nine muses, to Achilles, Occam, Aristotle, and the Hegelian dialectic and the Marxist paradox and the Botticelli Venus and twelve-tone music and Henry Moore and Chopin, all in wonderfully coherent sentences. He seemed like a trapeze artist flying over our heads with knowledge and elegant language, an Oscar Wilde, a Voltaire, a Mencken. His teeth were thin, bluish-green, tobacco-stained; his eyes, when he momentarily removed his dark glasses, were clear and ominous as a desert landscape. His long blond hair reached down his neck. He looked partly like a jazz musician, partly like an eighteenth-century composer. He was complicated, anguished, and absolutely articulate. Even though I didn't believe in it, how could I possibly have avoided love? Wishing as always that I were lanky and glamorous, I stayed close to his side, hoping at least that my wit would attract his attention. At four, when the White Horse closed, he picked up his books and said, "Well, I'm off to Brooklyn on the subway." The Prince of Darkness in the subway, all the way back to Brooklyn. I felt a stab of regret. He should live in a mansion or a bat-filled cave, not an apartment in Bay Ridge. "I'll drive you home," I said. Wilson leered at me: "That rich girl's got a car. Wouldn't you know it." I was ashamed. Jim led the way out. I bumped into one of the empty tables in my hurry to keep up with him.

The streets were very quiet. He stopped talking and was staring at me. "You're Marjorie," he said with sudden recognition. "You fell down," he added, "at the dance, didn't you? Why were you so clumsy?" I knew instantly that he wanted a graceful partner, not a ragamuffin in a torn people sweater with kinky hair, no matter how daring or devoted she might be. We drove across the Brooklyn Bridge, the only car on it, with the lights of Manhattan blinking behind us like distress signals. Below, barges drifted down the East River, a tugboat blew its horn, and the reflected red neon of a factory sign dipped in the dark water, shining like a promise of carnivals to come.

Jim was talking about a long story he had written about a student who murders his professor because the professor had logically proved that there is no meaning or purpose to the ways of humanity. "I don't think," I said, "people kill for such a reason. Jealousy, greed, yes, but it doesn't sound real to me to kill over a philosophical proof." "Doesn't it?" he said. "It's a matter, I suppose, of limited intelligence." We drove off the bridge and onto narrow streets bounded by factories, warehouses, and large waiting trucks. "Stop," he said when we came to an open White Tower hamburger joint wedged between a gas station and a huge Laundromat. It seemed like a lighthouse in a dangerous sea. "Every night I buy a hamburger and an orange drink here." Under the glare of the naked light he looked moldy. Like a man dug up from the grave, like Lazarus unwinding his shroud. "I don't have any money," he said. "Will you pay?" "Of course." I was happy he needed me. The onion and pickle spilled on the napkin and his eyes behind the sunglasses closed. When we got to his apartment house I stopped the car. "My grandmother's asleep," he said. "I can't ask you up." Would he kiss me, did he want anything else? "Thanks for the ride," he said, and chastely, like the purest of giraffes loping through the wild, he weaved out of the car and across the street, leaving me alone in a turmoil of feeling, far from my or any bed.

During the next six months, this trip was repeated almost every night in almost every detail. He would allow me to stay near him at the White Horse and to drive him home to Bay Ridge at the end of each evening. Our friends thought we were going together, sleeping with each other, but in fact each night was almost exactly like the first. Sometimes he ate two hamburgers at the White Tower and sometimes only one, but each night he left me at his door to make my way back alone in the dawn, climbing over the fence to my dormitory room on upper Broadway.

Wilson Harris was his good friend. Before the hour of the night when Wilson's conversation deteriorated to mere mumblings of curses, mostly attacks on women's private parts, he and Jim would talk about Rilke and his angel of death, or Dostoevsky and his guilt. Sometimes Wilson's girl, Sophie, who worked as a secretary at the Admissions Office at N.Y.U. and who paid for most of the drinks, would say, "Wilson, why don't you get a job?" and Wilson would grin. "Commie pinko," he would yell at the top of his lungs. "Don't you respect a veteran, an all-American American? You're nothing but an undercover Commie cutting at the underbelly of this fine democratic nation." And he would laugh. Sophie and I would say, "Shut up." "Hush." "Cut it out, Wilson, that's not funny." Loudly we would say to each other, "He's just joking, teasing." We didn't want somebody to go tell the Admissions Office that they'd heard Sophie was a Red. It was too easy to lose a job and never get another one. Wilson thought it was funny, watching her go pale and tense. So many hours without shape or purpose made him childish and he was the kind of child who might've tied a can to a dog's tail. Our friend Lenny Foss—who had dropped out of Andover after reading *Catcher in the Rye* and now at nineteen lived off odd jobs, odd girls, or a quick plea home to his grieving schoolteacher parents, who couldn't know that their son was only a premature example of a coming trend—Lenny came into the bar one night and said he was going to eat his last five dollars. Corned beef and French fries, I thought. Instead, Lenny took the five-dollar bill out of his pocket and began to eat it, starting from a corner and munching steadily till it was all consumed. First we laughed, then Sophie and I cried. "Here," she said, "let me lend you ten." "No," said Lenny, angry, "don't try to spoil my act." I thought of the germs he must have swallowed. I remembered my nurse, Gretchen, telling me that money was the greatest cause of contagion and epidemics, that germs were swarming across the faces of Washington, Lincoln, and Hamilton. But Lenny lived.

Our poet friend, Luke, who was built like an elf and had large ears that were never taped down to his head in infancy by a mother too busy with other children, had emerged from a Catholic boyhood in Jersey City with a developed sense of meaninglessness as fine as anyone else's. He would quote John Donne, Marlowe, and Pope. He was a defender of Ezra Pound and an admirer of Walt Whitman. One night he declared quietly to us that he was interested only in males who would whip him. Then he stood on the bar stool and tried to jump through the large window at the front of the bar. He didn't weigh enough even to crack the glass, though he was out cold. Wilson and Jim picked him up from the floor and poured beer down his throat.

ONE NIGHT IN APRIL, just after the spring vacation, Jim asked me to go to the cigarette machine and get him a pack. I was used to doing little things like that for him by now. I felt that somehow I was appointed by a force beyond my control to watch out for his comfort, his needs. Perhaps if I took good enough care of him he might return the devotion in some kind of currency. I was wearing tight white pants and my people sweater, with more holes in it now in April than in December. A crewcut young man carrying a slide rule got up from a table and stepped in my way. "Can I buy you a drink?" "No thanks," I said. "I'm with somebody." He wore a fraternity sweater. He was a stranger on our turf. Two more young men were sitting at the table, and on it were metallurgy, engineering, and applied-math textbooks. Watchers of Milton Berle, builders of future Levittowns and weapons systems. They would never understand "The Love Song of J. Alfred Prufrock." "Listen," said the one who had stopped me, "what're you doing with that fag?" He pointed at Jim, who was leaning on the bar, his dark glasses on, his eccentric hands fluttering like pigeons about to be fed. I turned my back, completed my errand, and returned to Jim's side. The engineering student came over. "Take your glasses off," he muttered to Jim. "Let's see what you look like." "Friend of yours?" Jim asked me. "You're the type we don't want around here," said the stranger. Wilson roused himself. "Get the fuck out of here," he said, and one word led to another. The future engineer took an empty beer bottle and smashed it on the bar. For a moment there was quiet and then the engineer banged the broken bottle on Jim's head. Wilson went for his throat, and the other engineers, all with clean nails and pressed pants, dove after Jim and Wilson and Henry Revere, whose large black body slowly rose to defend his drinking companions. Sophie picked up a chair and began to pound it against the shoulders of the enemy. I ran to the ladies' room and locked the door. Glasses fell, bottles crashed. I heard Wilson screaming, "Kill, kill," and I heard the bartender yelling, "I'm going to throw you out, all of you out, you're responsible for damages." I heard the police siren and then I heard running feet. Finally it was quiet and I came out of the ladies' room. Once when we were children I had hit my brother when he had poured salt in my chocolate pudding. Gretchen had tied my hand to the bedpost and I stayed there for hours. "Girls don't hit," she had said, and I had continued to believe her.

The police didn't want any part of it. They chased the slumming, tourist engineers out of the White Horse. They were ready to go, frightened by the possibility of blemishes on their record which might affect their eventual employment. Jim, pale and limp, was slumped in a booth. Blood was seeping from the back of his head down his collar. His dark glasses were broken and his copy of Yeats was bloodstained. "Let's go to St. Vincent's emergency room," I said.

In the barren hospital corridor, Jim sat quietly next to me as we waited. A pregnant Spanish woman was moaning in a rhythm that was nearly musical; a Chinese man sat with a coughing, wheezing baby in his arms. Jim took my hand. I was happier than I could remember ever being. Wilson and Sophie were with us and I felt that Jim had now acknowledged a connection to me. I was grateful to the violent intruders who had brought his hand into mine. I imagined him as a little boy running toward his mommy with blood on his knees. "Everything will be all right," I said, and I believed it. The young doctor on duty was contemptuous. "A fight," he said, "for Christ's sake." He shaved a lot of hair and I felt a kind of clammy terror at the open wound revealed. I held his hand through the shot and the stitches. "I need a drink, I need a drink," Jim said again and again. "Soon," I promised. "Soon, just another minute or two," and finally we were back in the bar talking it all over. Wilson and Jim were describing to each other every detail of the battle. It became an epic, making me feel for a moment like Helen of Troy.

I drove Jim home as the sky started to lighten and the bread trucks from the bakeries were crossing the bridge in the opposite direction. He closed his eyes. "I feel sick," he said. I couldn't stop on the bridge, but once in Brooklyn I pulled over on the silent, empty street. "Someday," he said, "I'm going to write about this." I wanted him to. I wanted my life as well as his to be used, not just endured, traversed, but be material for the poetry, a subject for the novels that would justify the passion that rose in me. He would be a great fish in the sea; I would be a small one, eating the crumbs that fell from his jaws, gratefully performing hidden services. Suddenly he opened the car door and vomit poured out of his nose and mouth and down his trousers and into his shoes. "You'll be all right," I said, "after you've slept." "Goddamn engineer, calling me a fag. I'll get a contract on him and get him pushed under a train." I took off my people sweater to wipe his face with and then threw it in the back of the car. "Someday you'll write about this," I reminded him. Calmer, he sank back into the seat beside me and began quoting *Para-*

dise Lost. We continued past a pizzeria, a lingerie store, and a discount appliance shop, up the hill to his apartment house. Helping him in, I entered it for the first time. The lobby smelled of cooked cabbage, wine, and Lysol. "What are you doing here? Why are you in your bra?" he asked me. The English accent was forgotten. I heard the voice of the boy from Brooklyn. I was embarrassed. I had no ready explanation. "Women are always falling in love with me," he said. I nodded. He went into the elevator and I called out "Good night" as the door clanked closed. At least this time I had gotten into the building.

On the way back to Barnard, through the long drive as the sun came up, fighting sleep at the wheel, I thought of all the people waking, having orange juice and coffee, getting ready for the day of work and school, and I was glad not to be among them. Zombies, walking dead, with safe-deposit boxes that held insurance policies and deeds to cemetery plots. I would follow my compulsion—and Jim Morrison was, I knew, a compulsion—wherever it would go. The city was beginning to stir. Mothers were packing bologna sandwiches in lunch boxes as I staggered up to my room. I would wake a few hours later for my class in "The Individual against Society," but first I would lovingly wash my people sweater.

JIM MORRISON'S GRANDMOTHER had a large and bountiful chest and she smelled of sweet cologne, of lilacs in the spring. Her hair was dyed to its original strawberry blonde and set in tight ringlets around her head. She towered over me in the small, cramped living room to which I had finally been invited. Amanda wore a flowered silk dress and support stockings and her hands were gnarled and red from arthritis, a heating pad for her shoulder resting on a lace doily that covered the worn arms of the high lumpy sofa. It was May and all the windows were wide open. She had fixed frozen shrimp cocktail and a Howard Johnson's fish specialty for the occasion. She was pleased to see me—so much of her grandson's life was a secret, just as her husband's had been. That man had prowled like a tomcat through the night streets of Charleston, Atlanta, Little Rock, Nashville, and New Orleans. He would be gone for days, and when he came home to the little house in Norfolk, where his wife and daughter counted pennies for a Saturday-night soda at the drugstore, he always told them he'd had a grand time and they were glad he'd been happy, even though there was always great distress and anxiety about money. "Jim's heard me tell it many times," said Amanda, and Jim's long, thin face sealed over—his mind adrift, thinking of the philosophy fellowship in Germany he hoped for, of new secret places where he would drink—while we women talked, shy and tentative, but united in a shared passion for the male in the room who seemed eager but unable to escape us both. "I could've had a very different life," Amanda sighed. "I would never have had to sell at Gimbels; not that I mind," she said, "it's interesting work, you know. A young man was courting me when I was eighteen and beautiful, and he brought flowers to the house every night, and then I met old Spike Mueller at the club. He had this mean glint in his eye and I just couldn't help but flirt with him, and this first young man, one night he came with a pistol and he and Spike, they drew on each other and Spike roared loud and angry and the other fellow, he must of just thought it wasn't worth it, 'cause off he slunk, and I married Spike, and you know what the other one went and did? He went and founded a soda company called Pepsi-Cola, and right now if I'd just

22

chosen with a little more wisdom I could be one of the richest ladies in America, but no use crying over spilt milk as they say." And I looked at her hard to see if she was bitter beneath the magnolia and honey, the arthritis, the corset, the powder and the lipstick. The soft brown eyes, so like her grandson's, seemed veiled with visions of other moments, and I saw regrets like blueberries on a bush, ripening and rotting in the sun. The apartment had only one bedroom, and when Jim's mother was alive the three of them shared it. I tried to imagine him, a tall, thin child with limp blond hair held like a closed-up umbrella on a sunny day between the full bodies of the two women, who tried in vain to hide from the intelligent boy the regular swellings and cycles of women's lives.

The television set, in a large old dark cabinet, stood in a corner on shaky legs, occupying nearly a quarter of the room. "I just love the television. I declare, I don't know what I'd do without Lucy and Desi," Amanda said. "Oh, Christ," said Jim. Amanda caught the sneer and knew that all she held dear was held in contempt by this strange boy, her only blood relation, who spoke with an English accent he had learned from the movies and from an education she had bought for him by selling lingerie five days a week for twenty-five years. "Twenty million people love Lucy," she snapped, "and who loves you? Practically no one." Jim turned his head away. She also liked the soap operas and the mysteries and the game shows. "If you're so smart," she said to her grandson, "why don't you go win $64,000 instead of staring out the window and flapping your arms?" When Jim was lost in thought he waved his arms in front of his face in a strange, hypnotic, repetitive gesture, like a bird awkwardly unable to take flight. When I saw him flapping that way, I felt pity for his aborted escape. I wanted it to be my mission to bring peace to whatever caused the constant trembling. Marjorie of Mercy, Nun of Healing Skill, Raiser of the Sick, Tender of the Wounded, nurse of nighttime bandages. How happy I would be to be a humble novitiate in the order of devoted women deservedly admired for their modest tenderness.

For the colitis that had hospitalized her once and might again, Amanda took a large, red pill. She also took several smaller pills for the arthritis that was curling her fingers. She looked me over carefully. I wasn't what she and her daughter had had in mind. I was Jewish. I didn't seem to be a ticket to the slopes of St. Moritz or the golf courses of Palm Beach. I was short and plump. On the other hand, she could sense my devotion, intensified now by my grati-tude that Jim had at last taken my presence in his life seriously enough to bring me home. She could see that I was concerned about him, that I had wanted him to eat more lunch. In an unpredictable world where a Southern belle could find herself living in a strange city without friends or kin, supporting her grandson in a hot apartment in Brooklyn near the Italians and Irish, whose many babies waited in strollers outside the five-and-dime on Sat-urday morning—in such an unpredictable world, holding on was everything, and she was proud of holding on, hardly ever grieving for what should have been or might have been. She would accept me, I could tell, just as she had the other peculiar apparitions that had unexpectedly entered her life.

Later, after a long conversation that wandered over various television personalities, Amanda fell asleep on the couch, her swollen ankles resting on a cushion. Looking at her feet and the redness of her joints, I found it hard to believe that she made it down the long hill each day to the subway, down the steps, and on to Gimbels at Thirty-third Street. When she was asleep, Jim pulled me into the

24

bedroom, where the green dirty walls and lace curtains suddenly frightened me. The sour smell of food cooking wafted in from the windows. I looked down the flimsy fire escape. "Let's go for a walk," I suggested. "No," Jim said. "I have a better idea." From under his pillow he took a bottle of Scotch. He lay back on the bed, pale, thin, one hand fluttering in its habitual way, the other grasping the bottle. A portrait of Bertrand Russell cut from *Life* magazine was Scotch-taped to the wall, a novel by Thomas Mann lay on the floor, and under his bed I recognized the box in which Jim had told me he kept the novel he had begun to write. I sat quietly on the edge of his bed. If only I could serve him well. Suddenly he opened his eyes, now pink. Staring at me like the vaguely malevolent rabbit that Alice saw beside the hole, he unzipped his pants, took out a long, thin penis, and began to fondle it. "What if your grandmother wakes?" I asked. "She won't, not for hours. Listen to her snore." And in fact her breath was steady and a wheeze accompanied each exhalation. If he made love to me, I thought, our connection to each other would become permanent. I had wondered why so many nights had passed with me waving him goodbye from my car. I drove him home, read and typed his papers, even often made comments about them that were valuable. He seemed to appreciate this. But nothing that resembled desire. Perhaps he wanted girls with long legs and straight hair. I desired him, I thought, but now when I saw his penis emerge I was confused. Jim seemed barely to notice me as he touched himself. "Just sit over there," he said. "Sit in the chair." I did as he asked. "Now," he said, "Just pretend you're going to the bathroom. Pull down your pants so I can see you from here and make, you know, grunting sounds." I hesitated, astonished. This was not normal. I had never heard of such a thing, though I had read Henry Miller's *Tropics*. "Come on," he called, "if you want to stay my friend," and he drank from his bottle. Yes, yes, I wanted to stay his friend, whatever the revelation was. My fidelity was strong enough to bear it.

So I pretended what he told me to pretend and his hands rhythmically pulled at his penis and his eyes staring at me grew wild and glazed. I didn't understand what he was imagining, what erotic pleasure my grunting gave him. Soon it was over. The white fluid, half the making of a human life, lay sticky on his shirt. I pulled my pants back on and sat still, puzzled. After he had silently smoked a long cigarette and drunk a little more, he said, "Now you know. That's all I can ever be for you. It's all I care to do for you. Sex doesn't interest me, except the kind I have in my mind—and I need some booze to do it. I am not your all-American boy." I had not expected this explanation for the chasteness of our nights together, but I felt deeply sad for him and fascinated by the odd tangents of his mind. He could be a great writer, I knew, and artists stand on the thin ice above madness and damnation. We had both read Mann's *Doctor Faustus*.

I could have pulled on my underpants and left the room in search of a man with more comprehensible sex habits, but having stepped into the fire, I was unable to do anything else but stay for the burning. It seems incredible now that I didn't then demand some pleasure for myself, that I didn't insist on fulfilling those urges that like the new spring were growing in me. I thought then that those impulses were not really legitimate, not feminine. I thought then that I was a servant in a holy task, like a nun married to Christ, or a priestess at the Delphic shrine. The honor seemed greater than the sacrifice. I understand now there was no honor. How important, after all, was sex? I thought later, driving back across the Brooklyn

Bridge. The creative capacity of a man was what mattered, and that his body was captured by impulses sordid and bizarre added only a dash of excitement to his soul, like a white scarf to a World War I fighter pilot's uniform.

I thought of the scenes I would write for my modern-dancer roommate: Persephone falling in love with the king of the underworld and hiding from her mother when Ceres journeys down to bring back her daughter. Persephone would be mute, catatonic, while sitting beside her powerful mother and would only come to life and find a voice of her own in her love for the ruler of the shades, the spirit of death. And I thought if I loved him enough, poured into him enough care and comfort and sustenance, I would heal the ulcer in his soul. Then, of course, we would have normal sex. I thought my moral powers, my goodness, would move this mountain, irrigate this desert. I was also still identifying with Glinda, the good witch of the North. It now seemed clear that I had been waiting for him since we had first met in those last cocoon years of childhood.

OUR CHRISTMAS 1952 Brearley class dance was held at the Cosmopolitan Club. I wore a yellow dress, and my date, a childhood friend, the best I could do, brought me a purple orchid that I pinned seductively to my hip. My hair had been straightened for the dance. All through those adolescent years my hair, dark and frizzy, was subjected to chemical rinses and sulphurous odors designed to hide what removed me from the cultural ideal. I would sit in a booth covered with foul-smelling plastic sheets while rubber-gloved hands massaged my skull with stinking chemicals. Next to me, women smeared with dyes admired newly painted toes separated by wads of stained cotton. Their hair was twisted in metal clips. As they sat flipping through the pages of fashion magazines, their breasts would flop out of their thin seersucker gowns. Often, a few days after my hair had been straightened, handfuls would fall out. Black hair would slide down my school uniform to make embarrassing tufts on the floor near my desk. Usually I could cover the patches on my head with strands of the remaining hair, and soon new bristles, stiff like a field of wire whisks, would begin to grow. The straight hair would lie on my head as if it were resting on a bed of nails. I didn't want anyone to touch me. They might feel the new kinky hair I was so deeply ashamed of. Even my good friends, who played with me on the basketball team, sneaked cigarettes with me in the park, and talked as much truth as we could share with anyone, called me Brillo-head. They couldn't know how deeply I hated my head of hair.

We had a Lester Lanin orchestra for the dance that year and small dinner parties at the homes of members of the committee before the dance. That was so every girl would have a chance to meet a few boys before the music started and the selection of partners began—an imitation, a microcosm of the cruel choices to come. At school, where we all wore white blouses and blue tunics, there was a certain prestige in being a good Latin scholar or a team captain, but we all knew that the real battlefield, where the stakes were success or failure, was located on some further unchaperoned ground where finally one would be chosen or not. We all knew this—those with acne and thick lenses and those with chestnut hair that hung in ringlets, the shy ones and those already rumored to have French-kissed or worse, those with knock-knees and those who towered Amazon-like above the Collegiate, Trinity, Choate, Andover, and Exeter boys, rounded up by our mothers for the Christmas dance. The very hint of failure was so unspeakable that we already talked with bravado of the kind of men we would pick and of the children we would have. I was lusting for a straight-haired blond Norwegian so that my children would have less chance to inherit my frizzy hair. At night alone, after my homework was done, after I had talked on the phone as long as my hand could hold the earpiece up, in bed with my most imperfect of imperfect, most definitely flawed bodies, I wished some Yale boy would give me his blue-and-white-striped scarf, which I would wear every day like a medal of honor, a promise of my golden future. In bed I faced the reality that many of my friends would have debutante parties where someone would signal for the right fellow to take the girl forever into an assigned silver slot; giving her his name would be like supplying oxygen, mouth-to-mouth resuscitation to a drowning victim. As a Jewish girl I would not go to those parties, but would have to hustle out from among my marginal group some male who would arrange my future. If only I had a Yale or even a Princeton scarf, I would feel less insecure and vulnerable on the cold winter mornings as I waited for the crosstown bus to take me to school. If basketball practice ended early enough, sometimes a group of us would go to the Automat on Eighty-sixth Street. We would put our dimes in the slots and the little doors would click open and we would reach in for chocolate cake or lemon pie, a little stale, more show than substance. My mother always told me before each date that I should remember not to order anything expensive, because the boy, home for the weekend or the holiday from school, might not want to spend all his money on me. I never ever ordered more than one rye-and-ginger and a glass of water.

Several hours before the dance I threw up. I had a short-lived hope that I would be too sick to go, but my mother, who had picked my dress and dyed my shoes to match, would have accepted only medically diagnosed meningitis as a sufficient reason to stay home. As I carefully blotted my lipstick on a tissue, praying that later it would not smear across my chin, I felt ashamed of how frightened I was. I didn't want to be left alone under the fake palm trees pretending I didn't care about being stuck with my round escort Peter Magus, who had been forced into taking me because his mother played canasta every Tuesday and Thursday afternoon with mine. I wanted just once not to be scared, to know what to say. "Make them feel important, talk to them about themselves, it always works," my mother said, but I knew how little help she could be when it came to success. I had a friend whose mother told her to look in the mirror every morning and say ten times, "I am a goddess."

Jewish boys didn't interest me. They didn't seem to be prizes in whatever game it was we were playing. They were too familiar. They had no exotic romantic powers. They were too much like brothers. They were reminders of sad histories and terrible destinies. They seemed round instead of hard, weak where they should've been tough. The Nazis had been defeated, but their image of beauty had survived the burning bunkers and affected us, male and female alike.

At the pre-dance dinner party given by Tootsie van Eyck, the girls, as self-conscious as if they were naked, had flounced and puffed the crinolines that kept the long organdy skirts in place. A few days before, I had badly scraped my ankle and knee on the gym floor trying a heroic save of a wildly thrown pass. The scrapes had become infected and yellow beads of pus kept sticking and tearing in my nylon stocking. I was glad no one could see the painful mess. I wondered if the metal clips of other girls' garter belts also left deep raw prints in the back of their thighs. Nibbling peanuts from a silver tray, I tried to look relaxed. Peter looked unhappy. His tuxedo seemed tight at the neck and he was sweating and his cheeks were tomato red. I couldn't think of anything to say at all. At last I thought of poor Vercingetorix, whom Caesar had so cruelly betrayed. I asked Peter if he agreed with me that Caesar was the Fascist monster of all time, the direct ancestor of Hitler, because he had promised the Gaul that if he put down his arms he would never lead him back to Rome in captivity, and then, going back on his word, he had placed him in a little cage and stripped him and humiliated and tortured the proud leader, who was carried crouching like a terrified animal through the crowds of cheering Romans. How I hated Caesar for that and how puzzled my Latin teacher had been. "Vercingetorix," she had said, "was nothing more than a barbarian who defied the higher civilization of Rome." "Then I am on the side of the barbarians," I shouted and was asked to leave the room. Outside in the hall, leaning against the metal lockers, I tried to feel sorry for Caesar. I tried to imagine with pity the moment the knife cut through the toga and split the white skin between the shoulder blades, but Vercingetorix had absorbed all my tenderness.

The butler gave me a ginger ale with a little napkin and a maid passed chopped-spinach hors d'oeuvres. I thought I was a socialist, of course, but there were times when politics didn't matter, and sitting on the silk- and taffeta-covered chairs in the turquoise van Eyck living room, I only hoped I wouldn't spill anything on my dress. I hoped I didn't look as nervous as my friend Bonnie, who was cracking her knuckles and blinking her eyes as if she were about to be asked to recite in French class. One wonderful afternoon Tootsie and I had drunk her stepfather's best Scotch while stretched out on her mother's sofas like lizards on cool rocks, telling each other true things about our faults. I told her about her habit of trying to bribe friendship and she told me that I talk too much and never listen. She was right, even though I knew the reason I didn't listen was that Tootsie was a little stupid. When she told me later that the cook had been fired for stealing the liquor I wanted to confess to her mother, but Tootsie stopped me because she was afraid they'd send her off to boarding school. I knew it was a kind of crummy beginning for a socialist, but after all, the ability to compromise with principle was a sign of my growing maturity.

During dinner my partner on the left, a fellow from Choate with black eyes and a nervous giggle, told me all about the school crew and his hope he'd make the team this year. We have a river near our school too. The East River runs right past our windows, and looking out from our homeroom, we can see the nannies pushing baby carriages on the walk, the old men playing checkers in the park, and the barges gliding by in the water, like hippos floating in the Nile. Sometimes on winter afternoons I walk alone along the boardwalk and, leaning against the high fence, wonder if there might be a river god with a garbage mouth and condom hair. I look down at the dark cold water. I feel a pull, a force of private gravity, as if the river god wants company for devious and inexplicit purposes. I can't understand why anyone would want to die. I cannot understand why sometimes I want to die. I wonder if the river by the Choate School has a demon god in it too, and does my dinner partner lean over the edge of his boat looking for him sometimes? Not suitable conversation, I think, and instead I ask him how he trains for crew and he tells me at great length.

After dinner we go into Tootsie's room to reapply makeup. I look in the mirror and see blackheads and red spots that have emerged through the layers of powder previously applied. If I don't allow myself to think about it, if I don't spend more than a necessary second or two in front of the mirror, I know I am not the ugliest person in the class. My post-orthodontia teeth make for a sweet smile and my face can have the appealing quality of a soft forest creature promising tenderness, no biting or scratching. And yet I put my hand up to feel the short bristles on the top of my skull, hidden but telltale porcupine quills.

Finally, after many compliments exchanged on each other's dress, shoes, pocketbook, and date, we—like seeds in pods, each carrying within a brittle protective shell the soft mysterious, oozing, gelatinous, pulsing possibility of reproduction—are carried on the wind of the social design down in the elevator, packed in several taxis, and arrive at last at the dance itself. "Just tea for two and two for tea/ Just me for you and you for me alone" were the words of the first song. Peter took me onto the wooden floor. Like me he had learned to dance at a school for Jewish children where the boys in white gloves and the girls in party dresses learned the fox-trot, the lindy, and the Mexican hat dance. Pinkie Fox, duenna of this second-generation upper middle class, dressed always in a purple ball gown (gold chains like so many jailer's keys clanking across her ample chest), supervised the proceedings with a loud voice and a marine sergeant's charm. "Darlings, change partners," she would call and a different boy would grab me by the waist. "Do you dip?" he would ask. Of course I dipped. Wasn't it required? Like sugar roses on a birthday cake?

Among the sons of pant and shirt manufacturers, of doctors and corporation lawyers, at Pinkie Fox's, there were also some Lehmans and Loebs, Warburgs and Schiffs, and my mother always asked if I had danced with any of them. All the boys were well fed; they were shiny and plump like the marzipan piglets in Yorkville at Christmastime. "Step, glide, together," Pinkie Fox would call out above the music. At the very moment we box-stepped across the floor we were being packaged for a future of country-club Sunday buffets, board meetings, tennis courts, ski resorts, roast beef by candlelight, charity balls. Our wild oats would turn into trees planted in Israel—a life I already knew was neither moral nor romantic, substituting comfort for real human experience. Sometimes lying in bed in pain from the menstrual cramps that came not only as a curse but as a punishment for crimes I would one day commit, a heavy weight pressing down like stones under the pubic mound, the room dark, the pain so sharp I would've been willing to cut off my body below the waist and retreat happily to some sensationless place in the middle brain—sometimes in the eight to ten hours it took for the spasms to subside I would think about escape, but I had not yet formulated any plan.

As Peter took me in his arms on the dance floor, I looked over his shoulder at the crowds of boys standing on the sidelines. Would anyone cut in? Anyone at all would have been welcome. They were looking us over: which berry in the bush to pluck, which puppy of the litter to take home? I smiled brightly as if Peter and I were having a wonderful time together. Someone else might find that promising.

I saw him sitting at one of the round tables on the edge of the dance floor with a long black cigarette holder in his hand and the most arrogant look on his long, pale, bony face. His hands were thin and fluttered about his punch glass. His blond hair hung longer than the other boys'. It feathered into a duck's tail in the back that spoke more of street gangs than prep schools, but at the same time he looked like an Englishman at the stables or a Southern gentleman at the slave mart or a dandy in front of a clothes display. He looked like a French intellectual who would never reveal the names of his fellows in the Resistance or a Polish count whose doctor had told him he would never live past twenty. I wanted him to notice me. I felt the kind of desperate certainty that might obsess a man on his way to the bank to withdraw all his savings and invest in Alaskan gold mines. "Charleston, Charleston," the band began to play. There in the wake of the war we had no music of our own. The rumbles of rock 'n' roll were beginning elsewhere, but we still danced to the rhythms of Gershwin and Berlin and Rodgers, like parasols keeping the true heat away from our bodies. Peter squeezed me closer. Was he being clumsy or did he like the feel of my crinoline, my garter belt? He squashed my orchid and the pin poked into me. "Excuse me," I said to Peter. "I'd better remove the flowers." He followed me off the dance floor to right near the table that now pulled me like the rock in the sack that pulls newborn kittens to their destiny. I pulled out the pin, a few drops of blood staining the folds of yellow dress. I put the orchid down on his table and caught his eye. "Will you sit with my flower?" I asked. He looked up and nodded. Peter took me back on the floor, but a moment later the guardian of the flower abandoned it and cut in. He was very tall and thin. I wondered if he had tuberculosis.

We exchanged names. "Marjorie Weiss." "Jim Morrison." The name was disappointingly ordinary. I had expected something like Cecil or Bertrand or Jean de Quelque Chose. He was, however, a magnificent dancer. We floated, we turned, we dipped, and I felt as if my body had changed from a thing weighted with stones once a month to a tern looping in the wind. I wasn't as naturally graceful as he was. I strained to keep up, to gasp out my vital statistics: name and telephone number. He wrote poetry, he said, and was about to recite a poem he had written that morning when the fellow from Choate tapped him on the shoulder. We did a lindy together while I watched Jim walking around the room. "Dogs. Dogs, don't look at any of them. Come back to me," I silently willed. I wanted to run over to him. "Tell me your poem, tell me your life," I wanted to say. I felt a kind of anguish, a bittersweet pain that was going to become all too familiar. Something was terribly wrong with him and I wanted to connect myself to it. Jim came back and cut in, but not before I got an invitation for the winter carnival weekend at Choate—a drooping feather for my featherless cap. At last, the poem he told me he'd made up while waiting for the subway: "Go, and catch a falling star,/Get with child a mandrake root," it began. Just what I had expected, mysterious, ominous, and brilliant. "It's beautiful, just beautiful," I said. "I'm glad you like it. I'll dedicate it to you." "Charleston, Charleston, come on, everybody, let's Charleston." The band was working itself up and we began, so wild and well, so remarkable a dancer he was that more and more couples cleared the floor to watch us. I saw my Choate boy's eyes flickering in the crowd. My ankle ached and I could feel the pus oozing into the stocking, but I decided to pay no attention. His long legs kicked like Gene Kelly's or Fred Astaire's. His face remained composed where I was beginning to sweat, powder and mascara making designs on my shiny nose. "Charleston, Charleston." I shimmied and I shook and my ankle wobbled, and suddenly I slipped and the heel of my shoe went through the hem of the yellow chiffon and I heard the tear as I sat on the floor with the music playing. Jim completed his spin and came and picked me up. "I'm so sorry, I'm just sorry." I wanted to be the kind of girl who never fell, who always knew where her pocketbook was, and whose makeup never smeared. I couldn't explain about my ankle and the scrape because I didn't think Jim would understand why the Brearley-Chapin basketball game had meant so much to me. He listened to Stravinsky records at night, he told me, and next to women, he reported, his true pleasure was drinking. He said it with a certain flourish of defiance that made the chaperones and the punch bowls and the other girls disappear, and it seemed for a split moment that I was with Jake before the running of the bulls at Pamplona—that my real life with its tragic patterns had at last arrived. I apologized again for falling down and limped off, my ankle now throbbing strangely, to the ladies' room.

Peter intercepted me on the way back to the dance floor. "I didn't know you could Charleston so well." They hadn't taught it at Pinkie Fox's. His father had wanted to be a violinist, he once told me, but then in a fit of pragmatism had given it up to go into the laundry business. When we were children we had played a game called laundry. Sometimes we pretended Peter was a violinist and I was an audience. We had also indulged in intimate games of doctor, once interrupted by his nurse, Elsa, and mine, Gretchen. The two women were tight-lipped, horrified, and offended; memories of our shared secret shame kept me from being totally friendly to him now. Our class had gone to the Museum of Modern Art, and when I saw Picasso's "Night Fishing in Antibes" I remembered Peter's little penis under the flashlight as we huddled together in the dark closet, while down the corridor in the kitchen the two German ladies were chatting away in their native tongue about relatives left behind. So much talk about relatives left behind. In some distant apartment our mothers were playing Mah-Jongg for high stakes, their long bright-red nails clicking against the pictured tiles. Peter and I started to do the Mexican hat dance. We were taught the Mexican hat dance but not the hora. That folk dance would have reminded us of times when we were real folk, not ethnic shoppers looking for curiosities, an attempt at ethnic pleasures by people whose memories had blurred like the eyesight of a man afflicted with a brain tumor. I looked near the punch bowl. Poor Sandy Alldon was standing alone. Like a pale, beady-eyed stork she shifted from foot to foot. Her escort was probably hiding in the coatroom. She had missed four baskets in Friday's game and I felt a nasty flush of pleasure at her being stranded. I leaned my cheek against Peter's. After all, something was better than nothing.

Jim cut back in. He had forgiven me, or so I thought, for falling. Behind a potted palm he poured some Scotch from a hip flask into his ginger-ale-punch glass. "Do you know," he said languidly, "just before the last Brearley dance I was invited to, I was nearly arrested. My good grandmother saved me." I was intrigued. In my world the police were there only to help you cross the street, but of course I knew about the other universes. "Why were you arrested?" I asked coolly. Already the first seeds of maternal protective feeling were rising in that place in my soul where respect for law and order ought to have been. Jim had firmly hooked his minnow and was calmly reeling in the line. He lived, he told me, in Brooklyn, out in Bay Ridge, with his grandmother and mother, who were once fine Southern aristocrats from Georgia, but his grandfather, old Spike Mueller, was a riverboat gambler who had lost everything, including the old house and grounds, and his mother at seventeen had run away with a piano player who came to the grand hotel in Athens with a traveling band and had landed divorced with a baby in Brooklyn. His grandmother followed her up North and supported them all by selling lingerie at Gimbels department store on Thirty-third Street. His mother had gotten him a scholarship to a city prep school because she wanted him to meet the right people. He had been invited to the last dance by Nancy Alldon, Sandy's older sister. He knew he had to have cab money and money for a flower and he wanted to buy Nancy a small bottle of perfume to impress the Alldons with, but there were no extra funds in his pockets that week. His mother was out on a date herself. His grandmother was working overtime, and so after a few quick drinks he went into the bedroom and took her jewelry, a garnet necklace and a pair of diamond earrings she had managed to squirrel away out of reach of the riverboat gambler, who had stripped her of everything else. He took these few poor pieces of jewelry to the pawnshop near the subway stop. The pawnbroker had looked him over, a tall, thin boy with a pale face and bloodshot eyes, and excused himself. In the back of his shop he had called the police. This pawnbroker was no fence for stolen goods. As Jim stood there admiring the violins and tubas, the multiples of watches and silver cigarette cases, cracked platters and dusty gravy boats, the sirens sounded in his ears and he was grabbed from behind and hustled down to the local police precinct. He told them his grandmother had given him the jewelry. "Were you scared?" I asked. "A drunk had vomited all over the floor of the station house and the smell of vomit and Lysol was making me ill, but I wasn't scared, because I knew when my grandmother came home from work it would be all right." The police went to the apartment building, down the green corridors that smelled of oil and cabbage, and knocked on her door. "Are you Jim Morrison's grandmother?" She said later she thought he'd been killed, a gang fight or something, pushed in front of the subway train. She was relieved he'd only been arrested. She went with them, a lady with dyed blond hair, an ample chest, and the voice of magnolia blossoms and Corinthian columns, a stranger in a foreign country. She looked the police straight in the eye and said, "Yes, yes, sirs," she had given the jewelry to her grandson to pawn for a little extra money. "Why," she added, "didn't they catch some real criminals instead of harassing innocent boys out on a family errand." The police took them both home in a car and the sergeant kept apologizing, his sister-in-law was from Georgia too. "Was your grandmother mad?" I asked. "She understood," he said, "that I needed the money. She adores me, of course." I looked at him leaning against the wall. He seemed like a cross between a hoodlum and a ballet dancer, a poet and a punk, and somehow I wanted to be with him, whatever the price, and welcomed the fact that there would be a price. I'd never known anyone from Brooklyn before. The chaperone, Mrs. Brownell, came from behind the palm. "Don't you children want to dance?" she asked, a question that sounded like a command.

Back on the dance floor he whispered in my ear a question so vulgar and crude I was amazed: "Are you rich?" "Just middle class," I said. "Jewish." I looked at him carefully. "My mother," he said, "intends for me to marry someone very rich and socially prominent whose father is in steel or oil." "Is that what you want?" I felt my ankle throbbing for the first time since he'd cut back in. "I want to stay drunk," he said, "till I die." I looked in his eyes, brown, flat like the tar roads leading to the swamplands of New Jersey. "I wrote a poem in French. Would you like to hear it?" he said. I would, even though I was only a middling French student with something of a dead ear and an impatience with grammar. He began, "*Hypocrite lec-*

teur—mon semblable—mon frère!" Peter cut in for the final dance. Familiar, like the oatmeal and farina of childhood mornings, like a brother, not a boy. Gretchen and Elsa and their friend Schinke talking German on the park bench while Peter and I played house on the grass, and now he was dull, pudgy, too comfortable. I had other thoughts. The band was playing its last song and Lester Lanin himself was handing out hats with his name written in white script across the soft rims. Peter gave me one and jammed another on his curly head. The music turned soft and the lights dimmed. He pulled me close. I could feel the pus from my ankle oozing into the top of my satin shoe. All over the dance floor couples were hanging on to each other. From above it must have looked like a field of mushrooms. Was it true what Plato had said about man and woman once having been a single creature, a lumbering awkward thing with all the necessary organs in one body and now split apart, spending a lifetime searching for reunion? I didn't really want the kind of union the chaperones buzzing noisily at the edge of the dance floor were there to prevent. I wanted a Yale scarf. I wanted a Choate weekend, and at the edge of those social concerns I wanted Jim Morrison to call me, because like a mole I felt I had tunneled to the edge of my mother's country club, my father's athletic club. I could sniff a wonderful freedom beyond. What was it like in Brooklyn? Only the dead knew it, Thomas Wolfe had said. And I had decided sometime during the evening that poetry was a means of escape—like tied bedsheets. I would have a poet to transport me. I took my Lester Lanin hat and held it like a particular treasure from the sea. It would always remind me of this night, which had been so much more promising than I had anticipated. Tootsie van Eyck whispered to me on the way out that she had an invitation to Deerfield's winter weekend. She was glowing and warm as if she'd been in the hot sun. "See you Monday in math land," she called. We both laughed. It seemed so ridiculous to be studying math when the tournament, the jousting, complete with colors, was here on the dance floor.

Jim Morrison came out on the street just as Peter's dad appeared in a taxi to pick us up. Jim looked me over carefully. I wasn't at all sure he liked what he saw. "Go, and catch a falling star," I said again to myself as I got in the taxi. He must be a kind of genius. Peter took me upstairs while his father waited for him in the taxi. He put his hand on my breast or, rather, on the stiff lace of the corset. I didn't know I was supposed to feel anything. I thought it was some mysterious pleasure for him. We kissed and I smeared lipstick all over his face. He didn't mind. I didn't really mind. He was entitled to the kissing because he took me to the dance. I understood that perfectly well. Finally I said, "Good night, Peter, see you over the vacation." I tried to sound sincere. He was rubbing his face with his handkerchief as he rang the elevator bell. Had I given him enough? I didn't want to be impolite.

THE FOLLOWING MORNING I woke up in the same familiar bed of my childhood on which Gretchen had grumblingly changed the sheets I had wet each night far past an acceptable age. My torn dress was slung over a chair and my shoes rested on the bookshelf with my collection of miniature china animals. When I stood up I could hardly put any weight on the leg with the scraped ankle. I hobbled in to see my mother, who was having breakfast on a tray in bed. I looked quickly at her eyes to see if they were puffed from crying. I looked at her face, which I could read in a second. Had they been fighting? Had she faced some new truth? Had the seesaw of marital discord tumbled again in one direction or another? She was exhausted, she said. Hadn't slept for hours and finally took pills, which made her groggy in the noonday sun. Her hands shook as she brought the coffee cup to her lips. She was in a hurry to eat breakfast because the waxing lady, Miss Himmelstein, was due at 12:30 and was I successful at the dance? I was. Had I been nice to Peter? I had. The canasta game was to start at two. Would I sit in for Helen since she might be a little late? I would. Would I start her bath? I would. Would I like to have the thin mustache that with puberty was growing over my upper lip waxed off? No, I wouldn't. Miss Himmelstein arrived. My mother slipped out of her pink satin nightgown and in her underpants lay on the coverlet. She was flabby and there were wrinkles in the thighs and folds in the belly. The dye in her hair had left a quarter inch of dark, and the cherry orchid color she had picked several weeks before had now a faint tinge of green in the daylight. She still wore last night's lipstick and the mascara stains seemed ingrained in her face like the nicotine smudges on her fingers and teeth. A Chesterfield cigarette burned in the Limoges ashtray by her bed and another forgotten one—familiar lipstick stain on the end—smoldered on the edge of the sink. Miss Himmelstein plugged into the wall a round electric burner. From her pocketbook she took a small pot and placed in it cubes of mustard-colored wax. They bubbled and melted into a sticky hot sauce, and then with a rubber spatula Miss Himmelstein smeared the hot wax in strips over my mother's legs and patted it into her underarms. My mother winced from the heat, grimaced, reached for the cigarette, and dropped ashes down the folds between her breasts. Five minutes for cooling and the wax stiffened on

45

my mother's body. Rip. Miss Himmelstein's firm hands tore a piece of wax away from the skin, and with it came the hairs now protruding from the wax strip, which was thrown in a paper bag. Rip. The skin beneath was pink and there were tears in my mother's eyes. Miss Himmelstein lived in the Bronx with her invalid sister and she told my mother of the indifference of the doctors and the number of times at night the sister woke up and needed care. As she talked on, I watched the wax bubbling. My mother finally said, "That's enough, it's enough. I can't stand any more." But Miss Himmelstein, who had large bony hands with red knuckles and big feet in sensible shoes and once in Austria had been trained as a physical therapist, said, "Now, now, don't be a baby. We're nearly done, just a bit more." And finally my mother was sitting at her Chinese mirrored desk writing out a check. "Darling," she said, "fix me a little drink, would you?" I walked into the bar; Bella had already put out the ice. Suddenly I felt a sharp pain traveling like the summer's shooting stars up my leg. I opened my robe and saw a thin red line that ran from my swollen ankle straight up my leg, stopping just short of the curly pubic hairs that spilled out from my pants, still another sign of my imperfection.

Lying on the black couch in the doctor's office, I heard him explain to my mother that another few hours' delay and the blood poisoning might have forced him to have the leg amputated. He couldn't understand how I could have neglected an infection like that, why I had continued to play basketball several days after the initial wound. Antibiotics, leg rest, total rest. "I think you should get her to take better care of herself," he said. "Imagine walking around without a leg because of a girls' basketball game. What is she, some kind of tomboy?" I lay on his couch feeling small and childish, helpless and vulnerable. I knew that Gretchen, who had retired just two years before, would not have let this happen. I thought of how I would look without my leg. Unmarriageable, I would take up social work and amaze everybody with what I could contribute even as a handicapped person. If there were no antibiotics, as ten years earlier there had not been, the four red streaks now running up my leg would have ended my life. Lying there with a slight fever, I felt the tenuousness of my existence. My heartbeat stopped as I tried to listen for it. I thought of infection as an army of marching ants consuming sweets on the ground. While I was frightened of the finality of what might have happened, I felt another, contrary sense of growing pleasure. The red streaks, the pus, the throbbing were real and proved in some way that I was more than a mass of turbulent feelings. I was real and my not-so-beautiful body was governed by laws of biology that I shared with everyone. I was in fact no freak at all, but could die, like anyone else, of blood poisoning.

The doctor's office was all done in gray and black, and pictures of his wife and grown children hung beneath his diplomas as if to testify that he too was in fact a normal functioning man. His one green plant turned out on closer inspection to be rubber. He didn't understand why I loved to run as fast as possible, passing, dribbling the two bounces we were permitted and making the quick shot from under the hoop and hearing the cheering of friends. I loved the sweat pouring down my blouse and the constant wearing, pushing against my own physical fatigue, the alertness to a teammate's desires and the forgetting of self that happened out there on the basketball court. My pleasure was perhaps a perversion, a childish thing to be outgrown, like making sand castles by the edge of the ocean, or collecting fireflies in jars in the twilights of July. If only

I could have blocked myself, plugged myself up, sent the menstrual flow back up to become no more than a child's nosebleed. Why, then I could resist them better, the forces that were piling years on me. My mother came into the room. Naturally her mouth had twisted into that bitter smile I knew so well, the lipstick, in the crisis, had smeared across her top teeth, and her eyes were puffy now in anticipation of the tears to come. My mother, whose life I was, whose future I would determine, who seeped (like water into sand) into my body and my blood and planned to be carried into happier days on the powers of my charm, sex appeal, common sensibleness—my mother, whose dissatisfaction with herself, her self-dislike and self-disgust, gave her ulcers, heart palpitations, anemia, boils, and once when she had lain in bed for three weeks unable to face the demands of running the house, bedsores, which she treated with cotton pads soaked in warm boric-acid solution, my mother whose placenta had reeked of Scotch and nicotine, of wrath and rue, looked at me now with ordinary rage. It scared me to have her so angry.

When I limped home bandaged and shot full of penicillin and recrimination, Bella told me that a boy named Jim Morrison had called. My mother was somewhat mollified by the news. I was overjoyed. I felt a trembling somewhere between the large colon and the right ovary. I interpreted the feeling as excitement, but perhaps it was an alarm system, an adaptive response that had lost its power to warn under the compromises of civilization. But I couldn't go out with Jim because I had to stay in bed all through that week and the next. In February I was still waiting for him to call back.

Through the Christmas vacation I lay in bed, my leg raised on a pillow, antibiotics landing like the Marines in all my blood cells. Gretchen—with sensible shoes, no makeup, gray hair, and a wart on her face, clearly a servant, a woman whose urges and impulses had been subdued so that she could serve better—came to visit. She had knitted for me another pair of mittens. The nurse of my childhood, the true mother of my character—it was strange to be unable to talk to her. Our conversation, slow and forced, was about her sister, about her apartment in Washington Heights, where she had retired. With her sitting near my bed, I was inarticulate, awkward with a failed love, as in the memory of a painful romance everything between us had become blurred with time.

AT CHRISTMAS Gretchen always grew morose because at home in Bavaria the holiday had been a time of such glory. Here she was, in exile in New York in the apartment of a Jewish family all during the dark years of the war where the enemy of the family was oneself. And yet they could not cope, not even for an afternoon, without her or her cousin Marie, who came and substituted on Gretchen's day off. Christmas for her was memories of evergreens and snow and Mama and Papa dipping strings into the vats of wax, making holy candles in red and green. Gretchen was not against the Jews, even if they were rich. War had come and made summer visits home impossible—made it even forbidden to write letters and get news of Mama and the cousins and the aunts. Christmas now meant visits to Yorkville, where the German-American Bund had held its last legal meeting in 1941 and where all now claimed to be Austrian or Swiss. The stores were nevertheless under constant surveillance by a nervous FBI, which expected East Eighty-sixth Street to provide sanctuary for Nazi spies. But at Christmas the windows were filled with gingerbread houses and heart-shaped cookies pasted with stickers picturing blond boys in lederhosen smiling behind Yule trees and fluttering angels with embroidered wings that said in medieval writing if you looked closely, "Deutschland." The Café Geiger had jelly beans and *Katzenzungen*, milk chocolate in the shape of cat's tongues. Our afternoon walk was part of a daily routine through the winter in all but the most hazardous weather. At 3:00, after a nourishing lunch, an enforced nap, we were bundled, my younger brother, Irwin, and I, in the leggings, straps, and English coats with velvet collars that kept up Gretchen's status among her friends. Irwin was pale with dark circles always under his eyes. Thin arms and legs moved anxiously around in nervous patterns. His full lips were damp from the constant restless movements of his tongue. We were not allowed to leave the table till every morsel of food was consumed. We were not allowed to sit at the table till every finger had been individually scrubbed and we had eliminated the potential danger of germs from hand to mouth. We ate everything, and we washed before all three meals and after each toileting, because disease, believed Gretchen, Elsa, and Schinke, was as omnipresent as sunlight, dust and dew, dirt and earth, soot and cement. Every man-made object, every natural thing was a repository of the invisible germs that would ultimately get us, reduce us to no more than a memory in our governess's scrapbook, if we didn't wash our hands diligently and if gloves weren't kept on in public places so that our hands could not rove where other hands had been. Our bodies, if we weren't careful, would go home from the butcher store, the five-and-ten, the playground, warm with polio, meningitis, rheumatic fever, measles, ear infections, mumps, arthritis, nephritis, scarlet fever, bronchial pneumonia, roseola, diarrhea, gastritis, all with fatal complications—a litany I knew by heart at the age of five.

We went to Yorkville to buy new additions to the Christmas scene that Gretchen made for us each year. The pieces were packed away in newspaper, and when the box reappeared and she began unwrapping the little miniature houses, the tiny figures of a skater and a snowman and a group of one-and-a-half-inch carolers with bright red scarves, each year I felt again anguished that I never had an adequate way to say thank you, no real present to give her in return for what was to come. Soft wads of cotton were spread like new-fallen snow over the top of the bureau, little mirrors from pocketbooks became frozen ponds and little evergreens dotted the landscape. The miniature houses nestled in the snow and a tiny skier rode down a hill made by books piled beneath the cotton. Near one corner miniature reindeer nibbled on pretend corn, and then in the center in a little wooden hut (from the five-and-dime we had bought the figures of Mary and Joseph, the shepherds, the wise men), cradled in painted straw, the baby Jesus. Gretchen would never allow me to touch the crèche but placed it herself in the center of the winter display.

One Christmas Eve, just before leaving for her sister's apartment on upper Riverside Drive—the sister, also unmarried, worked as a typist for a Wall Street firm—Gretchen stood looking at the Christmas scene on the bureau for a long time. She was very quiet. "What is it, Gretchen?" I asked. "Go to sleep," she said, "and keep your hands out of the covers. You know you are not allowed to put your hands under the covers. Seven years old and you still have to be reminded." And she added spitefully, "The day after tomorrow we must put it away."

51

"No," I cried, "please, no, let it stay just a while. Just through New Year's, just a little while." "Nonsense," she said. "What is past is past and there's no sense in pretending it isn't." I wanted her to smooth the blankets, to fix the bed, to come a little closer. We could have shared the passing of Christmas, but instead she put on her wool hat, turned out the lights, and slammed the door. I wanted to put my hands under the covers, but I was afraid she might come back in the room to check. Downstairs on Park Avenue, the doormen in uniforms like policemen were blowing whistles for taxicabs. My mother in her long mink coat, which made her look like a pregnant bear, was waiting in the lobby to go to a party. She was wearing a red satin dress and a diamond necklace. (Years later I would happily give it away.) Gretchen would go down to the basement, walk through the long stone corridors past the laundry room, where the laundress, whose name was Roswilla Brown, worked Tuesdays and Thursdays, exit from the side of the building, and walk to the crosstown bus. In the little room off the kitchen Emma the cook was listening to the radio. She had wanted to go to church on Christmas Eve, but Bella was going to visit a cousin, and someone, after all, had to stay home with my brother and me. Gretchen didn't mind walking in the cold. Her head tucked in against the wind and her brown cloth coat and brown hat made her look like a winter sparrow, hurrying across the ice, eyes searching for the miracle of a crumb, not expecting much but living nevertheless. I thought of her sitting in the dingy light of the bus, clutching her pocketbook, her galoshes covering the shoes I had watched her polish that afternoon. In her pocketbook was the gold-plated watch she had bought for her sister for Christmas. I had helped her pick it out. I had helped her wrap it. I wished I could see her sister's face when she opened it.

The wrapping paper with its pretty white bells and red ribbons would be smoothed out and folded up, put away for future use. That much I knew about those two ladies. I wanted to put my hands under the covers, but although I thought enough time had now passed for her to certainly be across town, she might have been tricking me. She might have delayed in the kitchen for a while talking with Emma or Bella the maid, and then in a little while come back and open the door to see if I was asleep the way I should be. If I'd dared I would have quietly gone through the bathroom we shared and into my brother's room. He would be asleep now, wheezing gently as he always did, his pale face looking haunted even at night by the rages of the day. I couldn't help him, of course, but I wasn't trying to poison him either, as he was always claiming, making me take a bite of everything on his plate before he touched it. I finally went to sleep that Christmas Eve excited about the presents Gretchen would have put under the tree. The tree, a sign of the Weisses' legitimate place in the melting pot, was given a place in the long hall between the gilt candelabras and the red taffeta chairs. Gretchen would help us unwrap the splendid toys, and later when my parents woke up everyone would say "Merry Christmas." My Uncle Louis, my mothers' brother, left money in our stockings. Every January I wrote him a thank-you letter.

On Christmas morning we went for a walk along Park Avenue, Gretchen, my brother, Irwin, and I. Outside, it was silent, as if all the people had died mysteriously in their sleep. The doormen huddled behind their thick front doors staring glassy-eyed at the empty streets. Few cars were traveling. The lights changed regularly but only the wind was crossing the avenue. Silver wrapping paper blew against the side of a parked car. Irwin reached for it. "Don't touch," came the command. "It doesn't belong to you." From underneath his padded snowsuit my brother's thin frame emitted a long, low, complaining wheeze. His nose ran, as it always did, and his black eyes turned on me with familiar reproach. It was not my fault that the air flowed freely in and out my lungs and I did not spend many of my waking hours immobile, bent over a kettle of steam, huddled under a makeshift tent of sheet and chair while Gretchen read stories hours on end. The doctor did not make weekly house visits to see me. I would hand the doctor a towel after he had washed his hands. He would never notice me even if I curtseyed before and after I gave him his towel.

We walked down the avenue past the Brick Church, whose doors were shut. The morning shadows cast strange shapes on the side streets. Burglar-proof iron bars shone in the clear sun. Pigeons roosted and cooed on the little grass islands in the center of Park Avenue. "I wish we had some bread to give the birds as a Christmas present." "Nonsense," said Gretchen. "Those birds with their dusty feathers just spread disease." Later on we saw a doorman sweeping a dead gray mottled shape, feathers flying, into a dustpan. "See," said Gretchen, "they're diseased." I started to run over to look at the dead bird. I wanted to see if its eyes were open or closed. "Stop that," said Gretchen. "Walk like a lady, don't run like a pack of devils were chasing you." My legs felt tired from walking. "I'm tired," I said. Her lips tightened. The wrinkles in her face pulled taut, expectantly. "Maybe you are getting sick," she said. "All right, let's go home." We got to Ninety-second Street. A doorman opened his door. "Merry Christmas," he said. "The same to you," said Gretchen. "The same to you," Irwin and I echoed. There were at least four of us alive on Christmas morning. Near our apartment building we met Elsa and Peter, also walking in the near-empty streets. The two women stopped and the familiar warm glow of German swirled like a May breeze above our heads. Peter held Elsa's hand. I could barely see his face beneath the muffler. His cheeks were red. "What did you get for Christmas?" I asked. "Everything," he said with a sigh. I knew what he meant. Something unknown was missing. We shifted foot to foot. We got tired of standing still, but we didn't dare run on the street. We wanted to go home. My brother arranged it with a long continuous hacking cough that turned into that familiar wheeze as if a fetus were imprisoned in his chest, unable to work its way up the throat to begin some kind of life. Now unbuttoned, at home, I felt Gretchen feel my forehead. "Warm," she said. "*Ach, der liebe Gott,*" she said, not without a trace of gentleness. "You are coming down with something." I felt panic. "No, no, I'm fine," I said, but already I knew germs were invading my body and I would in a few hours' time be in bed with worse things to come.

In bed in my pajamas I waited for the rituals to begin. My mother stood in the threshold of the door and waved. She wouldn't come into the room because there was no sense in her catching whatever it might turn out to be. Gretchen brought me a glass of orange juice and a cracker, and put them on a table beside the bed. "On Christmas too. Even on Christmas." She shook her head as if the injustices of her position came down like snowflakes resting in her hair. She carefully put Vaseline on the bulb of the thermometer. "Turn over," she ordered, and obediently, accustomed as I was to the endless matter of fever, I lay on my side, one leg bent at the knee. Quickly she found the small opening and I felt the smooth invasion. A shiver of anticipation went through my body and Gretchen pulled the covers over me for the sake of modesty, decorum, and warmth. She stared at her watch. "I told you yesterday," she said, "not to stand around after your bath. I told you the slightest chill carries with it sickness. Who knows where this will end? Do your ears hurt? Your throat?" I felt a dryness in my throat, but I wasn't sure if it was sore or not. "Maybe," I nodded. "Of course," she said, "you forgot your muffler. You went to school last week without your muffler and I told you that was dangerous. When my sister was just your age she got strep throat and was sick for eight weeks with a burning fever that we all thought would surely take her to God. Just when my uncle was starting to nail together a box for her little body, our prayers were answered and she recovered. But who is there to pray for you?" She shook her head again. The covers were quickly pulled back by her sure hands, nails short and scrubbed, smelling always of soap, moving about my body with the authority that comes from repetition. The thermometer snatched away, I felt my anus contract in relief and regret. But the red line, the line I could never see, no matter how hard I squinted and twisted the thin glass, showed 100. A possible disease, a contagious childhood illness. It was, thank God, I reassured Gretchen, not after all the season for polio. "Yes, but you need to be cleansed now before the fever builds. We may be able to prevent this from becoming anything serious."

I lay in the bed unable to protest, trying to think of pleasant things to distract me from what was now certain to come. I stared at the Christmas scene on my bureau— the deer and the skier and the little houses like Gretchen's village in Bavaria, I thought, where her mother was making cookies in the kitchen, waiting for her daughters in America to come home. Gretchen came out of the bathroom wearing a rubber apron over her starched white uniform. Gretchen did not like little girls who cried. And the tears that might have been flowed inward to form a secret river that, like the Mississippi and the Colorado, would one day suffer seasonal floods. I closed my eyes when I saw the familiar brown bag with the long hose and the white nozzle in Gretchen's steady hand. "Not on Christmas, not on the Lord's birthday," I tried to deter her, but health was more important than holidays, and besides, Gretchen knew that the angels were applauding, a chorus of hallelujas was echoing around her dedication to this little corrupt, unbaptized Jewish child who Jesus himself knew picked her nose and did other unmentionable things. A child hardly worthy of such good care, but each human soul must accept its destiny. Those were the eternal laws and Gretchen was never a subversive. "Take off your pajama bottoms," she ordered, "and fold them on the chair." As I did that she spread a white rubber sheet on the bed and I felt each moment frozen in ice, time at slow motion, as I lay on my stomach, my backside unprotected, naked, trembling with involuntary contractions and spasms that had already begun out of memory and habit. I felt as if a thousand eyes were staring down at my opening. My opening, which I could no longer cover by any means whatsoever. I saw the jar of Vaseline opened and the white nozzle dipped quickly in the jelly, and I pulled away to the wall, not quite daring to turn over, just as later I would open my mouth to the dentist while pulling my head as far away as the headrest would allow. "Over in the middle," she ordered, and I came, meek and exposed as if I were in the center of a ring of Indians looking for scalps, or my bottom were made of the very precious mineral the mad scientists wanted. My bowels were my treasure and I was powerless to protect them. "What's the matter with you?" said Gretchen, pulling me nearer her. "Do you

57

want the fever to worsen, you want to get complications of the liver or the brain?" "No, no." I wanted to be well and have my mother come into the room with a book or a puzzle as she might when the contagion had subsided. "Now then," said Gretchen, holding the rubber bag high for maximum flow and pushing the white nozzle through the tight rejecting muscles of my anal wall. The outside force was stronger and resistance useless. Greased and glistening, the nozzle with its multiple holes reached into my body, resting just beneath the small beginnings of my uterus, the tiny indications of my ovaries, the mystery of myself that belonged to the nozzle and the hose and the hand that held the bag of water and never belonged to me, impaled now on the bed, like a butterfly on a pin. A moment of rage. If I were a witch, a wild animal, if I were a vulture, I would pluck out her eyes, and my beak would snatch at her genitals, till she was a bleeding hole. A bare moment of rage quickly overcome by an ecstasy of pleasurable sensation that rocked the entire nervous system, into the mouth, the ears, the roots of the hair, pleasure that contorted the entire body into a scream of rejection: "Take it out, take it out, stop it," a scream ignored by Gretchen, fulfilling her duty, standing above me impassive like the Statue of Liberty, holding a bag of water instead of a torch. The Statue of Liberty which had welcomed my grandfathers to this country—"Give me your tired, your poor, your huddled masses." And after the moment of unbearable pleasure so violent I might be set on fire, the strong thumb released its hold on the stream of water and the water flowed into the colon, like a flood in a tunnel. Nothing inside could escape drowning, and then came the pain of pressure, the pain of my fear, the pain spread from my colon to my stomach to my vagina to my ears and my throat and the top of my head and I was only a spasm.

"Please, please," I screamed. "Help me, help me," though I knew my protector and torturer were one, and the thumb would come down again on the hose. For a second the pain would stop and then it would start again. "I have to go, I really have to go," and I could feel the now brown water backing out, dripping between my thighs. "Not yet, not yet," she would say. "A job worth doing, is worth doing right," and again the thumb would come off the hose and the water would flow. What if I burst like a balloon and my insides blown to smithereens? "Stop!" I would scream as the pain mounted. I cried. "I don't like tears," she said. "By now you should be used to this. Nothing to carry on about like that." I watched the bag out of the corner of my eye. Implacable, she would not stop till there was no more water in that bag at all, till the hose itself had been drained inside me. "I have to go!" I would scream, but she never would believe me till the last drop had disappeared inside my violated body. Then she would release me, pull the nozzle out. For a second I would feel relief and then the spasms would increase in intensity. What if I didn't get to the toilet in time? I was humiliated by the wet drippings that slid onto the rubber sheet. I stood up, but the pain, the pressure made my legs shake. I slipped to the floor. "Hurry up now," she said, "get right to the toilet." I could see the brown liquid trickling down my legs. It must not get on the carpet, not on Christmas, I knew. I crawled and pulled myself into the bathroom, up on the cold clean toilet seat, and exploded out the brown water, a volcano of waste matter, a sickly sweet noxious gaseous smell. The pain subsided and I rocked myself back and forth, shivering from cold and sweating at the same time; I waited for what I knew was the second wave of water deeper down, higher inside me, spasms that seemed to make me want to vomit from the pain and another explosion—the world turning into earth-colored pools, mud and rain and the dangerous wastes mixing in the white bowl like the first days of creation, before the amoeba, before the paramecium, when the entire globe was swirling dirt. At last the pain subsided. I sat quietly, dazed, on the seat, disgusting, repulsive, foul-smelling. I rested above what had been in my bowels, glad that it could no longer make me sick, urge my fever higher, spread new germs and complications through my blood system. I wanted to trail my fingers in the bowl, to touch, to bring to my mouth what had been mine, soon to be flushed away to join the cosmic rot from which new life, not my life, would spring. Gretchen had somehow saved me. I called to her. "I'm done," I said and she came. "Clean yourself," she ordered. I could see from her face how unpleasant it was in the bathroom with me. I used paper after paper. "Don't waste it. Use each piece thoroughly," she insisted. She was at the sink, cleaning the nozzle and the bag, putting it away for next time. Remnants of the wet brown mud stuck to my bottom, got on my fingers and under my nails. She ran warm water in the tub and ordered me in. She bathed me, soaping every crevice, using the bristles of the nailbrush on the mouth of my sore anus. She dried me and put clean pajamas on me and a bathrobe and my pink slippers with fuzzy pompons, and I was shining inside and out. I was exhausted and somehow happy. It was over, and if my temperature went down tomorrow it would not have to be done again. "Back in bed," she said. I could tell she was pleased with me. She had forgiven me for crying. I had, after all, made it to the toilet. "Gretchen," I said, "couldn't we keep the Christmas scene up just one day after Christmas?" She hesitated a moment. A special softness came over her face. "Just one day," she said, "just this Christmas. I don't promise for next year." I loved her then, she was my protector, my universe was bounded by the compass of her moods, by her memories of the hardness she had endured as a child. I loved her as my savior who would not let me die, who saw to it that I ate and was clean and clothed, and who nourished me at her dry breasts, even if in fact she hardly ever touched me, except for cleaning purposes. She had knitted mittens for me with little blue flowers marching across the knuckles. She had made me a cap to match, and I knew, I trusted she would always do her duty. She was that kind of woman. My brother came to the door. "Read to me, Gretchen," he said. "I'm tired of being alone." "Don't come in here," she shouted. "You don't need to catch another thing or you'll be carried away to the Lord before the spring thaw." My brother stood uncertain in the doorway. "I'm coming," said Gretchen, and I knew as always she would leave me for him.

NEITHER GRETCHEN nor my mother would have approved of my deepening involvement with Jim Morrison. My mother would not have been pleased that I was spending my nights in the White Horse with drifters and multicolored outlaws who sneered and joked at the very things she held most sacred. She suspected my disaffiliation, however, and on my rare visits home she would look at me with bitterness and pain as if I were the final nail on her cross. I was no longer presentable to her canasta-playing friends (my people sweater), and on several occasions I heard her announce to the guests that I was back at school when in fact I was hiding in the kitchen, eating the cook's chocolate cake, a childhood passion I indulged myself in from time to time. Once I came home from college to find my mother as usual lying on her bed, the familiar cotton pads on her eyes, trying to soak away the swellings of tears from the fight the night before. I saw my mother's lipstick half eaten away, her familiar Scotch-and-water on the French provincial eighteenth-century night table that the decorator had selected along with the gold Chinese screen in the living room and the white vinyl chairs in the dining room, where so many fights had taken place that winds of mutual hate seemed to fill the empty room. I saw the puff in my mother's stomach flesh that dieting and exercise class only temporarily removed. She gave me the look of a disappointed child. "I'm going to leave him," she said. "This time I really mean it. I can't stand his indifference any longer," and she put her short arms up to me, like a little girl fallen while roller-skating in the park. I took her in my arms, smelling the sulphur of the hair dye, the hormone in the cleansing cream, the nicotine that clung to her teeth and facial skin and stained the fingers that were digging into my back. In the half light from the half-drawn shades, fringed and with a tassel pull, I saw her feet under the pink satin nightgown. The toes all twisted under from pointed shoes and high heels meant to disguise her true growth achievement, toenails painted red in case a prince should come to try on a slipper, in case she should meet a foot fetishist at a party. Underneath the toes I saw the blood-tinged bandages where recently the chiropodist had been at work cutting out the corns that grew unwanted on the pads of the foot. "Leave him, Mother," I said. "I will, I will," she cried on my shoulder. "You're all I have." She sniffled and wiped away the mascara stains that ran like bruises over her cheeks.

But even as I held her, patting her back rhythmically, soothingly, filling her drink with new Scotch, fresh ice, even as I saw her closing her eyes, sliding into an afternoon nap, and I took the lit cigarette and smashed it out in the ashtray, I knew nothing dramatic would happen at all,

and this scene and the one the night before that had pre-
ceded it were just steps in a continual minuet they danced
with each other, a game incomprehensible to all including
the players themselves but nevertheless with rules and regulations and rematches and replays and daily reports to
friends and relations. Nothing would change, in that I felt
secure.

Every fall my mother lit a long-burning *Yahrzeit* candle
for her mother, who had died of bone cancer long before I
was born. I had watched that candle flickering on her
makeup table. My mother would paint her long, oval
nails, which never touched a dirty dish or a soiled child.
The light would glow and I would try for memories of a
grandmother on whose ample bosom a string of perfect
pearls rested, in the only photograph I knew. They had
attempted X-ray cures. The doctors, ignorant but daring,
had set her bones on fire, my mother told me, and I saw
the smoldering cartilage, embers glowing within a skeleton
that went on changing into charcoal even after burial in
the damp moist ground. Sitting carefully on her bed, so
my shoes would not touch the neatly ironed dust ruffles or
the satin spread, I played Oklahoma and double solitaire,
twenty-one and gin, and my mother, clicking her nails on
her shiny kings and queens, could remember every card
that had already been played and its suit and knew the
chances, odds, of the next draw. She needed me to play
games with her so she wouldn't become anxious as the
creeping dusk fell over Park Avenue and the uniformed
doormen changed shifts, joking with each other in the
basement beneath us, I held a grudge against God for leaving my needy mother, who cried at night, was afraid of
thunder, and was too often alone, without her mother.

One afternoon on a warm sunny Saturday, I was thinking how dingy the White Horse looked, how strange it

was to sit under dim electric bulbs when outside there was a real spring. We looked like characters in Sartre's hell, drinking the daylight away. My parents had a summer house in nearby Larchmont. I had spent long, lonely weekends there as a child while my mother slept the night before away and my father played golf or tennis at country clubs. The house was on Long Island Sound, and my brother, wheezing and coughing, would climb around the rocks looking for horseshoe crabs. Those ugly creatures with long tails and brown-plated backs would wander about our cove, and in low tide we could reach a hand down and pick them up by the tail and watch their multiple soft claws scrabbling in the air, terror contracting the one or two muscles they seemed to have. The baby horseshoe crabs would ride on their mothers' backs, like Indian papooses, like a game of piggyback, but it was no game, because the mother fed them while they traveled on her shell. She protected them from predators, and without this saltwater ride they would have been as helpless, as near death, as a human infant abandoned on the mountains of Sparta. My brother's great pleasure through those long boring weekends, while Gretchen sat on the porch writing letters home, was to catch a mother crab whose baby's shell was still soft. He would hold up the mother crab, tear off the baby, and then place the mother back in the water. He would climb off to some distant side of the rocks and release the baby and then watch the mother frantic, blind, but trying with primal energy's desperate force, with claws and flashing tail, to feel her way back to the baby for whom she bore total responsibility, whose life's destiny was hers. Instinct, of course, not thought, drew her frantically over rocks and pebbles, through seaweed, orange peels dumped from cruising boats, mussels; minnows scattered as she would turn in hopeless search this way and that. Meanwhile, the baby, hardly able to propel itself forward on its soft claws and unable to steer with its small thin tail, was turning in desperate circles— understanding nothing, but experiencing the beginning of death. My brother would dash from one side of the rocks to the other, watching intently the furor of the hopeless search. The baby would tire first and sink still to the bottom. Sometimes the high tide would bring its shell up on the ramp of the dock. The sun would dry it brittle and it would smell of decay. Once or twice I tried to bring the baby back to its mother, but my brother would go furiously red in the face and scream for Gretchen to stop me. Finally I accepted it, without of course understanding that he was engaged in a necessary ritual. I could not stop his compulsion and I would sit on the grass overlooking the water and wait for the ceremonial vengeance to be complete, so that he might play a game of checkers or badminton with me.

Suddenly I wanted to get out of the bar and into the country. Out of the Village, where every head had earrings and every pair of feet wore sandals just like mine. My father spend his Saturdays at this house in the country. He would play tennis in the morning and rest with the newspaper in the afternoon. My mother, who hated the country now and always had, stayed in the city, playing cards or going to the movies. My mother hated tennis and swimming. Her body, cramped by corsets, high heels, and hair that had been carefully set and dyed, could move only cautiously, awkwardly about. She loathed bugs and other animals. She was afraid of chills and heat. She was more at home with the painted porcelain flowers in her china cabinet than with the real things the gardener planted and weeded in her country home. Eventually she stopped coming. It seemed natural at the time to take a group of friends in my car up to the house. We left the bar, eyes blinking in the bright daylight; Sophie was holding Wilson up because he was already staggering. Lenny Foss, Jim, and I were talking of our summer childhoods. Jim's memories were of the street in Brooklyn where he played marbles and blackjack for pennies and nickels. Lenny remembered the beach resort his mother took him to, where they sold candy apples and saltwater taffy. I remembered summer camps in Maine with color wars and bunk inspections—where I had made my own bed and lived free of Gretchen for the first time, happy as I might never be again. It was good to be in the car with friends. I felt so comfortable. When we arrived, I saw two cars in the driveway. One was my father's, the other I didn't recognize. The front door was open. We went in. First we walked out to the porch and looked at the blue water and the rocks that shone silver and damp in the low tide. My mother had ordered matchbooks for the house in gold with Boulder Shore (the name she had given the house) imprinted in silver on them. "Wow," said Sophie, the daughter of a Brooklyn dockworker. "What a great time you must've had here as a kid," and I felt guilt for inequities beyond my control and for memories of sitting on the rocks praying for a typhoon, a tidal wave to break the monotony of the day.

After a while I noticed Jim had gone into the house. He and Wilson had gone to the bar. The gold corkscrew with the head of a cow amused them. The bar glasses with painted gold coins on them brought great howls. "Come on," said Sophie, "let me see the rest of the house." My father was nowhere to be seen. I figured he must be out walking. He was a constant walker. When he wasn't at his city club playing squash or his country club playing tennis or golf, he was out briskly walking. The condition of his body was, after all, his artistic contribution to the world.

We went through the downstairs, Jim noticing the *Reader's Digest* novels that had absorbed my mother on rainy afternoons, old copies of *Life* magazine, and a backgammon set in the den. We walked in a bunch through the empty rooms. At the head of the stairs the door to my parents' bedroom was closed. I flung it open, expecting to see the rose chintz bedspreads, the dressing table with a thousand and one bottles, and the shutters drawn to the little balcony that looked over Long Island Sound, whose blue depths were filling that very moment with waste products natural and chemical from the sewers of nearby factory towns, but instead of the empty room, the battlefield of my parents, the room where my father would rage and stamp like a bull at my mother and she would simultaneously stick needles by the hundreds into the bull's precious hanging parts—instead of an empty bedroom, we saw my father naked in bed with a woman. I recognized her. A friend, a tennis partner, a woman eight inches taller than my mother, considerably younger, but with no other important differences. (Her hobby was breeding tiny poodles. Once, she had told me, four hairless newborns, each the size of her little finger, fell from the edge of the sink where she had been feeding them by eyedropper and were sucked into the drain—$1,000 of infinitesimal dog traveling down the pipes.) Her husband must have thought she was off having a massage. Her children were probably with the Austrian governess. The interruption was, of course, totally unexpected. I quickly closed the door. "Wow," said Sophie as we hurried downstairs, "does this happen often?" "I'm not sure," I said, "I suppose so."

My father was not a happy man. He had migraine headaches once or twice a month, and sometimes, sitting outside the closed door to his room, I could hear him scream as if his brain were being torn apart by a pack of vicious dogs. He wanted to be richer than he was, to be more powerful than he was, and he wanted to be openly and constantly admired without the burden of returning the attention. He believed that women were pampered by foreplay and made neurotic by too much concern with their feelings. He was happiest at his club, where he was massaged and he sweated and exchanged information on the stockmarket, where servants called him sir and he was admired for a good game of handball and an aggressive style on the squash court. He smoked his most expensive cigars and kept changes of underwear at his club. I don't think he liked the smell of women on his skin. I imagined that after intercourse he immediately took a shower. He was a very clean man whose freshly ironed handkerchiefs and fine silk ties were kept in neat piles in immaculate drawers. His after-shave lotion was bracing and his hair was smoothed with just a touch of oil. He seemed to believe that if he could avoid ever being sticky or moist, dirty or rumpled, he might protect himself from decay and disease. It was a kind of self-freezing process meant to preserve the body for all time.

We left immediately. No one really wanted to talk to me. I knew there was nothing left to defile and the little secret would stay with me: I would not tell my mother, who must already have been told many times before by one well-meaning friend or another. Why should a man not enjoy his Saturday afternoons? I could think of no persuasive reason why not. Yet I wanted Jim to hold on to me, to take me away to a Shangri-la in the mountains where I could trust that today and tomorrow would be similar and that the fabric of deceit and indifference had been left behind. Jim was suddenly touching Sophie's tight small breasts, pretending a lust I knew he didn't feel. I heard him tell her his new idea for a story and in the rearview mirror I watched his hand wander up under her skirt. This was only a public display. I knew, by now, what his sexual appetites were, but still, I was uncomfortable. Wilson was asleep and beyond caring anyway, but I felt a grief as wide and indefinite as the Milky Way.

ONE SPRING NIGHT Jim Morrison took me out to Brooklyn to meet his father. "Be prepared," he said. "He's not what anyone would suspect. In fact, it seems unlikely he's my real father at all. It seems almost biologically impossible." As I drove across the Brooklyn Bridge in the twilight, shadows of steel beams passed through the car. The East River stretched out beneath us; on little islands below, the mentally retarded, the criminally insane were settling into bed. We drove past rows of tenements, their windows fencing the highway, past abandoned warehouses and into a no-man's-land of parked trucks and broken windows.

Jim told me the story of his father's appearance in his mother's life. She had been reading movie magazines, setting her hair and doing her nails, and flirting with the boys at the local drugstore when a traveling band booked into the Essex Hotel, the only hotel in town. It was 1932. Saturday night everyone who could get a date showed up after dinner for the dancing. It only cost 25 cents admission. The fat piano player sweated in the heat and jumped up and down on his stool. His pudgy, dimpled little hands were banging away on the keys. She caught his eye. He smiled at her. He seemed like a visitor from far away, like a man of the world. He hadn't spent his life in a dinky little town like this one. He was short; when he stood up at the break she could see he was very short, round, maybe five foot two. He looked cuddly and kind of cute. He must have been with women in New York, New Orleans, and St. Louis. That's where the sign said the band had been.

During the break he went out on the veranda to smoke. She pretended to pimply Rufus, who worked at the gas station and smelled of soap, that she was going to the powder room, and under the moonlight, with the crickets chirping, she spoke to Donald Morrison. He played drums too, and the harmonica and the accordion. He was a Yankee from Massachusetts. Being a member of a traveling band gave him a magic that like Alice's drink made him seem much taller. She had never thought a piano player, a real musician, would be putting his arm around her waist. They were good family, she and her mother, but poor. Her daddy had gambled the inheritance away and she wasn't invited to the bigger homes in Athens and she wasn't a member of the club up on top of the mountain and none of those boys would look at her twice and she could see clearly even though she was only seventeen years old that there must be a better place—if you took a train somewhere, who knows who'd fall in love with you and buy you all the things her mother always talked of as being nice for girls to enjoy—a natural God-given right for a pretty girl.

When he came to her house after the dance, they kissed. She had to bend way down, of course, but it was thrilling—a man of the world he was—he had seen and desired her and nothing would ever be the same again. The next night and the next she went to the hotel, and hiding behind the high potted palms, she would watch him play, and one night he brought her up on the piano stool, seating her by his side, and he sang right into her eyes and she could feel something unusual, fateful, was going to happen between them. Her mother, Amanda, had scrimped and saved and pawned what was left of the family silver. She didn't want the town to know what of course they all knew anyway, that Spike Mueller had probably scraped the bottom of the barrel and was never coming back to his wife and daughter. Respectability, the job at the bank that her daddy had gotten for him through a cousin, that respectability had proved just another spur driving him fast and away into nights with ladies of the street, club gamblers, and card players, the drinking men who roamed over the South like horses so wild no lady could gentle them, foxes so fast the dogs couldn't hound them.

At the end of the week the band was to leave for the next town. Donald Morrison, whom no girl anywhere had taken seriously before, dared, pretending to himself it was sort of a joke that was on him, because he was basically a good-natured fellow, to ask Lily to run off with him. He knew she wasn't the kind of girl who would just take up with a guy, so he asked her to marry him. To him she was a queen. He loved the lilt in her voice, the way she patted him on the top of his head, as if his shortness, his little arms and pudgy fingers, were really an asset. Lily didn't tell her mother, because that would have been too hard. They had been together so long—her mother sewing her dresses, listening to the radio each night, putting away the dishes, and waiting in vain for old Spike to come back— the two of them had grown into one flesh and it was hard for Lily to leave her mother, knowing what all the talk would be. Even when she got married, Lily knew there'd be gossip. But there was a part of Lily that was her daddy's girl. She knew you had to move, take the gamble, leap or die, and she wasn't about to flatten like so much Coke left in the glasses on the drugstore counter. Enough

73

gossip was buzzing on her just because of that little episode the summer before with Wesley, who, like an old lady, went clacking all over the place, and her best friends dropped her from that intimate circle she had no intention of spending the rest of her life in anyway. Spike Mueller's daughter could certainly take a risk when it was offered her, and though she worried about breaking her mother's heart, she knew this was her moment. The band had brought Donald Morrison to her. Fate had a hand in sending him and she wasn't going to be passed over by events, growing crotchety like the woman who picked rags out of other people's garbage.

They slipped out of town at three in the morning. The trumpet player carried one of her bags and she was packed in the van with the instruments; the other musicians slapped Donald on the back. "Good deal, man," they said, and laughed and drank all the way to Harrisburg. Lily came to regret her impetuous grab at the gold ring, as she called it, but she never regretted that night packed in with Donald's friends, drinking Scotch till her eyes whirled in her head, shouting goodbye and sticking out her tongue at all the despised memories of her childhood that later she would dredge up, treasure, and repeat to her son in a strange and unfriendly city.

Maybe it was really the trumpet player, or a hotel clerk, or a midnight customer at a bar who knocked her up, but she never admitted anything to Donald, and if there was a true father, a man with a little genius, a flair for language, and a height of six feet or so, she never let on to anyone. When they landed in New York and the band broke up because the bookings were drying up and bigger names were willing to go to smaller places, and anyway the dry rot of musicians who had spent too much time together had set in and the sax was always jamming his elbow into

Donald's ribs and the drummer crashed a cymbal down on the small man's pate, and Lily had realized that in Atlanta, Wilmington, Trenton, and New York, Donald Morrison was just a short, fat man who tinkled on the keys in an ordinary sort of way and wasn't anyone to reckon with at all. But by the time she picked up all those facts her belly was out to there and back and she couldn't get a job and support herself, and she didn't want to go home with her stomach the way it was and have everyone say what she knew they would say. She called her mother and explained that Donald was boring and small-minded and the other guys didn't even think he was a very good piano player, and he was sweet all right and kept trying to please her, but he just wasn't much. "Even his thing is tiny," she whispered into the phone so the operator wouldn't hear.

After that phone call, Amanda Mueller emptied her icebox, packed her bags, and took the Greyhound bus up to New York. She was a beautiful woman not yet forty and men still looked at her. She had been waiting at home for Spike Mueller long enough, and even before she grew discouraged about his promises, which like Confederate money were only souvenirs, she had pinned all her hopes on her daughter. Lily would marry the fortune she had missed, would go to the country-club dances and buy her clothes in Paris once a year, and Lily would have the happiness, the success, that had somehow drifted off, even though her youth had promised so much. Lily had been a fool to use her trump on this piano player. Now came Lily on the phone and this divorce was a big-city word with the hint of sin and the pain of loneliness, and it seemed as if nothing in her life would ever be the way she had planned it. She cried into her lilac-scented handkerchief all the way up the Atlantic coast, but when the bus pulled into the terminal at Forty-second Street and Eighth Avenue she knew that she would do whatever was necessary simply to survive.

Donald Morrison was allowed to visit his ex-wife and his ex-mother-in-law at their apartment in Brooklyn every Sunday. He had been devastated when Lily walked out on him. He knew, of course, that he had always had very little hope of keeping her, but he also figured no other man would ever wait on her hand and foot the way he had, bringing her Cokes at two in the morning and giving her all his money and not practicing at all until she woke up from her long, languid sleeps. He hoped after the baby was born she would go back to him. He got odd jobs in bars in Queens and Corona, in Red Hook and Bed.-Stuy., where he would play for the inattentive customers (background music by a background man), and they would leave, at least the regulars would, a quarter or two in the ashtray that always rested like an open palm on top of his piano. He never drank more than a beer or two himself; otherwise, he said, he'd never make it home. Either way he had that strange green pallor of washroom attendants and bartenders. He slept while the sun shone and had breakfast at five in the afternoon. At four in the morning he would be alone on the subway platform, his good suit over one arm, the *Daily News* in his hand. Sometimes he would fall asleep in the subway car and ride all the way into Manhattan. Once or twice he reached Grand Central Station before he woke.

As his boy grew year following year, he kept coming every Sunday afternoon. First he bought a tricycle, and then a baseball glove, a kite, a boat, a model train. He took his son for walks with all the other families pushing and shoving, shouting and crying, drinking, sucking on pacifiers, dragging on cigars, cigarettes, chewing on candy, crunching french fries, pizza, nuts, pretzels, and all the time, each Sunday, more than the one before, he searched desperately for things to say to his child. Nervous and skinny, by the age of four the boy could beat him at checkers, by six he could add and subtract faster, by nine he was listening to Beethoven and no longer wanted to go over to his father's apartment in the project on Eighty-ninth Street and hear "Mairzy doats and dozy doats and liddle lamzy divey" and other songs that the customers called for night after night. By ten he was inches taller than his father and was openly bored by the necessity of keeping company with a man he seemed to regard as a joke or an imposition. His vocabulary was larger than his father's, and already he was planning how to make a fortune so he could take his mother and his grandmother on a world cruise, on a safari to Africa. He was convinced that this fat man who earned $62 a week and ate hot dogs for dinner at five in the afternoon could not possibly be his real father. Jim believed himself to be the illegitimate child of an English lord or of exiled Russian nobility. It was clear when he looked in the mirror that his thin nose, his long face, and his high forehead spoke of distinction, breeding, and wealth. He could not be the seed of poor white trash, of a man who had been an accordionist in the high-school band in a small town in Massachusetts. Sometimes he tolerated his father as one might the court jester or the dog trainer, but then, at other times, he found the fawning attention unbearable, his father's wish to communicate with him, to be a pal, a near-impossible presumption for a man whose fleshy stomach bulged with mediocrity and mocked his son with a kind of threat, a claim on his destiny.

After Lily's funeral the three mourners sat alone in the apartment digesting the suddenness of the loss, which had occurred before the dessert was served. Amanda's friends from the store, ladies with long stories to tell, had left, and Jim's English teacher, who had insisted on coming, though Jim hadn't wanted him to see his home, so unlike those of his schoolmates. Donald Morrison had worshipped Lily from ten blocks away all those seventeen years that she dated and played and dressed up at night and grieved because nothing extraordinary happened to her: no bankers with an island in Greece fell in love with her, no movie star saw her on the street and took her away to his retreat in Palm Springs. Bachelors grew hard to find and they were all ordinary men and she had had enough of the ordinary, the mundane, the dreary part of life. She wanted champagne and Dior dresses. She took care of her amazing and prodigal son, she helped her mother prepare dinner when she came home from work. She told her son bedtime stories of all the glories that might have been and might yet be for him. Now she was buried and Donald tried to find something comforting to say to his son. He looked up at him, smiled in the cringing way he had developed over the years, and said, "The angels have a new friend now, sonny," and Jim, whose love for his mother as he walked about the burned-out plantation of her life, poking at the weeds that now grew where her grand illusions had once given color to the seasons, couldn't repress the negative images, moments that she heaved about the living-room couch with a partner brought home from the local bar for a little fun —times when he would find her drunk and smelling on the bathroom floor. Suddenly the love spilled into rage and Jim took his penis out of his mourning clothes and urinated right on his father's pants—a long arc of urine, a spray of contempt that spilled down on his father's newly shined shoes. "Grief," said his grandmother, red-eyed herself, and helped him get undressed, as she had when he was a little boy, and tucked him in bed. "Grief," said his father, washing his pants in the sink so the cleaner wouldn't think he'd lost control.

Jim took me to meet his father at his apartment. Donald Morrison had given up smoking because of his skipping heart. He chewed on peppermint candies all evening. The stale mint smell hung about his clothes. He could not stand up for too long, and from the washboard of his lungs scratching sounds filled the air. He didn't mind that I was Jewish. "Hebrews are smart people," he said. He played for me on the piano some songs from the thirties, from the dance marathons, and then in a croaking voice he sang, "just around the corner there's a rainbow in the sky, so let's have another cup o' coffee and let's have another piece o' pie," and he smiled at me as he did at the customers, when he could find work, when he wasn't too sick to take the subway and climb up the stairs. His heart beat irregularly under the heavy fat of his chest. I smiled warmly at him. Everything connected to Jim had for me a magic, a drama, a special role in the mythology into which my growing obsession, my deepening affection, was leading me.

IT WAS GETTING toward June. My mother had decided I should go to Europe for the summer with a group of college friends. We were going to travel around France and maybe go to Rome and Florence. When I got back in September I could finish my last year of college, but after that, she insisted, I must get a job and not go to graduate school, as I hoped to do. She wouldn't pay for it. "Enough hiding in the ivory tower," she said. I must come to terms with the real world, where capital was dominant over talent and safety lay in belonging to a group. Clubs, friends, the world—they had not made her happy, but they were all she knew: the Emerald City of accountants, corporations, golf clubs, restaurants, department stores, Parke-Bernet auctions, Palm Beach hotels, embroidered linens, teacups, and diamonds. My father was not interested in my future; he was like a remote Himalayan mountain range, impervious to invasion. I had given up believing in Lost Horizons. For me, that world didn't exist. Sometimes, in the few hours I would spend in my room at Barnard, I would wonder if there was a place, a space, a niche where I would live out my life. Could I run to a farming community in Vermont, or take up public nursing in Appalachia? Was there an ideal I could struggle toward, or was I destined to live without God, grace, or reason for the rest of my life? My roommate believed in the transmigration of souls, or so she said from time to time. As a child I had believed in Santa Claus. I had believed in the Allies marching triumphantly across the map of Europe. I had believed we won because we were good. I had believed in the Zionists and in Henry Wallace, but I had not believed in Elijah's coming at once to all tables of world Jewry and sipping of the wine. I had not believed in my brother's manhood, which had been celebrated at his bar mitzvah, where my parents and all my relatives made a great fuss over his ability to learn by rote what the rabbi had taught him. It seemed an adequate way to preserve a history, but nothing to believe in or marvel at. If God was good he shouldn't mind a girl's hand in his ark, and if he objected to the anatomy connected to the hand I wouldn't believe in him, and so I scoffed at my brother's bent head and all the presents they gave him. All right, I was jealous too. At fifteen one still envies other people's gayly wrapped packages. For days afterward he sat in his room counting his money over and over again, adding his assets, figuring his collateral. The bar mitzvah was all a flimflam sham to hide my mother's weeping through the long nights, my father's temper that had smashed the mirror in the bathroom and lay waste my collection of glass animals, which had once decorated a bookshelf.

Every culture, we had learned in school, has a system of beliefs, customs, mores, ways of dealing with time and the inner chaos of loss and fear and the disappearance of the sun and the coming of spring and the demons of death and disease. As I lay in my room at Barnard, I felt as if I were an anthropological impossibility, cultureless, defenseless, like an albino in the tropics. I was simply too aware to believe in anything. Even Martin Buber, whose promise of a happy I and Thou flowing toward each other seemed as childish as Dorothy's awe of the wizard. When my mind turned to Jim, it somersaulted away. I couldn't subject my feelings toward him to a reasonable or rational accounting. He could stand in a vacant lot, beside rubble, wine bottles, abandoned candy wrappers, graffiti on the exposed stones, and the broken glass debris of a long-ago fight, stand reciting verses he told me he'd written the night before. What could I do but call him my Daddy Grace and follow him wherever he went, hoping to be of some small use? Jim planned to spend the winter in Munich if he won the philosophy fellowship his department had proposed him for. If he left for Europe without me, I knew I would never see him again. Someone else would slide into the position I had made for myself: nurse, editor, friend. I couldn't allow that to happen. I knew I could not manage a loss of that dimension.

One night in the White Horse near the end of May, with the future unresolved and everyone high with a sense of the year ending and the web of friendships tearing down, Jim more pale than usual staggered over to us. "I've been rejected, I don't have the fellowship. I have no money for graduate school. I have no way of living. I cannot take a job—a nine-to-five filthy job." He was drinking more heavily than usual. It was unthinkable. Could Count Dracula work at Saks Fifth Avenue? Could Robert Browning sell shoes on Eighty-sixth Street? Could Lord Byron himself wash dishes in the back of a greasy spoon? Would Oscar Wilde peddle encyclopedias? Would James Joyce or Dostoevsky sell over-the-counter securities? Melville may have worked in the customs house, Eliot may have been a banker, but we all understood that was not the kind of endurance test Jim Morrison could be expected to pass. A job was out of the question. We were stunned. How was it possible that he was turned down? He stood on the bar and spread open his arms. He looked like a condor sweeping down a mountainside to chew on the flesh of a donkey that had missed its footing on the perilous trails above. "I am, as I always knew, a failure." He smiled and strangers in the bar quickly paid their checks and hurried out. "Don't worry, don't worry. We can go to Europe together," I whispered in his ear when finally he climbed down from the bar. "I'll get the money and take you to Europe and you can work and then you'll see what you've written and everything will be all right. I promise you," I said, "I will make it all right." After I took him home, drunk as the lord he sometimes pretended to be, weaving, staggering, burping, waving his hands in front of his face, carrying on a dialogue with inner voices that apparently had designs on his life, I went to my parents' apartment instead of returning to college. It was 3:30 in the morning. I knew I had no money to take him to Europe. My allowance of $50 a month had bought us drinks all winter but could do no more. I had promised and the promise had to be honored if I was to keep him close. In the outside hall, where my mother would never let me drop my books because they would get dirt on the satin fabric of the chaise, I hesitated, but my conscience was dismissed by the pressing circumstances. Besides, the baubles I would take were all insured and replaceable. Their value was nothing next to the salvation of an artist, of the man I could not be without. I carefully opened the bedroom door. My father was sleeping in his striped Sulka pajamas. He had pulled his body as far as he could away from the second bed, in which my mother slept. His suit hung on the wooden valet, neat and pressed for the morning. He had a clean pair of socks and a white pocket handkerchief waiting for him on a chair. I walked past his bed, glanced at my mother, Scotch glass empty by the bedside, a romantic novel of the gothic variety on the floor beside her pompon slippers. In her bureau I fumbled around till I found the sapphire ring, the turquoise, the diamond necklace that had been my grandmother's wedding gift to her daughter, a gold bracelet with amethysts studded in large gold lumps, and the pearl necklace that my mother never wore. She always put on the imitation jewels, saving the valuables for an occasion of grand proportions. I had taken only things I knew she wasn't in the habit of wearing, for the discovery of their loss would be weeks if not months away. I tiptoed out of the room and went to sleep in my childhood bed, my loot hidden in my book bag, neatly put away in the closet.

In the morning I left long before my mother had rung for the maid to bring in her breakfast tray and after my father had begun his thirty-block constitutional walk to his office. I called an older cousin of mine who had gone into his father's sweater business. "I'm in trouble," I said. "I need $500." "An abortion." He sighed with distaste. I didn't say yes and I didn't say no. "Please, I really need it and one day I'll pay you back." "All right," he said. "I'll send you a check right now." I was grateful.

Around six o'clock in the evening I was waiting in the White Horse. I had enough, I thought, to enable Jim to spend five or six months in Europe. I would give it to him because I wanted to, because his well-being, the time and the opportunity for him to write, signified something momentous. I wasn't consciously thinking of it as an opportunity to be a footnote in literary history, but if obsession has a rationale, that was part of the truth. Certainly the love that I felt was no simple, pure, altruistic emotion. It was the bitter fruit of my life—my newfound purpose explained the years of waiting that had gone before. I would appear in the doctoral theses on the works of a twentieth-century novelist, philosopher, satirist, essayist, jack-of-all-literary-trades, Jim Morrison.

When at last he came into the bar I couldn't wait to tell him my news—my promise was to be kept. He looked better than he had the night before—the haunted look was gone. "Well, everyone, I have big news." He called for mass attention without greeting me specifically first. "I heard today. I won the fellowship." "What do ya motherfucking mean?" said Wilson. "Last night you said you'd been turned down." "Well," said Jim, "I knew I wouldn't hear until today, but I thought it would be a good idea to practice what I would feel like if I had been turned down. Miraculously, incredibly, most fortunately, there was no need to practice." He smiled at us all. The outrageousness of the emotional comedy overwhelmed me. I was awed by a man whose practice sessions were so real and consuming—whose fragility was so great that he feared rejection and baited it at the same time. A kind of horror filled me as I realized, somewhat dimly, that we others, our emotions, our reactions, our empathy, were all bit players in his drama. "Congratulations, I'm so happy for you," I said, thinking that if he went to Germany without me I would, like a counterfeit, talentless sham of an Emily Dickinson, lock myself up in a room and write oblique poetry that no one would publish. Despite my plump form, which sweated beneath the people sweater I still wore night and day despite the change in the weather, I felt thin and ghostlike, an apparition that could appear or disappear at someone else's whim. If I could not be with Jim, I would haunt the world, a spirit of regret searching for revenge.

I told him on the drive back to Brooklyn. I handed him the turquoise, the sapphire, and the diamond necklace. I told him about the $500 check that was coming from my cousin Michael. He was delighted. He hugged me easily, without any self-consciousness. We were deep friends. There was no doubt about that. "All right," he said. "I'll tell you what. I'll take the money and leave for Paris mid-June, and you and I can get an apartment and live together this summer, and in September, when I start my fellowship in Munich, we'll see then." At the White Tower I bought us both hamburgers and orange soda and I floated in a glorious victory, yet I also felt the fatigue that follows great effort and a cold, indifferent distaste for the faces of the itinerant truck drivers, the tight-lipped, padded-bra waitress, and the harsh lines I saw on the faces in the tawdry glare of the cheap lighting that turned the most romantic of feelings into fried eggs floating in grease and a side order of soggy bacon. I thought that Jim and I were, by virtue of his way with language, his love of words and precision of thought, exempt from the process of embitterment, that we would create the picture and never be a part of it. I rejoiced that I had maneuvered myself so close to him. We pulled up beside his apartment house. His grandmother, heating pad, swollen ankles, hair clips, and all, was sleeping in the bedroom he'd known all his life, only a block or so from the trains carrying commuters every four minutes into Manhattan. Tonight he lingered in the car with me, talking about the price he'd get for the jewelry. "You're a good girl," he said, "even if you fell down at the dance." I winced. "Why do you keep mentioning that?" "Thomas Mann, *Tonio Kröger*," he said. "Read it and you'll know exactly what you mean to me and always will. How much I would have given to have written that story." He sighed, his pale, long face and thin blue lips looking unbearably beautiful in the lamplight. "I would give anything to be Thomas Mann," he said. "You could be," I whispered quietly. "Oh, God," he suddenly moaned, "I'd rather die, I want to die, rather than be a mediocrity, a failure, a drone, a workaday buzzard, to be my father banging the ivories in a cesspool bar in the city dump, a jump ahead of the bill collectors, hiding 50-cent tips from the tax guys, who know a little sucker when they see one. I must be better than that." "You are, you are." I dared to stroke his high forehead. Sweat had begun to pour off him.

Sure of me now, he took his pencil-thin penis out of his pants. "Pretend," he said to me, "pretend for me that you are being screwed in the behind by a large bear. Make the noises, make the motion. Pretend for me. It would make me happy." I recognized that I had slipped away from the shore and was now in the pirate ship—an outlaw, a social outcast, a demon had possessed me. A dybbuk took over my larynx and I uttered the unutterable sounds he had requested. No one came by, no early-morning dog walker, no patrol car investigating suspicious types. Why, I wondered, did he want it this way? Why did he avoid touching me? My breasts had filled with anticipation, but then, subdued by the charade, I felt no sex in myself, only curiosity, as I watched him bring himself to fulfillment. The peculiar look of the religious fanatic illuminated his face. I could see from the flickering wildness in his eyes that sex and insanity were related. Finally, he took off his tie, wiped himself clean, and saying, "Cheerio, good sport," disappeared across the street into the maw of his grandmother's breakfast and the closet where he kept the pictures of his mother which he would never show me.

At the airport I kissed my mother goodbye, guilt and shame making me unctuous and overly solicitous about her welfare. She had given me ample traveler's checks for this trip I was taking with my girl friends. As soon as the wheels clanged into the body of the plane and I could see clouds down below, I felt a kind of wild grief, a sense I would never wipe away the smears from my mother's lipstick again, and an exhilaration, a joy so profound that it made me tremble with excitement. The joy lay in the hope that I had seen the last of her, that the distance of the Atlantic would make me free, help me to escape at last. I went into the bathroom and changed out of the spike heels, nylon stockings, and little pink traveling suit my mother had bought me, and slipped into sandals and a dirndl skirt my roommate had made from an Indian cotton bedspread she'd spilled green ink on. My friends recognized me again. When we got to Paris, I gave them the pile of glowing letters that I had already written to my mother about all the sights they, but not I, would see on their travels. They had careful instructions to mail them from the appropriate places. I was now untraceable, unknown, responsible only to my chosen responsibility, Jim.

On my second day in Paris I rented an apartment in Montparnasse, with a long studio window, from a painter and his wife, who were off to visit his parents in Toulouse for the summer. They wanted all the rent in advance. I signed my name on the traveler's checks with growing terror as the pile in their hands grew larger and my black folder began to look like a shriveled pea pod. That afternoon I met Jim at Orly. He was pleased by the apartment and his pleasure made me forget the small store of checks that remained with me. Leaning against the high window, he looked at home, like a member of Gertrude Stein's salon, perhaps, like someone who belonged in the Paris of Hemingway, Rilke, Camus, Gide, Cocteau, Montherlant. The sun was warm on the window seat and we sat together and ate *fraises des bois*, and I knew this was the perfect environment to connect into the ghosts of *belles-lettres*. The perfect place for new creation. Jim would equal Mann, equal Joyce, could even if he chose challenge the architectural gothic solemnity of Proust himself, whose experiences resonated in our heads with more power of conviction than our own. Neither of us suffered from lack of ambition for him.

I can hardly believe it myself now, but that first night Jim went out alone. He didn't want to have a girl along on his first evening in Paris. I bought a sandwich at the café across the street, took it home, and watched from my window people strolling up and down the boulevard. I knew Jim could not be kept in the house and he would not want me following his tracks into bars and brothels, but he would have to come back to me at dawn, because his clothes were all in a suitcase on our bed. I carefully hung them up, feeling the extraordinary sense of the distance between objects, the indifference to physical weight, the closed shutters of neighbor's windows, and the comfort the voices from below seemed to gain from each other, from my seclusion and exclusion.

Jim told me later that he started by drinking in a number of cafés. He spoke elegant French and he bragged he was often through the night taken for a visitor from the provinces. He watched the Parisians and instantly adopted the gestures, the intonations that would promise the most. He told a young woman he attempted to draw into talk that he was a Polish aristocrat, orphaned by the war. He sat at a table at the Deux Magots, drawing attention to himself by drinking flamboyantly. He searched the streets for Sartre and inwardly challenged him to a duel of talent, of brain. The young American, hands poised above his holster, had ridden into town. "All right, Big Jean-Paul, it's high noon in your career and Bad Blond Jim Morrison has come to get your laurels." Very drunk as the long night went on, Jim staggered into Montmartre, down into the nightclubs. Lautrec was a cripple and Degas a dwarf, and the affliction of artists, the brotherhood of the wounded, brought a tear to his eyes, already pink from Pernod and loss of sleep and nervous excitement.

Far from Bay Ridge, Brooklyn, where the mediocrity of life poisoned the very air above the rumbling subway, where the stripes of sunlight were like bars on a cage, Jim Morrison renewed his pledge to himself that he would fulfill the dreams his mother had had while lying in her bed reading *Vogue* about parties, balls, places she would never get to see. "Somewhere over the rainbow," as she would say to herself in her Southern drawl, and Jim was going to prove it could be done. In the nightclubs he drank some more. He watched the French country girls, full-breasted, sequins in their belly buttons, gyrating to the music. He felt as if he were the only man in the room to understand that second by second he was getting closer to death. The lights shimmered on the greasepaint on their cheeks and the breasts spoke a language you didn't have to learn in school. Down from Montmartre he loped, an American with money in his pocket, my mother's diamond, sapphire, and ruby all turned to traveler's checks. Down the hill from Sacré-Coeur into the red-light district. The girls were singing like babies calling for milk. The lampposts, like branches of the tree of knowledge, were hung with ripe, forbidden fruit. They called out to him as he went by, "*Ici, ici. J'ai la chose que tu cherche.*" Odysseus among the sirens. He was full of the exoticism of French, the fatigue of translation, and alive with physical urges, so irregular as to need the blurring of alcohol, the fantasy of the winding foreign streets, and the release from daytime reason. "Will you," he asked in his most perfect grammar, "permit me a small amount of whippery, a little moment of tying you up? Nothing serious, you understand." "*Mais oui, mais oui,*" the voice of too much experience sang out. "Fifty American dollars." And despite the naggings of reason and conscience that fell like leaves into the onrushing river of his desire, the deal was consummated. In Bay Ridge he had eaten hot dogs bought from the corner vendor. He had played baseball, not very well but willingly, with his friends in the vacant lot behind the florist's. He had gone through all the motions of childhood, flying a kite with his father on Sunday afternoons on the beach at Coney Island. He had won the spelling bee and the English poetry prize at P.S. 171, and because he was the tallest he had played Uncle Sam in the class play in fifth grade, but now in Paris that same childhood became like a broken mirror with fragmented, ragged shards of glass that no one could piece together.

I didn't want to hear about it and yet I had to hear. I listened intently as he told me (half confessing, half bragging, enjoying the devil in himself and despising it at the same time) that after he had finished his party, the girl, in a kind of pain she was willing and able to accept, seemed not to despise or fear him, only to be indifferent, as if pain were not after all so different from pleasure and she had ways, secret ways, of protecting herself from both. After he had left her, as he was walking back to Montparnasse to the apartment that he did not yet think of as his, where he knew a stranger, a kind stranger was waiting, face probably pressed against the window watching the French night for signs or clues of his return, he felt a kind of shudder, a terror at the cyclones inside himself beyond understanding or control. But, ah, he comforted himself, as he heard his footsteps on the unfamiliar cobblestone streets, Rimbaud, Baudelaire, Degas, Lautrec, Gide, and the others, they had peculiarities also—demons of greater or smaller size, gargoyles of the brain that caused the body to move in spastic and convulsive ways. Now as he rounded the corner and could see the lights in the apartment, she was waiting, and he was glad. He wanted a hamburger with onions and pickle and a Coke. The Scotch and Pernod caused a wave of nausea to nearly make him lie down, right there in the strange street. A hamburger would stop the nausea. He lit a cigarette, and the Gauloise shook in his trembling hand.

"Tomorrow," he told me he had sworn, looking up at the dark windows and the shuttered doors of shops and cafés, "tomorrow, when I've slept off the booze and I've taken a hot shower and she's fixed me breakfast, then I'll start to work, I'll write." The words like pistol shots were meant to destroy any other talent that might be nearby. Like the gorilla's *grand cri* it was meant as intimidation of other males who might dare to trespass, to steal.

I opened the door and saw that he had come home just the moment before collapse. I was relieved that he had returned from the belly of his whale. I led him to the bed and tenderly took off his shoes and socks, pulled off his clothes, and while he slept on the bed I covered him with the blanket. His pale face looked ravaged, the liquor had made dark circles under his eyes, and shadows of beard and dirt gave him the look of a prisoner whose time will never be up and whose hope has been teased beyond revival. In the early dawn as I watched him sleep I wanted only to protect him, to cover him with a magic sheet that would spare him the vulnerability, the unbearable tension of his internal life. I wanted to make it possible for him to be the artist, the writer I knew he was. I wanted to go with him, as a governess or a caretaker, a gardener or a scullery maid. I wanted to be a part of his household. As he lay sleeping, I did what I might not have dared had he been awake. I undressed and lay down in the bed beside him. I knew there was no use in trying to arouse him. It had all been spent, soaked in booze, and now he could only sleep. But I had hopes that once we were living together he might turn to me with ordinary lusts. I believed my love would change his sexual habits. That night I kissed him tenderly on his high forehead and stroked him gently as one might a child with a high fever during the watch through a long, critical night.

Late in the morning he woke asking for an American hamburger. Only on the Right Bank, a twenty-five-minute bus ride away, could I get a hamburger in an

American roll. I had suggested a croissant or a patisserie from the local boulangerie, but he wanted a hamburger and a milk shake, and so as he showered and dressed I took the bus ride over to the Pam Pam, the imitation-American restaurant on the Champs-Elysées, and took the hamburger on the bus back to the apartment. I sat down in a seat with a sign beside it—*mutilés des guerres*—reserved for disabled veterans of the wars. Everyone, including the bus driver, yelled at me at once and I couldn't understand what was the matter. Finally someone explained in English. I muttered apologies in French and English and changed seats, staring red-faced and mortified out the window for the rest of the trip.

After he had eaten his breakfast, we got into bed and entwined our arms and legs. "I like having you with me," he said. "You know, I almost can't remember not having you around. You're a funny thing, but I'm getting used to you in bed with me." Suddenly he bounced up. "I know. You need to be tickled," he said, and he began despite my screaming, wiggling, futile attempts at escape. He tickled and tickled and I laughed, drenched with perspiration, twisting and turning, pushing him with my legs, flailing at him with my arms, and finally I cried. At last, exhausted, he put his arms around me. "Stay close, funny face," he said, and fell asleep. Things were going well.

Soon our days in Paris found a certain routine. Jim spent the afternoons writing at the desk he pulled up in front of the studio window. In the morning I waited for him to wake up, and then I made motions at cleaning and straightening up. I missed my college roommate, who had despairingly taken over those functions. I missed Bella the maid and I missed Gretchen, who had always picked up anything I had dropped on the floor and who had provided clean surfaces and neat drawers and hygienic bathrooms all my life. As June slid into July, I began to see that things I had always taken for granted were in fact the result of someone's time, energy, and skill, and I was reduced to tears of frustration by frying pans full of grease and sheets that stayed dirty and towels that did not fold themselves away. We ate mostly sandwiches and chocolate milk, bananas and ice cream. Dust and disorder turned the apartment into a kind of parody of *La Belle France*. I knew it was not right, but I could not begin to think of what to do. Jars of juice, unwashed glasses, cigarette butts on plates, wilted, rotting flowers, cake crumbs on the floor, and cobwebs swinging from the high ceilings took over. When I allowed myself to think about it, I was puzzled. The money began to run out. I could see it would never last through August. After we'd had a drink together in the local café, Jim would go out for dinner, and he would spend the long nights in confrontation and adventure, off on expensive binges while I read alone in our bed, guarding the pages he had written that day. I became in my dirty underwear the symbol of his intellectual conscience, prod to his gift, muse to his mind, tender of his physical self, friend of his better self, irrelevant and unwanted by the nighttime Dracula-Hyde who emerged from the liquor and prowled the red-light streets in search of strange satisfactions he now wouldn't even describe to me. I had told him how beautiful the story he was writing was—a story about a young painter whose work of empty canvases finally so depresses him the artist hangs himself, proving that there is no meaning or order to life, only the dark laughter of absurdity, or the cosmic hilarity that passes as indifference. The death of the painter was painfully moving both intellectually and personally. I encouraged him to go on to complete the projected collection of short stories. We stood together on important literary ground. I picked up the scraps of paper with false starts and notes of outlines for other stories. I was convinced that one day the Yale or Harvard library would be glad I had known enough to save these beginnings.

We were resting on the bed together early one evening before Jim left on his usual prowls. He was already elegantly dressed for the evening. I was in my bathrobe. I reached over to him and kissed him on the neck and stroked his blonde hair. He reached for me and pulled me to his chest, rubbing my back as if I were a tabby cat, a familiar friendly tabby who had slept on his feet on cold nights. I reached down and unzipped his fly—to touch the penis I thought might be waiting for some gesture of mine. Jim pushed me away, jumping to his feet. He was white and his hands shook as he adjusted his pants and tucked his shirt neatly inside the belt. "I thought you understood me," he shouted. "I thought you cared for me." His eyes were empty now like the winter sky at teatime. "I do," I said. "I do." "Then leave me alone." He left, slamming the door. It will take more time, I told myself, less disappointed than afraid my boldness might have driven him away.

I WALKED through the streets alone, then sat in the Tuileries watching the children play. I walked to the Seine past Diderot's house, past the studio of Descartes. I looked at the sculptures of Rodin and the windows of Notre-Dame, and with each passing day I felt more and more like a waterbug skimming over a dark pond in search of sustenance, avoiding enemies, randomly circling and sliding—a life cycle unnoticed, unconnected to the rest of the organisms in the pond. Something about the buildings in Paris, the rooftops dipping up and down, leaning against each other on sloping hills—it seemed as if each street teemed with a secret I could not know, that my role as tourist underlined my rootlessness. I had nowhere to go, belonged to nothing. I was like foam in the sand. I felt the enormity of the planet, the weight of time from the dinosaurs to the present, and the insignificance of my survival. I consoled myself with memories of more solid times when I had felt as if I belonged and was able to construct illusions of self-importance that served to protect me from too large a vision, too wide a scope, a perspective that would bring about only my internal psychological destruction. I sat in the afternoon Parisian sun with the chatter of strangers around me remembering when I had been on the Yellow team at camp and we had a treasure hunt and my team won the trip to town for ice-cream cones. I remembered when five of us from school went shopping downtown and my friend Wendy had picked up a scarf from the counter and stuffed it into her pocketbook and we went running up Fifth Avenue, till finally ten blocks away at the Plaza fountain we sat down, casually smoking and watching the parade of people, the tourists taking a horse-and-carriage ride around the park, the hot-dog vendor and the pretzel man exchanging Spanish curses, and we were such a solid clump in our friendship— It was hard to believe I hadn't seen any of them for many months. Maybe by now they had been pinned or married, but they too were strangers in another country.

Finally I thought about the fall. The return to college seemed irrelevant now, confining like a playpen when I already had begun the real business of living and had made choices that placed me outside the world of golf and big-board blue-chip sunshine my mother hoped to head me toward. I realized we had little money left, that one or two more major nights out on the wild streets and Jim would

have used up my mother's sapphire, turquoise, and diamonds and have barely enough left for a daily Coke. My
traveler's checks mostly had gone to pay the rent, and food
and carfare were rapidly consuming my cousin's remaining abortion money. We would be broke in a couple of
weeks. Jim looked panicked when I explained this to him.
"Sell something," he said. But there was nothing to sell.
His fellowship money was set aside for him in Munich
and his first check could be picked up at Ludwig Max-
imilian University on September 15, but the question was,
how was he to survive till then? "Cash in your plane
ticket," he suggested. "I could do that, I know, but how
would I return?" "Stay with me, come to Munich with
me," he said. "I need you this year." It wasn't a declara-
tion of love, it wasn't the proposal that a childhood of
proper programming had led me to expect, and yet it filled
me with joy. It was more than acceptable, it was beautiful. I felt as if a direction had been given me. I could do
nothing else. Of course I knew it would be cold in Munich, it would snow and I would need my winter coat,
and I would need money, because the fellowship was for
one not two. The next day I did two things. I went to Pan
American and returned my ticket, and they gave me so
many francs my wallet bulged like a frog swallowing air,
and I wrote a letter to my mother confessing that I had
never gone on the trip, that she had been receiving letters
from me written in the Barnard library months before.
I told her about Jim: that I loved him and intended to
live with him through the summer and into the following winter in Munich. When I mailed the letter I trembled
with excitement. The stakes of the game I was playing
were getting higher. A delightful sense of wickedness, of
rebellion and defiance, practically made me dance down
Boul Mich and home to our pigsty in Boul Montparnasse,

not far from where Allen Ginsberg and Gregory Corso and Jack Kerouac had not long before flamed in fury against the gray suits, the split-level ranch houses, the Howard Johnson's flavors, the America that made exiles of its most talented sons—the frontier that dared so little in matters of mind and imagination. What would my mother say when she read my letter? Would she cry for the canasta games I would never play? Would she cry for the social rules I had broken? Would she weep for the promise of fiscal security I had abandoned? I knew that the fact that Jim was not Jewish would be an additional pockmark on her already scarred soul. Would she be able to understand that I had to escape the turquoise satin chairs, the Chinese wall decorations her decorator had chosen; would she understand that I was running for my life, so that it would not imitate hers? Would she feel betrayed by my duplicity and my rejection; would she tell Gretchen, whom she still spoke to now and then, that I had done something dirty after all? It came to me in a wave of anxious remorse that I didn't want Gretchen to be disappointed in the results of her life's work. She had tried hard and she had done time, being the nourishment, the soil of our growth. I waited in eager terror for my mother's response.

MY BROTHER had made his own escape from the family drama. He had chosen an ironic route. Not long after his bar mitzvah, Irwin began to take seriously what he had been taught for perfunctory social reasons, in his Hebrew class. He turned to the word of the Lord as it is written in the Talmud, to the rules and regulations of the Orthodox Jewish system of belief with the purity of heart and fanaticism of the desperate. Everyone in our family was appalled. To the casual high-holiday congregation of our synagogue real religiosity was nothing but bad taste. In Manhattan in the early fifties it was embarrassing, socially out of place, awkward, downright eccentric, and peculiar. But my brother persisted. His wheezing improved with his mastery of the Hebrew language. He refused to eat the non-kosher food served by Bella, cooked by Emma the cook, and eaten at the table of his parents. He closed his mind to all reasonable entreaties and announced that he would rather starve to death than compromise his religious convictions. I thought it would be no great loss to the world if in fact this dour, round, hunch-shouldered, heavy-thighed youth who collected money in a combination safe in his closet indeed did starve to death. He would be the only boy on Park Avenue ever to manage such a heroic feat. If he had died for his principles, I might even have been moved to sorrow, pity, or respect, but, as it was, my mother sent him out to a Jewish delicatessen where he bought his own food, eating off his own plates in peaceful solitude in his room. He grew long sideburns at a time when only Hasidic Jews wore them. He bought a black hat on the Lower East Side and wore it day and night, tormenting his father, who himself looked like an advertisement in *Esquire*, the most assimilated, handsomest of melted Jewry—who floated in his Sulka ties, his white monogrammed handkerchiefs, and his black silk socks in the American soup, like the upper crouton he wanted to be.

In my father and mother's world the spiritual side of life was taken care of by underlings—under because their financial weight was insignificant. The rabbi, the teacher, the college professor, even the doctor who might have his office on Park Avenue and belong to the same clubs, were all servants to those who had managed to amass sufficient capital to hire attentions—like barbers and beauticians, chiropodists and piano teachers, tutors in French and experts in modern or ballroom dancing, decorators, operators of the electrolysis machine, the facial masseuse. Rabbis and Sunday-school teachers and Hebrew tutors were necessary to maintain the Jewish identity and to assuage guilt. But to be taken seriously? Never. My brother was among the first in his generation to practice downward social mobility. He went tobogganing on the ice of his good fortune and developed a funny kind of speech with a strange singsong inflection, as if he were always translating from the Yiddish. He never went out in the sun and disapproved of all physical exercise as if it were an indulgence of the flesh, a crime against piety. As a result (besides the normal acne and purple blemishes of adolescence), he developed a proper pallor, the pasty white skin, the folds of inattentive, unused flesh that were common to his ancestors, who had spent fourteen hours a day poring over the Torah in the dimly lit rooms of Eastern Europe.

My brother decided to use his Hebrew name, Isaac, the name of a man who had come to America in hopes of abandoning forever the prison of ethnicity his grandson was rushing toward. Isaac continued to go to private school with other sons of Jewish businessmen and professionals whose fathers got them tickets to the Harvard-Princeton game each fall, but he made no friends and poured his energy into homework in mathematics, science, history, or English. Then he stayed up until the early hours of the morning reading Hebrew texts. Every morning he put on tefillin, faced east, and prayed, swaying rhythmically. He closed the door to his room at all times. He wouldn't go near me, afraid to touch me in case I was menstruating. He grieved for my atheism, staring at me with sad eyes. Sometimes, when I had done my homework and had a moment or two between phone calls to friends, I would open his door and taunt him: "Your God shoved little children into gas ovens. What kind of God allows that? What kind of God permits earthquakes and cancer and babies born with bad hearts?" And he would go greener and I could hear the wheezing start. "Everyone knows that God is dead," I would shout into his ear and then run and lock my door. I could hear him pounding on it with his pudgy fists. "Whore, whore," he would scream, because once he had caught me in the hall with a date simply doing what was necessary to receive an invitation to the Yale spring weekend. Sometimes, when I heard him choking with rage at my philosophical tease, I would feel a great guilt. We should be allies. We should be friends. His suffering should be mine. He should be able to depend on me to help him to a lifeboat, and the two of us rowing the mired waters should find a way of living beyond the china-closet island where my mother slept with restless melancholia. I should help him past the fiery breath of the dragon father who screamed and yelled and gave orders and fought with all comers, peddling influence, buying a judge here, enriching a juror there, a corporate captain who breathed fire if anything moved at all. A dragon who had forgotten how to sit down quietly with another person, look him in the eye, and say, "How are you? What do you think?" Our father's eyes were so glazed by combat that he looked outside himself only suspiciously, preparing for attack. He had never known about walking in the woods and recognizing mushrooms and fungus. He didn't know about hot chocolate on cold afternoons and collecting treasures of dead things from the side of the sea. My father went to his club and played squash, and he went into his bathroom and closed the door, and he read his newspaper and his legal briefs, and he went to his other club and played tennis and golf, and he went on trips out of town, and we managed, my brother and I, to be very little in the way.

I should have escaped with Isaac-Irwin to higher ground, where we could have laughed and he could have put his head in my lap and I would have touched his face, very gently, so as not to alarm him, and we could have made our way together. But it didn't happen. "Snob," he screamed at me. "Yid," I called him once and was ashamed, but after all, why was he sliding backward into superstition and repression? Why did he believe in God when God so clearly had forsaken us? Why was I ashamed of him—his walk, a shuffle imitated from his Hebrew teacher; his speech, sprinkled with expressions you could not and would not translate into English? Was he my private prophet, coming back from the wilderness of his social isolation and preaching my downfall, my destruction if I did not mend my heathen ways? We could not be friends, it seemed. Why did he wheeze and wheeze, sniffing at his inhalator, his head over a pot of steam? Was breathing immoral? Was air not kosher?

My brother talked my mother into giving him a summer's trip to Israel. She was ashamed of his religiosity, she was ashamed of his slouch and pallor, but most of all she was mortified by his announced intention of becoming a rabbi. At first she thought it was a childish thing, like a wish to be a fireman or a plumber, but gradually his firmness became more apparent. She was wounded by his nonconformity, a strange and sickly child who was always running to Gretchen when she came into the room to visit. He didn't like playing cards, her favorite way of spending time with children, and she never had known quite what to say to him when, bathed and in his little plaid bathrobe, he would come into her bedroom for his nightly talk and stare at the walls waiting to be released back to the safe world of Gretchen and his steam kettle, which hissed night and day in his room, making the air moist and clammy.

Now, in his seventeenth summer, the summer I was in Paris with Jim, he joined an Orthodox group traveling to Israel. On the way, they spent a day in Rome. The twenty-seven boys and three tour guides took a bus ride to the Jewish cemetery, looking at the ancient dates that testified to millennia of Jewish presence in Italy. They went to a synagogue down a little alley where the windows had been broken by Nazis in 1943, and they sat on the hard benches, listening to the echo of the heavy steps of the oppressor who would one day come again for them or their children or their children's children. They felt a connection to the dead Jews. They hurried, they pushed, they shoved to get in line themselves for this destiny, this history that like a giant boa constrictor, a vision from prehistoric times, strangled and swallowed everything in its path. The tour avoided the Vatican. They looked at no Michelangelos, and when they heard the vespers chime over the rooftops of Roman villas they closed their ears. Quickly they left for Israel, where they spent the summer planting trees in the desert. Because of his asthma, Irwin was given only the mildest of work; he spent most of the time reading in his bed in the kibbutz dormitory.

Once in Tel Aviv, just before their return, he had an asthma attack so bad that the tour director placed him in the hospital. Under the oxygen tent, he gasped and sweated, thinking he might die. "Gretchen," he called and called, puzzling the Israeli nurse who hovered anxiously by his bedside.

On the return trip in August the tour was scheduled to stop over in Paris to visit Villejuif and the train station where the Vichy police had herded over twenty thousand Jewish children to the waiting boxcars of the SS. This was the reason Isaac-Irwin happened to be in Paris at the same time his mother arrived on her emergency flight to visit her disturbing daughter.

Isaac-Irwin loathed the sister whose atheism had brought her to the point of living in a small apartment in Paris with an impoverished Gentile. He knew she sneered at him behind his back, imitating his walk, mumbling in fake Hebrew. She was ignorant and impious and assimilated beyond reclaiming. She was not a Jewish woman, the kind who would light the candles on Friday nights and cook feasts for her hungry sons. She was a traitor, and in his mind he spit on her, he reviled her, and he hoped for God to show his disapproval. A sense of loss, as if someone had died, was gnawing at his guts, causing him to eat even more bread than he ordinarily consumed. He felt somewhat as he had when Gretchen had packed her clothes from the closet they had shared his entire life and announced that now he was too old for a nurse. "Never," he had screamed, although he was twelve years old and ashamed of her when she waited downstairs for the school bus to deliver him home. He had thrown his arms around her and dug his fingers into her back, but she had shaken him off. "It's enough now," she said. "I am going to live with my sister in the Bronx." "But what will you do all day?" he wailed. "Whatever I want," she said, and smiled the smile of a servant who would have many days off. He could tell from a childhood of experience there was no use in further pleading. "You can take care of yourself now," she said. But no one is really ever ready to lose the person who fed and bathed them, who poured castor oil and sulfa drugs down the unwilling throat, who constantly cleansed and daily purified, who played an occasional game of Parcheesi or checkers, and helped with a stamp collection. No one wants to be alone, each of us (then I understood my brother's refusing to go to school or to come out of his room unless Gretchen returned) needs a Gretchen to turn to in the night with stomach pains or earaches. No one wants to be a bird, nudged, pushed out of a nest, forgotten the minute his wings are spread and a draft carries him out of sight. Now in Paris, hearing the news of his sister's living conditions, my brother felt again a loss. This time it was only theoretical. It was the loss of a love that had never begun but remained in the dreary way of inherited family furniture, hidden in closets, disguised as enmity, fenced in with rivalry and fear, but existing nevertheless, a possibility of tenderness, respect, a knowing of each other, a closeness of brother and sister who were in fact the only survivors of the same catastrophe—the marital frailty and the human incompleteness of their parents.

I MET MY MOTHER at the Hôtel Maurice. The wood-paneled elevator with fancy grillwork was itself a work of art, a monument of taste, a piece of the Europe I wanted so badly to belong to. My mother had come to Paris with her brother, Louis, the only male in the world she loved and trusted. The president of a pajama company, a golf player who also danced the meringue, knew what he liked in the way of art and didn't get to see it very often. He was the love of my childhood because he always remembered to tell me I was pretty, and I realized that had my mother been killed by tobacco, alcohol, automobile, germ, fatigue, or heart failure, he would have absorbed me into his family, not joyously, but at least dutifully. When it was cold and windy on Fifth Avenue and I was waiting for the bus to take me home from the orthodontist, I half expected this uncle to come past in his limousine and bring me warmly home. I knew he was fond of diamond cuff links, of Herbert Hoover, and admired Rockefeller over Roosevelt, but still, up until that summer in Paris, I dreamed of him, my good uncle Louis, bringing me ice-cream cones on hot afternoons. When I learned to ride a bike I wished he was there to see me, and now he was sitting in the Hôtel Maurice, helping his sister through the ordeal to come. My father, of course, was indifferent to my deviations from the social norm and was delighted by the freedom provided by my mother's hasty trip to Europe. I waited for my mother's voice and felt torn, defiant, and ashamed. I thought with a twinge of relief that she would insist I pack my suitcase and we return to the Park Avenue apartment, the frigid golden turquoise womb that had spawned my current uncertainties. How could I not lie to her? How could I explain Jim to her, my need to live with him, a need I couldn't explain to myself? "Help me," I wanted to say, but how could she help me?—she who had embalmed herself while still breathing, mummy-like she rested—the bandages of recrimination, regret, the sensations unfelt, self-hatred and barely stifled rage bound her to this world. My uncle was stern and disapproving, disliking my sandals, my lack of lipstick. "And who," he said, "is going to support you? Not your mother, that's final." And my mother's eyes filled with tears and I wanted to say "I'm sorry," but instead I offered her back the string of pearls she had given me for my eighteenth birthday. I put them on the hotel coffee table and watched my uncle pick them up and slip them into his pocket. "If you want to go to Munich," said my mother, "you'll have to get married, that's all. You must be married. No one else would want you now." And she faced me with the crumbling of my virtue. She thought, of course, that I was more of a woman and Jim more of a man than in fact was the case. What would she have thought if she had known the truth, that Jim and I had never had anything that could be called normal sex? She couldn't have imagined what we did. Would she have considered it better or worse? If I had been "ruined," it hadn't been by Jim. "All right," said my uncle, "bring Jim to dinner tonight at the Tour d'Argent and let us know if you're getting married or not." He put the pearls back on the table.

"Married!" said Jim. "Why?" "Well," I explained, "my mother can't just give me the money to go to Munich. She has to tell her friends where I am and what I'm doing, and you know she believes that respectable people get married." We of the bohemian world, of Paris and Bay Ridge and Hudson Street and Barnard, we didn't believe in respectability. We saw the con and held on to our goods, and still, in truth, there was nothing more in the world I wanted than to get married to Jim. I would have a slightly stronger claim, a reason to follow him around. He would keep me with him a little longer, and with that thought I felt a great happiness, like coming to the top of the mountain and looking down on all the sides and seeing distant peaks, far trees, and wildflowers on nearby hills, breathing hard from the climb, sweating, legs trembling. "We wouldn't have to tell anybody we know," I said, meaning the few friends we'd picked up at the local cafés—an old translator of Rilke, a concert violinist getting over a breakdown, a few American girls from Vassar. "We don't have to tell anybody in Munich," I said, "maybe the landlady, but nobody at the university. We'll do it just to get the money for next year." "Why not?" said Jim. I knew he wasn't fond of the charade. Lord Byron should not marry a dumpy Jewish girl with dark eyes, frizzy hair, and a good memory. Rimbaud went alone into his jungle. Why was he being pursued by this refugee from the petite bourgeoisie? Why was she in his bed every morning, willing, eager to fix him breakfast, always waiting for the sexual moves he couldn't, wouldn't, make? Somehow he had begun to think of her as he did of his grandmother or his mother—someone he owed a little time to, while his real life was out on the streets beyond the home door. Nevertheless, he might not like the thought of her leaving, going back to New York with the mother and the uncle who had come with the shotgun from a continent away. A kind of panic overcame him. The toughest tomcat in the world appreciates a bowl of milk placed out for him in the morning. If he has to rub against someone's legs a little to get it, well, then so be it—rub he will. Besides, he felt an appreciation, a gratitude for her connection to his work. It was not that she was responsible for his creation but that her belief in him was becoming one of his own addictions. He now needed to read his daily output aloud to this critical but totally partisan audience of one. Marriage like other forms of social intercourse was just an illusion, a dissolvable arrangement that altered in no way the basic nature of man and his naked vulnerability before the spinning galaxies of indifferent space. So why not get married if it meant they would have enough money? "But promise," he insisted, "that nobody will ever know." "What about Amanda?" I asked. "I'll write and tell her. I'll tell her I'm marrying the rich girl I introduced her to—that'll make her happy. Maybe she'll send us some money as a wedding present."

That night at the Tour d'Argent my mother fell rather in love with Jim. I could feel her brightening with each passing moment. She saw how brilliant he was, how beautifully he spoke French to the waiter, how elegantly he ordered wine. My uncle Louis refused to deal with the

French menu and Jim explained it all to him. He quoted poetry to my mother, who hated poetry but found herself charmed when it was spoken right into her eyes by such a beautiful youth. She understood why I loved him. He dropped literary names she had never heard before but she realized that they must be important. He told my mother he was a first-rate card player, having learned from his grandfather, who had been a riverboat gambler, and he would be happy to play a little double solitaire with her any time. He told my mother she had beautiful eyes, sensitive and gentle. He complimented her on her diamond ring. She told him sadly that some of her jewelry had recently been stolen. She'd fired the laundress. "Who else could it have been?" And they were collecting the insurance. "A nuisance." She shrugged. My uncle was bored all through dinner. He complained of the rudeness of the French taxicab drivers, who pretended not to speak English. He complained about the board meeting he was missing. He agreed to arrange through the embassy the necessary details for our marriage. My mother grew fearful. She had always imagined a large wedding at a hotel with a rabbi and bridesmaids and a dais on which she would sit, and she had always imagined a groom with connections in industry or banking or stocks that would insure the future as they had the past. But nothing was perfect, she knew, and as she looked at Jim, images of Leslie Howard drifted through her mind. It could, in fact, have been much worse. She sent a postcard to her sister from the Tour d'Argent showing a sparkling duck next to a deep red wine, and outside the window the lights of the Ile de la Cité glowed like the most promising of stars. All wishes might just come true.

After dinner as we parted, my mother slipped a handful of franc notes into my pocket. "Here, darling," she said.

"Buy yourself something pretty to wear for the wedding."
As we were walking home Jim took the money. "I need to
go out," he said. "I need to spend that." I wanted to protest, and yet how stupid to care about a dress. His needs
were primary. I gave him the sheaf of money and we said
goodbye on the next corner. I knew as I climbed into bed,
tired from the emotional battles of the day, that my
mother was imagining us together. I was ashamed for the
few seconds before I fell into a deep sleep.

When he woke the following afternoon, Jim looked
green and white, like a ghost, like a person waking from
electric-shock treatment, like a man who's been very sick
greeting the first feverless morning. I had been sitting by
the bed watching him. Asleep he looked like a child, a
thin, sensitive child who understands more of the ways of
the world than is healthy. He looked, as I fussed with the
covers, like a large white bird wounded, lying in the grass,
forsaken by the rest of the flock, a kidnapped prince, a
changeling child, my love. A sense of renewed tenderness
and caring rose in me. I felt frantic with the desire to make
his life happy, to help him in his work, to cool the heat of
his ever-burning inner hell, and to bring peace where I
knew a thousand doubts pricked and bled the soul, sap-
ping his strength, sometimes driving him into the nights of
alcohol and sexual fantasy where I could not follow, my
very sanity preventing my entrance into the extremes of
his nightmares. I was immensely proud that such a man, a
mind whose language dipped and soared, made images,
designs, thought patterns more intricate than Aztec medal-
lions or Gothic cathedrals or Persian miniatures or Orien-
tal rugs, had allowed me to be included in his life. I must,
after all, be worthy. I warmed myself with the illusions,
the elaborate constructions of my shameful love.

My brother came to the apartment, picking his way

over the dirty dishes I had left on the floor. Jim was a fallen aristocrat. He imagined himself in Tolstoy's circle, a heroic young soldier who gambles and drinks too much, who loses heavily at baccarat because he is not at peace with God. Isaac-Irwin pictured himself in the same Russia, swaying in the synagogue at his daily devotions, chanting the chant that united him in time with the processions of Jews leaving Egypt, Babylon, Jerusalem, Madrid, Constantinople, Rome, Moscow. The long slow line of prayer that led directly to the showers at Auschwitz. It was an awkward meeting. Isaac-Irwin's face was puffy; his payess curled and kinked around his half-shaved cheeks. "Traitor," his nearsighted eyes blinked at me. "I didn't know your brother was a kike," Jim said to me later, and I looked at him horrified. "Just a joke." He laughed it off. "It's the kind of joke," I said, "I can make but you can't." "The trouble with Jews," he shouted. "You always think you're so superior, smarter, better, and have suffered more than anyone else. You look down on the rest of the world from some self-righteous pedestal. Secretly you think you're better than I am, don't you?" "Of course not," I reassured him. I too wanted to be beyond evil, whatever that was.

The wedding was arranged within a week. The ceremony would be at the nearby *mairie*, where the local mayor would perform the rites. Afterward my mother would take us to lunch at Maxim's, and then we were to go on a honeymoon, five days in the *château* country. She would arrange to send my winter coat and a monthly allowance to American Express in Munich. The night before the marriage, after our passports had been changed at the American embassy, after we had waited in line for the proper pieces of French paper, pushing our way through throngs of angry Algerians who had been rounded up by the police for visa violations of one sort or another, Jim went out to get drunk, this time to rid himself of the fear of the union he had been trapped into. As always, I recognized his need as real. His psyche used alcoholic excess to release the tensions of a soul that might otherwise mount and blow, volcano-like, the entire brain to kingdom come, to madness never undone. I ached with love and sadness for him. I understood he was an artist and had no other choice. Early in the morning he came into the apartment, stumbling, a long-wounded jack rabbit. His eyes were pink and raw from the Scotch, the Pernod. He hoped, like Degas, like Lautrec, to go a little blind for his sins. He had been hours in the little cafés, the prostitutes' beds. He had swaggered through Montparnasse quoting Keats to the blank faces of the tarts and pimps of the nighttime hills. His shirt was wet with sweat and he flailed his arms about as if all the devils of medieval memory had come to haunt him. He lay down on our bed, still mad, possessed, as if the booze had eaten away, rotted away the barriers most of us contain, the high-water levees that keep insanity from overrunning the internal geography.

"Do you want to know what I do to them—what costs all those francs?" "Yes," I nearly shouted. "I want to know everything." "Why should I tell you?" He pulled back to the other side of the room, where the artist who owned the apartment had turned his unfinished canvases to the wall. I was quiet—the way I always planned to be if suddenly faced by a wolf in the forest. "Please," I said, "nothing could change my feelings." "Really," he said, "don't you know that saints and martyrs are ugly—as twisted as sinners, without having any fun." I knew he was right and the knowledge hurt. "I can't help myself," I said. "Can you?" And then he told me of taking the prostitute (he liked them tall, he liked them blonde, but would settle for the first one that said yes) up the stairs of the dingy hotel and waiting in the room while she went into the W.C. and then undressed. When she took off her clothes, he would put on himself whatever he could—holding her bra between his legs, a blouse over his shoulders, and stockings pulled up his legs as far as they would go, and then he would tie her up with the bed sheets and, taking his belt, would slash at her body. If she didn't cry he would do it longer. "There's something wonderful about it in French," and he imitated the girl: *"Ça suffit, ça suffit!"* Then, he said, he would ask them to open their mouths, and he would urinate, directing a long bow of piss into their mouths. "Bad teeth, missing, rotted, they have," he told me—and the yellow water would drip down their jowls, and then their eyes would look wild and the urine would run over the tops of their breasts and they would finally look like the gargoyles on the cathedral rooftops in the rain. Into their underpants was where he liked to come most. When he finished talking we were quiet for a while. At last I said, "You could have my clothes if you like, my underpants too." "I don't want yours," he said. "It doesn't work like that. I don't want yours at all. You don't have to marry me," he said. "You could go home with your mother." "I want to marry you," I quickly answered. I wouldn't run away from my responsibility even if it meant wiping the running backside of rational thought.

He lay down on the bed and I could see that his room was spinning. "What if I'm no good? What if I'm not a writer, if it's all pretense, illusion, if I'm a mediocrity tinkling with words like my father in fifth-rate bars in third-rate boroughs." "You're not, you're not," I cried. "You're really a genius." He relaxed a little. His breathing became a little more steady. To love, to be responsible for a sick person, was a special taste of human pain I had not known before. It was exhilarating. "Take off your clothes," he said. I was numb with a kind of fear. He was and was not the Jim Morrison I knew. There was now a strange kind of calm as if he had slipped to an even lower level of psychic organization. I stood naked, plump, my roller-skating scar on my shin, my basketball scar on my ankle, my kinky pubic hair sprawling like urban blight over the tops of my thighs. "All right, now," he said. "Pretend I'm hitting you—scream," he ordered. I waited. "If you love me, you'll do it," he said and stared at me, a glaze of sexual fantasy coating his eyes. "Like you're getting beaten with a paddle," he howled as I stared at him unmoving. He took his thin penis in his hands and watched me pretend to pretend in the land of the bizarre. "Pretend twenty men are watching you," he shouted. "Urinate! Piss on the floor!" he screamed. "I can't," I begged him. "If you love me, you will," he said between teeth clenched over an image I couldn't see. I tried. I succeeded a little. At last he sprayed himself with his sperm and sank back exhausted, peaceful on our pillow. As I dressed he fell asleep. I looked at him carefully. He looked normal again. The demon had finally been exorcised. He looked again like a shy and vulnerable child, an intelligent child recovering from an illness. It was a few hours before we had to get up, get dressed for the wedding.

The district mayor had twenty-nine weddings to perform that morning. The couples sat on benches waiting their turn to be called forward. There were young girls in long white dresses who were going after the required civil ceremony across the street to the church, where the priest would repeat the vows. There were middle-age couples with children, widows and widowers, and a bus driver in his uniform, and relatives, aunts, uncles, parents, nieces, and nephews crowded into the room, all listening quietly to the vows of the couples before them. Smoking was forbidden. Jim was nervously tapping his foot. He had no desire to marry, only a whim to keep me with him a while. My mother was sniffling into her Kleenex, her nose swelling with each additional weeping thought. What was for others a major moment of life's drama was for Jim only part of the con, the ruse, the pretense at normality. He was telling my mother that he had had malaria as a child. It had made him very thin. That his mother had taken him with her boy friend on an anthropological study of Haitian voodoo rites. He had nearly died of fever and still had bouts of it occasionally. My mother was caught in the drama of his life. I could see the sympathy in her eyes and the fascination with such an adventurous childhood. None of it was true, of course. Except for army service in Washington, he had never left Bay Ridge.

The mayor called our names. My uncle stood up as a witness. The mayor sat behind his large, high desk, a small civil servant, a functionary of a fussy bureaucracy, and smiled down on us. *"Bien, bien, Americains."* He smiled, a little meanly I thought, but then I thought most of the French were sneering at me because my accent wavered between imperfect and dreadful. "I have never had a divorce in my arrondissement. All my marriages have been happy." Now he stared down at us. Were we foreigners to be an exception? I felt a quick wave of guilt, a knowledge that this marriage was not quite like the others he had performed. My brother believed that this intermarriage was doomed, that the Arabian horse of a Gentile I had decided to ride would throw me back to the gilded ghetto in no time at all. He despised the entire proceedings and kept his eyes on his large clumsy feet. My uncle was pleased with himself for doing his family duty. Times were he had worried that this niece of his with her bohemian ways might end up never getting married at all, be a burden to the family all her days. This marriage was not made in heaven, the boy was poor and Gentile, but after all, his niece was an oddball too. Good thing they'd found each other.

My mother, who knew that marriage was the beginning of war, that the battle lines were being drawn, the bloodletting beginning, felt relieved that her daughter would now be socially respectable and depressed that this was all that was going to happen to her. She now gave up her ambitions for her daughter. To go to bed with a man each night, she knew, was not in and of itself such a wonderful thing. She had not wanted to take care of the baby girl and boy who drooled and wet and fouled and screamed and needed constant holding. She was even afraid she could not do it right. That's what nurses were for, and on the nurse's day off she had hired a substitute nurse so that the physical realities, the basting of the chicken, the peeling of the onions, the making of beds, the washing of clothes could be left to menial hands, hands she slightly envied for their competence and despised for their unfortunate position in life. Her daughter, as she grew, became her confidante. The mother sat on the toilet seat and told her daughter sad tales of male perfidy, stinginess, rage, and brutality. As she bathed in the morning her daughter would sit beside the tub and soap her mother's back and listen to the woes that made the air turn black with dissatisfaction. But there was always the hope that mothers place in daughters, the hope of a second chance. They live not only their own lives but their daughters' as well. They slip their soul into their daughters' pocketbooks and travel with them to dances, parties, to first kisses and ultimate penetration. My mother was crying at my wedding because she could tell that, charming as Jim was, he would make a future for me not so different from her past and present. I was her last chance for happiness, peace, and fulfillment, always promised and never delivered.

At Maxim's—where fancy ladies of the night entertained their keepers, where monied internationals dined on quail and grouse, where Camille had been taken by her lover and Katherine Mansfield had eaten before that final trip to a tuberculosis sanitarium—my mother, originally from Riverside Drive, New York City, looked at me, raised her champagne glass, and stared at me as if to say, "I was wrong to expect so much from you." My brother refused to drink or eat anything. Because the food wasn't kosher and the glasses had been washed by unclean hands, but also because the occasion was clearly not one he approved of.

We said goodbye to my family and got on the train in downtown Paris with our overnight suitcases. We were going to Chantilly. My mother had had the travel agent plan the trip and had given Jim traveler's checks to pay for it. The train stopped at Montparnasse, a block or two from our apartment, and we got off. Jim didn't want a honeymoon. He wanted the money for evenings of pleasure. He cashed the traveler's checks at a local bank and we went home. As he lay in bed, exhausted from the night before and the events of the day, he put his arms around me. I took it for a sign of affection, though it was more the gesture of a man in the water hanging on to a life preserver. But I was content. I had arranged, manipulated, designed a deepening of our connection.

WE ARRIVED IN MUNICH in time for the Oktoberfest of 1957. The city was also celebrating the birth of its millionth citizen. I had tried to clean up the apartment in Paris before we left, but I seemed only to shift the crumbs, the brown plates, the stained slipcovers from one place to another. The owners of the apartment later sent us an angry letter demanding $150 for damages.

Now I rented an apartment in Bavariaring, on the top floor of a town house on the meadow where Hitler had massed his cheering crowds, whipping them up to frenzies of devotion. A large statue of Miss Bavaria with torch in hand stood at one end of the meadow. She looked a little like the Statue of Liberty, the same large cowlike folds in her body and the same blank eyes that formed no opinion of what they saw. With Jim's fellowship money and my mother's monthly check, we were wealthy even by the standards of this economy, then in the midst of its recovery, *Wirtschaftswunder*. I spoke no German. Jim, again, was nearly fluent, often mistaken for a Berliner or a native of Hamburg. I watched the German faces carefully as they looked me over in the streets, in the restaurants, where it seemed everyone read their newspaper. The Bavarians were like peasants out of Brueghel's paintings, thick-ankled, heavy-thighed, wrists like necks and necks like loaves of freshly baked bread. They drank beer all the time out of steins I could barely lift to my mouth. I grimaced as the foreign malt washed over my Coca-Cola taste buds and caused culture shock and frequent nausea. They were friendly people who smiled when you bought a newspaper, who offered you pastries in sign language when they understood you were a foreigner. They were helpful with directions but I was often lost in the criss-crossing of the trolley cars as I tried to explore my environment, back and forth like a dog in a strange yard. Dachaustrasse was a mile out of town. The smells must have come over the gardens and the rooftops into the large beer halls, where maidens could dance all night with soldiers home on leave. "Don't be such a sensitive Jew," Jim said to me with more than a hint of contempt. "Christians were martyred by Romans, Moslems turned to compost by Crusaders, Armenians slaughtered by Turks, Catholics disemboweled by Protestants, Japs decimated by Americans. Don't forget Tamburlaine and Genghis Khan, General Custer and Cortes. Holocausts are common human dramas and someone has to play the part of the victim. The Jewish thing is just history now." I very much wanted not to make a philosophical mistake. Existentially he was right, and still, despite my reasonableness, my rational control, I felt a special anguish as I walked down Maximilianstrasse, where the trucks had been loaded with waiting Jews. I felt as if ghosts, my brother's friends, my people, were walking with me. I felt that I was sightseeing while walking on graves. But on whom and how should I take vengeance for the collective voices that spoke to me from under gabled roofs, on each and every corner? I tried to assuage my conscience, throwing it crumbs of Judaic satisfaction. I wrote my name in large letters in the dirt on our windows overlooking the Bavariaring meadow. We went to eat in the fine French restaurant in the Vier Jahreszeiten Hotel, where Hitler had once had his headquarters. I sat in his seat. "My body is alive and yours is dead," I jeered at him, but that was no real satisfaction.

It was very cold that autumn and my mother had not yet sent my winter coat. There was almost no heat in our apartment, and I spent more and more of my days in bed, under the wonderful eiderdown quilt. Jim was at the university only an hour or so each day. "German philosophy," he sneered, "is like tapioca pudding, like taking a mud bath at an Elizabeth Arden spa, like drowning in a swimming pool of Elmer's glue." They needed Occam's Razor. They needed the cold steel of mathematical logic. They needed to learn not to string too many large, long words together in lines that shuffled slowly along till at the last, like the false messiah, the verb appeared, an anticlimax, an irrelevancy. No verb, no matter how active or reflexive or passive, could redeem what had gone before.

Jim was writing stories. His mentor, his model was still Thomas Mann, who had lived in Munich before his exile. We read together: *Buddenbrooks, Mario and the Magician,* all the short stories. "If I am not as good as that bastard, I want to be a drunkard, a gambler, a corpse," Jim would say again and again. Each time I would put my arms around his thin shoulders and reassure him: "You are, you are, you will, you will. Today's work was the best, tomorrow will be better. You are what you hope." I believed with an absolute conviction I held about nothing else, I believed that the particular grace of his language, influenced as he was by the priests of French existentialism, German surrealism, and Italian passion, combined with the uniqueness of his critical brain, would produce the thing I valued beyond all else—the only thing I thought of as a meaningful goal—a work of literary genius. Primitive peoples have their totems, which if lost or destroyed seem to debilitate the tribe beyond resurrection. Everyone holds on to some kind of spiritual good, something that decorates the sun's unthinking circles with meaning and purpose. I had come to a form of worship, as fanatical and narrowly restricting as any other. I had given up my brother's God, who arranged celebrations for him and none for me. I had given up my mother's God, the mammon of the well-invested future, because it had failed her so badly. The political gods had been judged and found wanting. I was reduced to the last religious refuge of the determined acolyte—the prose and poetry of man, who might ruin everything he touched but who could describe it with such grandeur and precision.

At night, when Jim came home, often staggering from long hours of drink with the few Americans who also were studying at the university, he would lie in bed shivering with an inner cold that even our eiderdown could not ease. "I'm a failure," he would shout at me. "You've got to stop pampering me, I've got to face it, I'm a failure. I'm twenty-two and I've written nothing of value, nothing lasting. I'm still an apprentice. Don't lie." He would glare at me. "You know I'm nothing." Sometimes I would hold him and rock him in my arms, and the warmth of my body would eventually break through his trembling, and he would relax and fall asleep with his blond straight hair lying between my breasts. When he screamed I would get frightened. It wasn't the scream of a child having a tantrum, though there was some of that in it. It was the scream of a man and his devil, a man on the edge of chaos; a cesspool of internal pain and a stench of madness occupied our bed, a threat of insanity, if the work was not applauded and recognized. I had to keep him working so he wouldn't scream at night. His fear of failure might summon nightmares that would lead him into hallucinations and a trembling I could not always end with the simple offering of my love.

We had read Mann's *Doctor Faustus* and I understood that the artist was connected, twinned to the demonic part of Jim, the drinker, the lunatic who sometimes stood in a corner waving his hands before his unseeing eyes (a gesture I noticed years later in blind children who have retreated from human contact), who complained of a restlessness nothing could ease but sufficient booze and sometimes the sexual practices that I knew belonged in a case history and yet accepted as a normal routine of my life. I understood that creativity was permitted by the forces of madness, of sexual disease, that one without the other was probably impossible. His vulnerability and the enormity of his struggle, and his pain of being a man with a tumor of madness spreading in him, moved me to a tenderness and a love I had never known was possible. I was exhilarated by my love. I was happy. We visited the house where Mann lived. We held hands and were very quiet, like children wandering in the halls of the Vatican.

Each morning I listened to the friendly American Army radio station. They had a German phrase of the day which they repeated fifty times in an attempt to ease the G.I.'s into the native culture. The sounds of country music, of rock 'n' roll, of commercials for toothpaste and deodorant, all available at the enormous PX just at the edge of town, gave me a familiar sense of home in a country whose strangeness was not wearing off with each passing day. The army, the conquering army, first invaders and now allies, occupied a large portion of the city with barracks, administrative offices, training fields, schools. But most interesting to me was a section three blocks long just beyond the railroad station that had become army territory. There were bars and whorehouses and liquor stores in this area. M.P.'s patrolled there night and day, stopping fistfights, picking up young derelicts from Tennessee and South Carolina who had found themselves on their faces in the German gutter after a night to remember but not to write home to Mother about.

Our friend Bob, a graduate student in philosophy from the University of Kansas who was on an exchange program, told me to stay out of there. He'd been in Germany two years. He was Catholic, with a twenty-year-old wife and two children. He told me I'd be mistaken for a prostitute. His warning fascinated me. I would go to the edge of the area and hover about, peering at girls, younger than I, going off with soldiers to little hotels with shabby doors. I saw the M.P.'s strolling up and down. This was the real world that Jim left me out of. The real world of body odors, beer breath, false teeth, padded bras, money exchanged for discharges that were necessary if not honorable. I was naïve, an innocent. Many of the girls were from the country, girls who could have been Gretchen's nieces, who came from the peasant farms that the war had left without menfolk. They had come to town to find an American to marry. I wished them luck as I stared (pretending to study my map of the city) down the street I was afraid to enter.

Bob and his wife, Mary, lived in a tiny apartment. The

tub in the kitchen was the only place to wash out the diapers that hung on ropes crisscrossed over the small living room. The smell of urine mixed with Bob's pipe tobacco was not entirely unpleasant. Bob and Jim often argued Hegel or Russell till dawn, the beer bottles piling up on the table, too many to count. The babies had been delivered at home, ten months apart, by a midwife and Mary glowed as she told the story of their birth. Bob had stood at her head; it had been a beautiful, even a religious, experience. They were both from Kansas City. She, too, was Catholic, and I often stared at them, wondering how it was possible, a mile from Dachau, with photographs of childbirth (Bob had used his camera) on the wall, to believe in the divinity of anything. Jim didn't want anyone to know we were married. He thought he cut a better figure living with me in sin. Sometimes that hurt me. We were simultaneously living our daily lives and posing for the literary historians of the future, and Jim wanted to look like the young Shelley off to the continent, not like a Babbitt paying life-insurance premiums. Mary was fascinated by my Jewishness. She told me that in her high school the Jewish girls had had the best clothes and got the best marks and lived in big houses on one side of town. She was always jealous of them. She embarrassed me by talking about how she wished she were Jewish. In Munich it seemed to be a mockery or an invitation to disaster to wish that. Bob was tutoring English to a window dresser who hoped to go to the States and become a rich window dresser. His name was Johann. Because he worked at home so many nights and talked to Jim on others, Bob suggested that Johann go out with Mary to concerts, theater, and dance halls in order to practice his English. Sometimes I went with them. Mary was delighted to be freed from the constant and grinding work of caring for twenty-month-old and ten-month-old babies. She leaped into the Munich night with joy and innocence, but the innocence was soon lost when she began what became by the time the snow fell on Maximilianstrasse a major drama, an affair with her husband's pupil.

One snowy winter morning I walked into the living room, where Jim was working, his strong Roman face intent on the page in front of him. He looked like a philosopher-prince. His long, elegant hands rested on the tabletop. He was gentle and somehow wistful. His aristocratic head seemed almost ready for imprint on some new coin of the realm. The sun streamed over his desk, spilling onto the dust I never could get off the floor, gliding over the complete works of Heidegger he recently had carefully underlined. He was so beautiful that I was afraid to move. I wanted just to watch him concentrating. He turned around and saw me. "Come, lean against me," he said, "your fat should keep me warm." I put my arms around him. *"Ich liebe dich,"* I said, showing off my new German. *"Ich liebe dich auch,"* he answered. I was surprised and I knew my nose was turning red with some kind of emotion that might even be tears. "Come on," he said. "Let's get out of this cold apartment and go walk in the sun." We bundled in boots and hats and sweaters and walked down our spiral staircase into the pure-white, glowing world. The trolleys had stopped. Schoolchildren tumbled in the drifts. We trudged along, leaving deep footprints in the clean snow. From the café on the corner came the familiar smells of coffee and sweet pastries. The windows were steamed over, but we could still see the pastries, covered with mounds of whipped cream topped by cherries, that rested on a shelf. We could see the racks of newspapers already used and replaced by many of the early-morning customers. We walked past a block of bombed-out buildings that had not yet been rebuilt. In the snow they looked like Druid ruins. We began to climb in the rubble. My cheeks were red with cold. We held hands and tried jumping from cement block to cement block. Suddenly I tumbled. Jim came down on top of me. *"Ich liebe dich*, my funny face," he said in a soft voice I'd never heard before. Then he tried to tickle me. Of course I couldn't feel it through the heavy clothes, but still I jumped up and ran all the way back down the street with Jim chasing me. We went into the café and the old men at the tables looked up. I knew we were enviable with our youth and our love. Jim ordered a large piece of chocolate cake for me. "Don't worry about pounds," he said. "The more of you the better. I want you to be happy." And I was.

ALL THROUGH THE WINTER Jim wrote stories. Soon we began to mail them out to *The New Yorker*, to *Botteghe Oscure* in Rome, to the *Paris Review*. They were elegant, Mann-like stories. The snows came. Our apartment was so cold that when I had to get out of bed to cook I sometimes cried and whimpered and wondered if Gretchen had been frozen all her childhood. I thought often about Gretchen that winter—listening to the language of her homeland, looking at the piano legs of women in thick brown stockings who might be her mother carrying baskets of bread down the street. I was part of her. I was part-German. At Christmastime I saw the elaborate candles of my childhood in the store windows and the china angels with embroidered cloth wings that I had seen in Yorkville years before.

One afternoon just before the New Year I was trying to wash some dishes which had piled up in the tub, the only place in the apartment with hot water. I was frantic with the enormity of the stale stuck rotting food that clung to the plates, forgotten for too many days. Jim was at the university, where he had been asked to teach a class in William Saroyan and Thornton Wilder. (No German student wanted to read or discuss Mann or even Goethe or Schiller. They all spoke perfect English and they wanted copies of *Life* magazine. While we thought of ourselves as boors and innocents, characters from Henry James in search of cultural tradition, we were in fact the tail end of a conquering army. After tanks and Coca-Cola came Sinclair Lewis and Scott Fitzgerald. Sometimes I wasn't quite sure if we were students or colonizers.) The doorbell rang fiercely, as if it had been punched. I took a moment or two to dry my hands. Then there was a knocking on the door, the pounding of a fist, and I felt a memory jolting through me. I didn't quite know what it was. I didn't want to answer the door. There was more pounding. In movies I had heard that knock. I made myself go to the door and open it. I saw a tall, black-helmeted blond man with a black leather jacket and boots. I felt a wave of nausea. Memory had mixed with a fear I had been months suppressing and the SS man who stood before me was just the one I had always been expecting. I was on my knees heaving my fear into the toilet when I suddenly realized the youth in a black leather jacket was only the postman delivering a special-delivery letter from my mother with some extra money to have a good time on New Year's Eve. I was ashamed. The postman was my age or younger. He had been a baby when his father might have been knocking on doors to round up Jews. He was no more guilty than I, but his blue eyes, his Aryan nose, meant we were players in a game, hunted and hunter, and it was not, whatever Jim or logic said, the same as the Crusades or the Armenian massacre. There was between me and the leather-jacketed postman an eternal enmity that could erupt at any moment in disaster.

In February the first rejection slip crossed the Atlantic by air from *The New Yorker*. Mary and I had been out shopping. She stopped at every church and lit a candle. She was beginning a fever of guilt that would rise higher in the spring. She knew how to buy vegetables, how to cook veal and potatoes, and how to put a kitchen in order. "Put things back when you use them," she said; I needed her help, her advice, as I had never needed anything before. She envied my college education. She had had only secretarial training in high school, but I was beginning to see that the steps of humility of St. Bernard were not mere intellectual exercises and that if I was determined not to live my mother's dream I needed some skills they neglected to teach you in college. When she was trying on a dress, I held her baby and had a sudden sense of anxiety. Could Jim give me a baby? He would never want it. He would have to enter me and I didn't know if he could. This wasn't the time to think about babies. Now the day's main event was rushing down the four flights to the mailbox each morning hoping for good word from a distant publication. When I returned from the shopping trip I found Jim lying rigid in bed, staring at the ceiling and waving his hands rhythmically over his face. I saw the curt form letter: "We are sorry we cannot . . ." It could have been bordered in black; certainly I felt as if someone dear had died. "Don't come near me," he screamed as I attempted to hold his fluttering hands. I sat down quietly at the edge of the bed, rubbing my arms over my body to keep away the outer and inner cold. Finally he said, "I told you, I told you, and you've been pushing me and pushing me each day. You're driving me crazy." He was right. It was my fault. It was my certainty that he was good that forced him to the typewriter. What if I was wrong—if the balance between madman and artist had tipped and he was only an open sore of festering disconnections and irrelevancies? "All artists are rejected at first. If you were automatically, instantly accepted, you'd be a mediocrity. Hemingway was rejected by *The Saturday Evening Post*. Van Gogh, Degas . . ." I tried to reassure him. I knew he heard me and might find comfort in that later, but now he was over the edge of an unreachable desperation. "Give me money. Give me the traveler's checks. I'm going out on the town. I've got to go. I need champagne." He dressed quickly in his most elegant outfit. He looked so sad and beautiful, like a fighter pilot whose best friend has not returned from the last mission. He took so much money I was frightened. We would not have anything left till March, when the university and my mother came through again, but I couldn't, wouldn't, think of stopping him. I understood that he had to run to the bar with the same desperation one sometimes has to run to the bathroom. No amount of rational conversation would alter the urgency or ultimate destination of this trip.

I knew he was going to the cabarets where each table had a phone and you sat down and dialed a girl who was sitting alone at a table with a number prominently displayed. The girls were not always hookers. Some were looking for Americans to marry and some were just out for fun after a week of dreary work as file clerks or sales help. They all seemed tall and blonde, and though most had bad teeth or were missing some, they had a certain vitality I knew I had lost, as if I had become old at twenty-one, because I had a special mission, my own peculiar devotion. Jim went through the night, ending broke in a soldiers' bar where a fellow American punched him in the nose for reasons he didn't make clear to me. He came home at four in the morning with a strange, moldy, sad-eyed girl who hadn't expected to find me in the apartment. She spoke only pidgin English. She was, she told me, waiting for a G.I. in Arkansas to send her the money to join him. She had been waiting six months. Perhaps he had forgotten her. She shrugged. "Then I must find another one." They were both drunk, but Jim seemed wildly energetic. "Maria," he said, "come in the bedroom with me." They closed the door. I guessed he wasn't going to do much that I could be jealous about, but I felt betrayed, just as if we loved each other like the other Barnard girls and their boy friends. As if I had gotten pinned and married and was living in Scarsdale. I knew I had no right to be jealous or ashamed of my jealousy or ashamed that I couldn't comfort him better or ashamed that I didn't understand anything at all in this dawn where the sun was cold and pale on the dead winter grass of Bavariaring, and I wrote my name again and again in the winter frost on the glass pane. "I have survived," my name said, but I myself was not so sure as I heard Maria screaming in German, "Don't hit me, don't hit me." "Just a little. *Ein bisschen ist alles*," he was saying as, half-dressed, leaving her winter coat behind, she fled the room and the apartment, and raced down the four flights of stairs into the new morning, where she could forget but I couldn't. "Come, pretend you're being hit," he said, "just pretend." His eyes were bloodshot like an albino rabbit's, like the Mad Hatter's. He was in pain, and more than anything I had ever wanted before, I wanted to comfort him, so I pretended with self-conscious screams, and at last he came and fell asleep.

In the late afternoon when he woke I made fresh orange juice and fixed him eggs and sausages. I was beginning to get better with my hands. They were becoming useful hands, hands that made things, women's hands. It was better to be a cook than to be cooked for, of that I was certain. It was like the day after a funeral. A numb silence filled the space between us. I didn't dare suggest he go back to work yet but I knew that working was the only cure for the disruption that raged within. His long fingers, like a violinist's, I imagined, drummed against the table and his body under the heavy sweater that had been mine trembled with the cold. Why couldn't the *Wirtschaftswunder* heat an apartment properly?

A few days later he went back to work on a new story and our life returned to its proper, comfortable routine. Sometimes we went to Westerns with German subtitles. Often we went to Bob and Mary's and drank beer and talked all night. Sometimes we went to the theater, where, not understanding enough German, I would amuse myself by trying to decide who in the audience had been a member of the Nazi Party. We saw classic German plays, and Ibsen and Beckett, O'Neill and Saroyan, and a production of Lillian Hellman's *The Little Foxes*. Each day I rushed to the mailbox and then hesitated, wishing I had prayer to help, wishing I had magic to control the contents, and frightened always of what my hand would find inside.

After a few more rejections, at last in the early spring *Botteghe Oscure* sent an acceptance and a check for $50. I was wonderfully content. Jim was easy with himself for a few hours. We had dinner at an Indonesian restaurant. "Someday," I said, "we should go to the Far East." "Yes," he said, "we should travel to Hong Kong, Singapore. We should never be stuck, never be moored, but move all the time like gypsies." We who belonged nowhere should taste everything. I heard him say "we" and I was grateful as I had never been before. Later he took the check from *Bot-*

teghe Oscure and went out alone. I understood he wanted to celebrate. He needed room and freedom. I didn't want him to feel I was cramping him or hanging on too tight. He needed to enjoy his victory by himself. I went to sleep alone but happy. When I heard him come in I sat up just in time for the vomit to rain all over me and the sheets and the bedposts and the wallpaper, which would never be quite the same again. Some mixture of drinks had gone to the gut. His contractions lasted several hours. I held his head. I held him, shaking and screaming with pain. It seemed unfair for him to get sick on a triumphant night, but I knew fairness was not part of anything. I cleaned the floor again and again, nauseous myself from the retching and the odor. But I knew he would wake up all right and go on writing as he was meant to do.

The cold air came down through the mountain passes and the snow covered Bavariaring again and again. I learned from Mary how to make veal stuffed with apples and how to fry potatoes in yesterday's oil. I read *The Magic Mountain* in English and then tried to read it in German. I was learning more and more, and the sound of spoken German no longer made me think instantly of boxcars crowded with human beings. My landlady, whose two sons had died on the Russian front, brought Jim a bowl of beef broth when she found he was in bed with a cold. He sat in the bed with used tissues thrown everywhere, quoting passages of Spenser's *Faerie Queene*. He talked about getting TB and racked his chest in deep convulsions. I was a little worried but my sense of reality reassured me he was talking of TB only because he knew I was so involved with *The Magic Mountain*. He told me he preferred Naphta, whose world view was cold like the light of the most distant star. Did I agree with Jim that Settembrini was a fool, meant to be a fool? Sometimes, when Jim was sleeping curled up like a small boy, hand cupped protectively over his penis and eyes constantly flickering under the closed lids, restless even in sleep, I knew that my love was like an infection, an alien force that had possessed me. But maybe that was the nature of all love. Once, in the middle of the night, Jim woke, turned on the lights, and shook me. "I'm coughing blood. See, I told you," he said. "I'm coughing blood." And on his pillow was a large red stain, not a lumpy clot as I had expected, but certainly blood. The occupational disease of poets. I held him in my arms. "Whatever happens, I'll take care of you," I whispered to him. Would my mother give me the money for his medical care? I would steal it if she didn't. "We'll go to the doctor first thing in the morning. They have medicine now," I reassured him. He moaned and groaned and sneezed on me all through the night. In the morning he felt better, got up, shaved, and dressed for his class at the university. "But we have to go to a doctor," I said. His nasal passages had cleared. "Nonsense," he called to me from the bathroom. "You're a Jewish mother, a hypochondriac, get off my back." "But the blood on the pillow," I reasoned carefully. "Oh, that," he laughed, "just bleeding gums. I picked them last night before I woke you." I was relieved. It had just been a game. I waved goodbye from the window as I always did and then I wondered why I was almost disappointed that he didn't really have TB.

ON ASH WEDNESDAY in Munich it seemed as if all the city was smudged on the forehead. "Just wait for *Fasching*," Bob had told us earlier. "*Fasching* is the carnival season. In *Fasching* nothing anybody does counts. Even adultery is no grounds for divorce." Bob, of course, was still innocent of the playtimes that were tormenting Mary. "Anyone can be a fool. *Fasching* is time out of regular life." It sounded like the end of the world and I was eager to see it. The city authorities provided a special 4 a.m. trolley car, affectionately called the *Fasching* bus, and the conductors picked the drunks up off the sidewalks and took them home. The Kunsthaus, the modern-art museum, a postwar glass building, was the setting for the first night's *Fasching* costume ball. Everyone in the city who could pay the three-mark admission was invited. The music was heavy German renditions of American popular songs, while burghers in peasant dress and a variety of other costumes, which appeared to be a mixture of Halloween and Purim, clumped on the dance floor. Jim and I found a table with Bob and Mary. Soon Mary's window dresser, Johann, joined us, looking morose in a pirate's hat and earring. Bob and Jim had refused to wear costumes. Philosophers, they had agreed, observe but don't join in play. Mary and I wore cowboy hats. Beer and cheap champagne flowed. The mayor made a speech I didn't understand too well. It seemed to be about love. A student in one of Bob's classes came by. Her name was Renate von Schrag. She was blonde and tall and had eyes like blue steel. She wore a rhinestone tiara and claimed she was costumed as a Swedish princess. Jim asked her to dance and I went on smiling bravely. Bob lit his pipe and watched as Mary and Johann disappeared on the dance floor. Did he care? I wondered.

Gerhart Keller came to our table. He was also tall and blond, an Aryan of Aryans. He had been in the Hitler Youth and at seventeen was made an officer and sent to battle in France. He was too enthusiastic a soldier and within the first ten minutes of combat had been seriously wounded and taken prisoner. When the Americans brought him to the field hospital he refused to be operated

on because the surgeon, with what I suppose was under-
standable sadism, had told this perfect specimen that he,
the doctor, was Jewish and the anesthetist was Jewish and
the nurse was Jewish. Gerhart was operated on against his
wishes and sent to Nevada to a POW camp, where he was
indoctrinated in democracy. The result was that he loved
American students, loved to practice his English, and late
at night would tell you how Germany had destroyed its
finest talent by ridding itself of Jews. Although older than
we, Gerhart was always looking for something, asking
Bob and Jim deep questions about religion and art. There
was something touching in the puzzled look in his eyes. It
wasn't just bombed-out cities that needed to be rebuilt—
the interiors of minds had also been reduced to rubble.
Gerhart asked me to dance. Balloons tied to light fixtures
were all over the ceiling. Crepe paper and confetti were
being thrown about by middle-age women. Gerhart
started to do a rhumba with me. "In the summer," he
said, "I will take you to the top of the mountains and pick
flowers for you to wear in your hair. I'm sorry," he said,
"about what I asked. The war," he said, looking away.
"You are not supposed to atone during *Fasching*, you're
supposed to atone later," I said. Gerhart pulled me close.
"I will catch a trout in my bare hands for you. You will
see." I suddenly felt slightly dizzy from the beer and the
heat and the large number of people dancing to the loud,
heavy music. An older fat man bumped into Gerhart, who
turned around to demand an apology. The fat man began
to back off, but a crowd surged around us. Someone
shoved me and I tripped over the feet of the people behind
me. I fell to the hard marble floor and there was a lot of
blood and my front tooth was hanging by a thread. I
jumped to my feet. Jim and Renate came by. As I rushed
by to the ladies' room, Jim called to me, "I always knew

you were the kind of girl who falls down at the dance." Gerhart followed me and waited outside while I tried to clean up and stop the bleeding. Then he took me home. On the way, he gave me the name of his dentist. Then he told me that the greatest crime of the war was when the American soldiers came to Darmstadt and took the German flag and cut it in pieces and made bathing trunks out of it—loincloths of the flag—and then went swimming. "That was so insensitive," he said. Didn't I agree? I didn't, though in a way I envied Gerhart, because he had some magic that had worked at least for a while, whereas I had never expected very much in the way of spiritual comfort. My mouth was swollen and sore. In Mann's stories all the artists have bad teeth, bluish and thin. It's a sign of their difference from the healthy burghers' world. Now I would have not merely bad teeth but a false one. Not a symbol of inner decay or weakness, but an empty space, a false front.

When we got home, Gerhart asked to come in with me. "It's *Fasching*," he said, "and what happens between us tonight doesn't count—not to your Jim, not to God, not to anyone." Nothing counts at any time, I thought to myself. No one is keeping score. I thought of Jim dancing under the balloons with Renate. They looked beautiful together, like the blonde Inge and Hans from *Tonio Kröger*. I allowed him to follow me in. He guided me into the bedroom I shared with Jim. Gerhart reached over and kissed me hard on the mouth. His big head crashed onto mine and I felt more blood in my mouth. I swallowed and with the swallow I lost my tooth. After I had mopped up the blood on my lips and his, we began kissing again. When he undressed me I began to cry, but I continued to ache with physical yearning. "It's *Fasching*," he said. "It doesn't count." But the sharp erotic spasms made me sad even though it was Fasching. Gerhart was awakening feelings I wanted to share with Jim. Without Jim I felt like a blind beggar's cup, empty of coin, shaking in another's hand.

I had no protection, since I needed none from Jim's spilled sperm. I didn't want Gerhart's baby; in fact, I didn't want Gerhart. My erotic feelings, so used to being dormant, seemed to have submitted themselves to the discipline of my mind so well that they now were mere echoes of pleasure. Inside me he squirmed and pushed. I was disconnected. The Germans can conquer the body but not the spirit. It was a drama all right but I was in the audience. He came outside me, considerate and disciplined. I liked him better for that, but the truth was that pictures of Jim playing at Don Juan with Renate were always at the edge of my mind, and ordinary human fucking seemed pale and unimportant in the Fauves canvas of my fascination with Jim.

When Gerhart at last went home I was glad, and I began the long wait for Jim, who would only have pretended to seduce Renate. It was a bluff, for Bob, for himself. If he was really forced to go through with it, he would have found some way to back off. I was sure of that, but still—despite what I had done with Gerhart—I was a knot of jealous tension staring down the street, listening for the sound of a taxi, for footsteps on the deserted cobblestones. I heard a taxi, and relieved, I felt every muscle relax. But it stopped down the street. I went on with my vigil. At last I saw him staggering across Bavariaring. Looking like an upright eel, he weaved across the meadow toward our house. "Hurry," I nearly screamed aloud. I knew that if he wanted to see Renate again, in or out of *Fasching*, I would have to accept it. Possessiveness would drive him away—so would competition with a more functional man. I decided never to tell him about Gerhart. Only understanding and quiet, as with a wild deer in the tangled forest, would get the creature to come close and take some food from the open hand.

When I returned from the first of many sessions with Gerhart's dentist the next day, I learned that Mary had disappeared with Johann that first ball of *Fasching*, to begin the drama that absorbed all our energy the last few months we spent in Munich. Mary had finally confessed to Bob early that morning that she and Johann had been having what she claimed were beautiful, orgiastic afternoons of sex in the bedroom she and Bob shared while the babies took their naps in the same room. Mary had hoped that Bob would be angry, then forgive her, demand that she set matters right at confession, and forget it. But Bob, the mustached, pot-bellied student of Hegel, responded by going to the bathroom, vomiting and continuing to vomit for three days. We came to see him and he told us it made him sick to think of Johann's penis entering the same space through which his children were born. He said that he would never again be able to sleep with Mary. He told her that since they were Catholic they were married forever, but that the sexual part of their relationship was permanently over; then he fell silent. I was amazed at how romantic he was. I wished someone cared so primitively about the comings and goings of my genital activity. Jim was amused by the story. He took Bob out on the town, on one of his drinking binges. Jim bought a special notebook in order to record the story, which he intended to write some day. I spent hours watching the children, happy when I thought some passerby on the street might think they were mine, while Mary went from church to church, confessing and confessing, asking advice from one secluded priest after another. They all said the same discouraging thing: "You have sinned, my daughter, go back to your husband and be a good wife." We walked from one end of Munich to another, looking for a church we might have missed, one that might give a more satisfactory answer.

Mary grew pale. The children were getting wilder each day. Sometimes she forgot to feed them or to change their diapers, and one day the younger one smeared feces on the wall. Mary began to meet Johann secretly in our apartment. "Flaubert is not the only writer who can deal with an Emma Bovary," said Jim, making me promise to tell him everything that occurred between them while he was at the university.

It was hard for me to understand how it all had happened so quickly. At college girls were pinned and then they changed their minds and grieved in their rooms a day or so and then were pinned to someone else. Or a Yale or Dartmouth boy found himself straying and broke up with his girl and heartbreak lasted a few weeks, but it seemed like a moment in which the change of partners was a natural part of the dance and the pain gave you something to moan about with your moaning friends. And then all of a sudden it had become so serious, so eternal, so damaging. The little children, who now looked like waifs or refugees, showed that the game had a deadly side. The hard edges of one's life, the box of one's own design, were made so quickly, before we really were ready, before we understood what was happening. Mary and I agreed that our childhoods had not been long enough.

While waiting for Johann to come on his lunch hour (the children asleep on our couch, each with a bottle and a diaper that reeked of good use), I was tempted to tell her about Jim, how our relationship was a total fraud. We were not living in sin; we were married in a legal sense but not in the real sense—the kind that makes babies. I wanted to tell her. She confessed so much and I confessed so little, but I was too ashamed, and at the time understood my shame so little that I swallowed it down, to go on talking about her seemingly hopeless problem.

While Bob was swearing a lifetime of chastity, a monk-hood caused by a betrayal he couldn't forgive, Mary could not give up Johann, whose appeal seemed to lie in his sexual organ. One spring day Mary had an appointment with an ecclesiastical lawyer, a priest, whom she had found through the diocese phone directory. "Do you really think," I asked her on the way to the cathedral, "that you'll burn in hell if you get a divorce?" "I might," she said and her hands shook with fear. "I don't believe you could believe that. It seems so irrational," I said. Mary looked at me blankly. We had grown through the winter to love and depend on one another, but the differences between us seemed like a wide, alligator-filled moat. While she was inside, I waited in the nearby park with the children, filling a water pistol again and again from the fountain. "*Tot, tot,*" yelled Stephen, shooting his little sister in the head. She cried and I held her on my lap. Mary came out of the cathedral subdued, ghostly pale. "He said that because I didn't have sixteen weeks of bridal training, only four, he can arrange an annulment in Rome on the grounds that we were never properly married. I suppose," she said, "he's trying to help." It took Mary another few weeks to be able to tell me that if the rule of eternal marriage was bendable, skirtable, avoidable, then the entire structure of the religious prison, as she called it, could be knocked over with a feather. So she knocked it over and moved into Johann's apartment with the two kids and seemed happy and content and never mentioned burning in hell again. Now she talked about their plans to go to New York.

Bob would come to see us and sit puffing on his pipe as his sad eyes grew weaker and more watery. "If I lose my children," he said, "I lose everything." We were not quite prepared for what happened next. One night not long afterward he brought to dinner Ursula, the assistant window dresser who worked with Johann. Ursula was a plump girl who seemed to believe in serving men, not in talking to them. She had the secret, shy smile of someone who still hopes for good things from this world. Soon after, Ursula moved in with Bob, and she, too, became a part of our life as the religious drama subsided. I was beginning to learn that even disasters had rhythms. They built, they peaked, and they diminished as new adjustments were made. I had expected life to be more literary; in books climaxes were final and epilogues were explanations, not new starts.

I realized that I still did not understand very much of what was happening between Jim and me. I was reading *Buddenbrooks*. In it the decay of the family's psychological and financial fortunes resulted in a small boy whose sensitivities were extraordinary but whose physical and mental capacities to survive were doubtful. I thought of Jim. As a child, he, too, must have been like a raw nerve, conducting, attracting too much truth. If only I could change the inevitable ending. If love could redeem his suffering and release the wellspring of his talent, I would provide it. It was all I wanted for myself, to be the greenhouse in which the orchid, the cross-bred, prize-winning, original orchid could grow to full magnificence.

Late in the school year Jim had stopped going to classes. "I am a writer, not a philosopher," he said. "If I'm not a famous writer in two years, I will not allow myself to live. I will not accept a mediocre life. I will not teach logic to high-school students. I will be a Nobel Prize winner or nothing but dust." It frightened me to hear that. The distance between his present anonymity and the Nobel Prize seemed as impossibly far as the light of the Russian sputnik we had all gathered by the demolished war museum in Goethestrasse to track in the sky one fall night. "You will have whatever you want," I said, stroking his back. We had evolved a sweet kind of intimacy that I valued greatly, often rubbing and kissing like kittens in a litter. This was separate from the less frequent erotic sexual moments, which continued in the pattern that had been established from the beginning: Jim, drunk and depressed, bringing himself to orgasm, while I, at a distance, enacted his fantasy of humiliation. My nine-month marriage was still unconsummated, and it amused me to think how little my case would have exercised the ingenuity of Mary's ecclesiastical lawyer.

A little magazine in England named *Albatross* accepted another of the stories for $25. It looked as if the future were golden sunlight; nothing but admiration for my orchid lay ahead.

That spring I wrote my mother long letters. I was sorry for her in a new way. She probably had wanted to be someone else, almost anyone else, but the trap once sprung released no one, and like a hamster in a cage she had no control over her fate. No wonder she sometimes bit at fingers that came near. I agreed to let her give me a large party for all her friends when we returned from Europe. Jim agreed when I explained that we would get lots of silver and pots and pans and vases and other useful things.

It was just as well that we were leaving. I had had enough of Europe. Day after day, I hitchhiked to the PX on the edge of town and ate hamburgers and read *Time* and *Life* and *Newsweek* and the European edition of the *Herald-Tribune*. I wanted to go home. I had been a venturesome innocent abroad for as long as I could, and now I needed to go back home.

The fellowship money was coming to an end. In New York I would get a job and support Jim until the three cherries showed in the slot-machine. I missed my mother, whose face I sometimes could hardly remember. I knew she would help me find an apartment, furnish it, provide theater tickets, buy me new clothes, and help me get a job. First, of course, she would have to pay for typing lessons so that I might be employable. I had left America with more innocence than I was bringing back, but in retrospect it seems clear that I hadn't aged or ripened as much as might have been hoped. I had remained a large baby, only now I had attached to myself a still larger baby. To the outsider everything seemed in order; there was nothing unusual to be seen in the Weiss family. I was doing my part to keep up appearances.

MY MOTHER had hired a decorator for our new apartment on Central Park West. Jim especially liked the French provincial desk; when it arrived, he stood behind it speaking streams of French, playing Cardinal Richelieu. I clapped and laughed and playfully pounced on him. When Amanda came to see us, she was overwhelmed by the apartment's elegance and ashamed of her gift of plastic dishes. Then I, too, was ashamed and we sat about awkwardly. I told her I was going to get a job until Jim earned enough by his writing to support us. In New York I wore my wedding ring. Jim didn't mind. He didn't even mind the reception for 250 people my family gave us at the Hotel Pierre. He danced with me, holding me close, whispering, "How much did we get? How much are the people right behind you worth to us?" His vulgarity matched my mother's. The joke was on me (though I could not see it quite so clearly at the time): I had not traveled far from her after all. But I was so grateful that he seemed to accept our marriage, now a year old, that I labeled his interest in our gifts a kind of demonic cunning, an artist's prerogative, not mere greed—a splitting of hairs that would certainly have pulverized the hair. On the dance floor he again quoted the John Donne poem he had claimed as his own the first night we met. He now admitted that he had thought I was incredibly dumb not to have recognized it. "Go, and catch a falling star." We danced among the roses. It seemed to me that I was becoming more graceful.

My father danced with me that night—a cold, upright, handsome man, pleased that appearances were being maintained, that all was right in his life. His wife, his daughter, his mistresses, all well dressed, were here, bobbing among the red and white flowers. His tennis and squash games were still good, and if his investments were sometimes shaky, his wife's financial cushion would protect him from the effects of a fall. His daughter—still a little dumpy, her eyes clouded by shyness, a strange creature—wasn't exactly what he would have wanted. Too much education. But all right, married to a good-looking boy. He must have wondered what Jim got from me. His son had an exam the next day at the theological seminary and didn't come to the party. A rabbi for a son. My father grimaced. His daughter was looking at him so intensely he suggested they stop dancing and go to the bar for a drink.

I was looking at him, thinking how much I wanted to love him, to play tennis with him in the late afternoon and have him admire my game. How much I had wanted to hold on to his hand and have him really worry about which camp I went to, to care and notice and stay up at night thinking about whether I should take Latin or French. I had wanted an attentiveness I even then knew was impossible. Like a wax figure my father moved about the floor, his eyes never connecting with mine. When he went to the bathroom, he flushed himself all away. When he perspired on the tennis court, he sweated himself all away. When he looked for himself to sit down with his little girl, he just wasn't there, and it was a pity that only the appearance remained. I remembered a Christmas night before I left home for college, after the relatives had left and the glut of presents were open—the silver, red, and green boxes like empty shells abandoned on the beach by avaricious gulls—and the tinsel and the pine swept from the hall floor by the maid (who didn't have Christmas Day off) and the endless pile of sweaters from Saks, belts from Bonwit's, gloves, hats from Bergdorf's, robes, gowns put away in drawers, and my mother lying in bed drinking her fourth Scotch of the day. We all felt the pall from expectations that had turned brittle and hard—the unsatisfactory aftertaste of material glut, as if we were sieves through which gold charms, velour shirts, suède gloves flowed without ever filling or plugging the holes. By five in the afternoon we needed something else. "Let's go out for a Chinese dinner," said my mother brightly. "For Christ's sake," said my father, "haven't you had enough?" He wanted to go for a long walk alone and shake off the depression, the beginnings of a migraine that came from a day encaged in the bosom of his family. If he walked briskly enough in the cold air he might, he thought, leave his shadow behind in the hall where the flickering Christmas tree lights were reflected blue and red on the carefully waxed floor. He had no memories of Christmas. His parents had forgotten the Jewish holidays in their rush to Americanize, but they hadn't adopted the strangers' ways either. It seemed to him a mockery, as if the lights on the tree, like that snobbish salesman at Saks, were laughing at him, seeing through the vicuña coat and the monogrammed shirt to the origins of struggle across the ocean, as if the tree lights blinking on and off shone into the empty corners of his mind, exposing the lack of furniture, memory, or connection. "All right," he said, "if that's what you want, that's what we'll do." Isaac-Irwin had spent the day in his room boycotting the celebration. He wouldn't open any of the presents unknowing aunts and uncles had brought. He covered himself with his silk tallith, and when I opened the door to his room to sing "Deck the halls with boughs of holly," he put a pillow over his head and shouted at me to stop. But now he agreed to come out and accompany us to the Chinese restaurant, though, of course, he wouldn't eat anything there but the vegetables and tea. I was glad he was coming, although with his young adolescent fuzz on round cheeks and pudgy belly, with dark circles under his eyes, he looked like the ghost of Christmases spent in ghettos where Santa Claus flew over the rooftops without stopping and the three wise men knew better than to linger.

At the restaurant, up a flight of stairs in the East Forties, a waiter showed us to a table in the center of the room. Christmas bulbs from the five-and-ten decorated the chandeliers. The smells of wonton, moo shoo, and egg roll floated about the dining room. "There's not enough light here," said my father. "It's nice, it's intimate," said my mother. "Smells greasy," said my father, who never ate anything that wasn't lean and dry and spare. Isaac-Irwin looked at the ceiling. He looked at the floor. "What are you reading in English class?" I asked him. "Mind your own beeswax," he said. "Until you believe in God there's nothing you read will make any sense to you." "I don't know why I have to pay to have fat poured down my throat," complained my father. "Enter into the spirit of things," my mother began, a familiar edge to her voice. "It's a holiday. Be cheerful for the children." "When do I get a holiday?" said my father. "Now look," said my mother, "I know what your idea of a holiday is and it doesn't include anyone else." My brother absently began to pick at the largest pimple on his chin. I interrupted with an attempt at diversion. "It's been such a nice Christmas," I said. "I wish every day were Christmas." "You just want to get things. Gimme, gimme, that's all you can think of," said my father, his voice rising and the customers at other tables turning around to stare. "When are you going to grow up and stop being a parasite, a big mouth that stuffs itself?" "She didn't mean anything," said my mother, the beginning of a shriek in her voice. My brother pushed his plate nervously from side to side. "Whatever I give you," said my father, "is not good enough. You always want more." Heads were turning to stare. I continued to eat, mixing the mustard with the duck sauce in neat little pools. "You had your goddamn family around you all day. What more do you want?" "I want," said my mother, tears glistening over the mascara that had already begun its wanderings over her face, "I want a little bit of human kindness." "I am kind," roared my father. "If once you'd stop attacking me, you'd see I am kind. You're too dumb to know when you're being treated well." "You're arguing," said my mother. "I am not," said my father. "You're spoiling Christmas dinner," said my mother. "I am not arguing," said my father. "You are fighting with me." "Am I at fault or is he?" said my mother, turning to me. "Who started it?" "Be honest," said my father. "Nobody started it," I said. "Why are you asking her?" said my brother. "Only boys, only men can be judges." "She knows when your mother acts stupid just as well as you do," said my father. "Any moron can tell that." "If I were a lawyer," said my mother, taking careful aim, "I'd be a judge by now, or have some clients really worth something, not just the peddlers and pushcart jerks you work for." My brother took off his glasses and was wiping them with his napkin when my father, indifferent to the new velvet dress I was wearing, to the sanctity of the holidays, to the spirit of kinship, to the staring eyes around him, took the tablecloth and pulled it up, spilling moo shoo, water chestnuts, pea pods, hot tea, glazed shrimp, and little pieces of diced pork in every possible direction. Everyone in the restaurant was watching. My brother's glasses, caught in the tangle, lay broken on the floor. Only some of the thick plates stained by too many washings seemed to remain unbroken. The waiters were rushing around, my mother was trying to put powder on her tear-stained nose. My father had left the restaurant. There on the floor in the mustard cup was a $50 bill he had thrown down. I was grateful for it. On the way home in the taxi I kept reassuring myself that it had not in fact been my fault.

I held on to Jim in the reception line. He was more than just an appearance, he was a magnificent, even brilliant presence. Now I see it all as a farce, but it didn't seem like farce at the time. Then it seemed wonderful. I kissed relatives on the cheeks without a twinge of conscience. Their lives had secrets too.

I FOUND A JOB as a receptionist in a doctor's office. It paid only $65 a week and we were always broke. In the daytime Jim worked on his novel about our time in Munich; nights he went out to drink. He also developed a passion for pool and gambled on cards and horses with whatever extra money he could find. I pawned the silver we were

given as a wedding gift. I pawned soup tureens and platters. I stole ashtrays and cigarette lighters from my parents' house. I didn't really mind at night when I was
alone, typing the novel. We kissed and cuddled; he called
me his *"petite chose,"* and the bed we shared, though not
erotic, became a place of safety and warmth for us both.

After a while I became good at answering the phone,
relaying messages correctly. I could file well enough and
didn't mind the typing of a letter or two that came my
way. I enjoyed the other girls in the office. I relaxed over a
cup of coffee in the ladies' room with them. I was the
keeper of the key to the toilet. I had grown used to the
Muzak-filled elevators and the halls with glass windows
and gray carpets. I had become resigned to thinking of
myself as stale lemon-meringue pie in the Horn and Har-
dart slot, waiting for someone to drop in a coin and release
me from the glass prison. I had friends at work, and my
friends had interesting dates or crabby fathers or mothers
with hysterectomies, or bad childhoods of one sort or another, and we talked it all over at lunch, in the bathrooms
and the crowded elevators.

In a few months the novel was finished and we sent it to
Thomas Mann's American publisher. When it was turned
down later, I was ready for the enormous drunken binge,
recriminations that came and went. Then he sent the
novel out again. After another two months it was accepted.

Following a long and anxious wait of many months,
punctuated by swings of manic hope and despair, the book
was in the stores. Surprisingly enough, it was an immedi-
ate success. The first favorable reviews of *After Ludwig* and
the editor's excited calls and the insistent ringing of the
phone and the requests for interviews made us realize that
we had won. Jim Morrison was no longer a name like any

other but now belonged to a "promising," "talented," "highly gifted," "remarkable," "fluid," "Mann-like" writer who was going to make his way to the top of any list of the newest and brightest and most newsworthy of young writers in America. It seemed like a miracle, but I had always known it would happen. *After Ludwig* described the end of Bob and Mary's marriage. It became a parable of postwar Europe, as Johann was gradually Americanized and the philosophy student Bob was reduced to emotional, existential chaos. Mary was described as the biblical Eve whose impulsive sexuality signaled civilization's decay. The sexual scenes between Mary and Johann were written with such heat and passion that, reading them, I was weak with arousal and amazed that Jim could know so much. I was impressed with his art.

Jim was buoyant and exhilarated. He bought himself a green velvet jacket and a new, more expensive pair of dark glasses. My mother took us to dinner. It was gratifying that the fruit of art was the same as the fruit of manufacturing. It became in the end hard cash, and Jim appreciated and shared my mother's pleasure in the rewards. Baked Alaska and *crêpes cerises* arrived for dessert and my mother announced that she had bought Jim a diamond tie pin because the reviews were so good. Boss Jim, riverboat gambler, unwrapped the diamond from the Tiffany box. He stood up, tall, angular, brown eyes like chips of the Rocky Mountains, blond hair straight and soft. Oddly, he looked to me more and more like Bad Jim, the gangster, who got paid off every other Friday for deeds he didn't talk about with his wife or girl friend. After dinner we walked back to our apartment, arms around each other, enjoying the peace of the moment and the rewards of fame. Suddenly Jim said, "She could've gotten a bigger diamond. This one's the smallest she could get away with,

I'm sure." I was numb with a new knowledge and a new fear. Nothing would ever be enough. His soul was not, after all, like a pool that had filled with contentment but, rather, like a sieve. His needs would increase, and no diamond would ever be big enough for the boy from Bay Ridge whose doubts were as big as the Ritz and whose ambitions made the pyramids look like anthills. In his green velvet jacket and his dark glasses and his diamond pin (even if it was small), he looked like a many-splendored thing, like a bird of pleasure, a Chinese emperor's peacock. Beside him I looked like a city pigeon. At the entrance of our apartment house he said good night to me and went off down the street into a night of drinking, now at a bar with literary friends and their girls. He was entitled to enjoy his reputation and he needed to flaunt his colors without the dreariness of a wife, a domestic burden he had never really asked for. The donkey that carried Mary into Jerusalem was left behind when she entered the gates of heaven and was placed among the jewels of God.

I couldn't help feeling disappointed. I had been counting on success to cure the sexual malaise—to turn his attention away from alcohol, away from the running sores of childhood, and to bring him to an appreciation of my soul, which after all lived in my body. I dimly understood my body needed attentions it just wasn't getting. After the success, the vindication of my literary taste, I began eating more and more. I couldn't understand why just when I should be totally happy I was continually gaining weight. I decided he needed more time and more substantial success. I never mentioned to him my unfulfilled hopes. I was still afraid of driving him away.

Now there were interviews on radio and television and invitations to literary parties. A spread in a fashion magazine included Jim among a group of young writers photographed jumping out of boxes, each with his name on the lid. But Jim was not at all reassured by the publicity and the praise. Now he was churning in a new kind of storm: was his success a fluke, a mistake; would he be able to do it again? He was also jealous, angered, whenever another writer was mentioned or written about. "You're the best," I would say. "But then how come they put that incompetent on the show?" he would complain, and become silent and morose and wave his hands before his unseeing eyes in that strange, disturbing way of his. All this no matter how many new friends we made and how wanted we were. My mother's friends all invited us for drinks. Everyone asked us to dinner. We now knew people whose names had been part of the magic of the grownup world we thought we could never enter. It was hard to believe that they were real, people with lines in their faces and hands that trembled and dim memories of when success had first hit them. "What is it like to be married to such a brilliant man?" I'd be asked, and I would smile and say nothing. I would reach for another hors d'oeuvre. At home, when he was home, Jim was not so brilliant, anxiously demanding of me, "Why wasn't my name in print once this week?"

Amanda was proud of him and kept a scrapbook of all his clippings. But when she suffered a colitis attack and was in the hospital for a few weeks, Jim refused to go see her. "She's boring," he said, "and I hate hospitals. I won't be able to work if I go. I'll be too upset." The conditions that made it possible for him to work were of course the decisive factors of how we arranged our days. After work I would get some flowers and movie magazines and take the subway to Brooklyn to the small hospital where Amanda lay in a room with three other women. We had nothing to talk about, aside from her grandson, and I repeated everything wonderful that had been said and written about him. Then we would watch television, and then around eight o'clock I would take the subway home. Jim would be gone by the time I got there. I'd be so exhausted that I was almost glad not to have to listen to him read his day's work or hear about rivalries that a few months before had not even existed. The thing we had in common, Amanda and I, was an obsessive, total interest in Jim. I foresaw myself hospitalized, an old woman with white kinky hair, and knew that Jim, even an aged, arthritic Jim, would never bring me flowers or sit and watch television with me. I would probably have been forgotten long before. I began to think about having a baby, a child.

On Saturdays we would make trips to bookstores. Jim would stay outside, casually looking in the window, and I would ask the clerk for a copy of *After Ludwig*. Then I would pretend I'd left my wallet at home and promise to return later to make the purchase. If his book had not been prominently displayed, I would surreptitiously take a few copies and place them on top of other novels, blotting rivals from view. There seemed no end to this game. Jim could keep going for hours, watching me thumb through the pages of a book I knew so well.

Jim complained all the time that his success was an illusion, that he would be put in his place with the next novel. His mood was as black as before he'd been published. It was hard to understand.

Jim would often sit in the bathtub for hours, soaking out the booze of the night before. He would push the soap around, pretending it was a battleship that he would torpedo with the washcloth. As I watched discreetly at a distance through the half-open door, I was touched by these childhood games played and replayed in privacy. How amazing to be a little boy—"Bang-bang, got 'em, guillotine the villain, red blood splashing skyward from the severed vein in the neck, garrot the criminal, Adam's apple turning black, spittle running from the dry corners of the mouth— Ack, ack, ack" (the sound of a comic-book childhood), wipe out a company of soldiers or a covey of tanks, and again and again let the fires of death burn wide across the imagination. Everyone knows little boys are made of puppy dogs' tails, snake eyes, pig shit, mice turds, stomach bile, and nose boogies. They can't help themselves.

One morning I secretly looked at the soapy water rippling over his penis, like a sunken ship in shallow Caribbean waters, hiding a treasure he didn't give me. His long, thin body was pale white, as if the sun had never shone in Bay Ridge, as if his blood, aristocratic and blue, had thinned to the color of a late afternoon's winter sky. His blond hair hung limp just above his thin shoulders, scholar's shoulders, saint's shoulders, a ballet dancer's shoulders, delicate like the Chinese porcelain figures in my mother's living room. Now he lay back and closed his eyes, hands twisting in the water—Narcissus in the pool waiting for some unexpected experience. I gathered from his incantations he was waiting for the goddess of fame to appear before him. Then he spoke for her in a high falsetto. "You, Jim Morrison, Jim, Jim, Jim Morrison, have been singled out for global recognition, for worship from those you most respect as well as from those you hold in contempt. You will have Tiffany cigarette cases and gold-handled canes, invitations to the inner sanctums, to universities and royal palaces and Hollywood bashes. You will be admired for the brilliance in your eyes, the white of your skin, and for your brain tissue, the finest of its kind. Women will lust for you, men writhe in jealousy when your name is mentioned, and you'll be on the cover of

Time, and *Life* and *Look.*" The goddess he described in a narrator's voice picked up the small flaccid penis that was twining downward as if to hide from her stare. "And this dear shriveled abused organ, part of so special a man, will learn to stand erect on all occasions"—so much worldly love might bring it to attention. The Goddess of Fame, he declared, had feet of coin and the bathtub was filling with silver and gold as she wiggled her toes. "Stay, stay, I want you," Jim cried as the goddess (like the visions that came to poor peasant girls in the fields and orchards of Europe) obviously faded away. Jim's long fingers touched his penis. It was still there. Dimly, without conscious knowledge, he recognized that fame, even utmost total fame, would never heal that particular wound in himself, a longing for an impossible peace. "Marjorie, Marjorie," he screamed. "Bring a drink in here, right away," and I tiptoed off so he wouldn't know I had seen what I thought my devotion entitled me to see. When I approached the bathroom with Scotch in hand, I heard him talking again to this Goddess of Fame he had conjured. This time she must have been scowling at him. "You think you've got a chance to keep me, you skinny kid from Bay Ridge with hickeys on your ass, with balls made of oatmeal and a prick of cottage cheese." Then, in the tone of Dickens or Thackeray, he described to an audience he didn't think was there how the goddess pulled up her long white robes and squatted above the bathtub. "That's what I think of you, " he said again in the goddess's falsetto, describing how a soft long brown fecal spiral hung above him, suspended for a second, caught in the goddess's tense anal contraction, only to fall splashing into the tub, Jim yelling, "Don't let it fall, don't let it fall. Marjorie, I want my drink." Fame faded, temptress, taunter, tease, his heartless love, whom he loved as I loved him.

I came home from work one day to find him lying on the bed, waving his hands in front of his face. "Do you know," he said, "Thomas Mann had already written two novels by the time he was my age. Today I feel I could go out the window or push you out the window." He sat up and the color returned to his face. He got up, went to the window, and opened it wide. The satin curtains billowed out, and the room suddenly became cold. "Look," I said in a thin voice, "you need help, more help that I can give you." I could feel the six-story drop in the pit of my stomach. If he was serious, I wouldn't be able to stop him from throwing himself or me out the window. It was also possible, likely, that he was only making my adrenalin flow and my hands shake for the theater of it, that afterward he would apologize for scaring me. He couldn't bear the everydayness of everyday. The food, the TV, the desk, and the paper in the same place. Even his nightly drinking bouts had taken on a routine quality as frightening to him as a shroud or a winding sheet. "Look," he said, putting his head way out the window, "no one cares what happens to me." "I care," I screamed, knowing that my caring meant nothing. He needed beautiful actresses, famous publishers, international bankers to care. I was only a receptionist, a maker of appointments, a sender of bills and insurance forms, a woman who ordered her lunch at the corner delicatessen (one BLT down, two ham on rye to go). I was only his mirror and a mirror doesn't keep anyone from jumping out a window. As I looked at his back, tensed like a trapeze artist about to take a swing into space, I felt a curious surge of excitement. My nipples stood up and under my pubic mound there was a gurgling and a groaning, a pressing and a pulling that could only be sexual desire. "Make love to me," I said. "You might like it." He slammed the window shut and came away from it.

His face was white as a Kabuki mask. He sat down on the edge of the bed, put a cigarette in the ebony cigarette holder my mother had given him, lit it, and glared at me. "I am a man," he said, "who knows Spinoza, Hegel, and Heidegger. I can quote any passage of Shakespeare. I can deal with the work of Russell and Wittgenstein. The flowers of civilization. And you ask me to behave like any ordinary animal, to copulate with you as if I were just a plumber with a hose hanging between my legs. I thought you were more spiritual, more complicated than that. What do you want, to be laid every night like any woman with curlers in her hair and a flowered robe from the five-and-ten? The great accomplishments of civilization come from beating down the sexual impulses. You've read Augustine, haven't you?" I had, I wasn't sure that my impulses were tawdry and ordinary—possibly they were legitimate. After all, the world would end without such impulses, but at the time I would never have thought of challenging him. I even knew it was his madness, not his logic, speaking, but I didn't want to lose him—risk a confrontation which might drive him away. His hands started to flutter in front of his face and I felt helpless.

I knew that now he wouldn't talk to me again for a while. He drank so much every night and was in so much pain every day that he played with games of suicide and murder. I knew he needed a doctor. He needed more than I could give to ease the tension that seemed to be pushing him closer and closer to madness. If the artist patrols the electrified barbed-wire fence, the border between insanity and reason, then it seemed to me he was wandering away from his post, deeper into his madness, where I knew he would be tortured in ways more terrible than his present reality and where he would be lost to me, finally, totally. I knew I just had to get him to a doctor. First I had to get the money. Could I confess to my mother: "Jim needs a psychoanalyst. Will you pay for it?" I could just see her bitter smile turning in at the corners, exposing the lipstick-smudged, tobacco-stained teeth. "You had to go your own way," she would crow. "You didn't think a businessman with a future was good enough for you, and now here you are begging for money so we can send your lunatic to the doctor." Eventually, I expected, she would give it to me, but first I would have squirmed on my belly in the deep pile of her turquoise carpet and repented and repented my escape from the golf club, the dancing schools, the secure and comfortable world where maids brought breakfast in on trays and women could concentrate full time on decorating their empty spaces. I would have to apologize for sneering at her canasta-playing friends, for the sloppiness of my dress. But, in the end, she would pay for Jim to see a doctor because she was a part of me. I was a part of her. I was a tumor in her gut and she couldn't ignore the spasms I caused. I had no other way to get the money. Did Amanda perhaps have it somewhere, hidden in a box, in a vault? If she did, would she understand? I could see the hurt look that would come into her soft violet eyes. "What's wrong with Jim? He seems just dandy to me." A dozen pills through the day for her arthritis and sherry in the evening kept her going. She had worked hard enough and I hated to confront her with still another failed hope. I didn't want her colitis to act up again.

Several days later I got a windfall. An aunt, one of my mother's sisters, sent me a large package of old Dior gowns and Chanel suits. With change of life she had gained twenty pounds and had resigned herself to her new shape. I immediately took the clothes to a resale shop where I got $450 in cash that I hid from Jim. Now I had the difficult job of talking him into seeing a doctor. I waited until the following Saturday morning. "A psycho-analyst!" he shouted, sitting up in bed. He had come in drunk at four, awakening me as he stood over the bed. His eyes had turned bright pink. He looked like something from a Japanese horror film, maybe a rabbit crossed with human genes. "Pretend," he said, "that a priest of the high court of the Spanish Inquisition is interrogating you. He wants the names of all your Jewish family. He wants you to admit you are descended from Sarah, Rebecca, and Rachel, that you are an infidel whose soul is worth dust on redemption day. You deny his charge. Deny it!" he ordered. Fully awake now, I said, "I deny it. I'm a Christian. My family has always been Christian. I've been baptized. I have the papers." "I'll just bet you have the papers," said Jim with such contempt that I pulled the blanket up over my shoulders. He ripped it away, then tore away my nightgown, a leftover flannel from college days. "We'll see," he said, "how long it takes you to confess." I was ashamed to be naked before him. I was round and soft where I should be hard and firm, my breasts did not hang the way they did on calendars. Now I know that I was not without a kind of appeal. Then I did not have the courage to affirm my own body and face. I treated them both with undeserved contempt. Jim looked at me. "I know you're a Jew. I can see the fear in your eyes." "No, no, I'm not," I said, trying to cover myself with the bedspread. He pulled it away from me. "Now," he said, "let's think about the Iron Maiden, the rack." He took off his belt and began waving it wildly, flailing at the pillow where moments before I had been sleeping, dreaming of playing field hockey at camp with the sweat rolling down into my shin guards. "This is ridiculous," I said. "You're acting mad." "I am the Mad Inquisitor," he shouted, "and I can smell that you're a Jew. Please," he said in a small voice, almost a whine, "let me hit you once or twice. Let me just tie you up a little." From between his legs, out from behind the zipper, like a machine gun hidden behind a curtain, came his erect penis, pink and expectant. I went numb, my mind separating from my body, like a ghost at a séance. I felt his tension as if it were mine. How gripped by fear he was, how possessed by pain and sexual energies gone haywire in a mass of despair and rage. The lurid patterns of his sexuality were impressive, like the intricate tissue of a worm seen through a microscope. If I loved him enough I should let him hit me to relieve his anguish, which I almost admired, so real and passionate did it seem. "I am the Grand Inquisitor," he said. "I am the master of all the instruments of torture in Granada, Madrid, and Barcelona. I can put out your eyes with a hot poker if I want to prove you're a blind Jew. I'll stuff a rat into your vagina and let it eat its way out," he shouted. Suddenly he stopped yelling and lay down on the bed. Milky semen splashed on his tie and over his alligator belt. He stared empty-eyed at the ceiling. I put my nightgown back on, awed by what had almost happened. "I want a hamburger," he said softly. I went into the kitchen; out the window I could see the pale gray of dawn, the empty streets with icicles hanging on the traffic lights. I made a hamburger and put it in a bun with ketchup and tomato. When I brought it into the bedroom on a tray, he was fast asleep. I sat on the bed, staring at him, eating the hamburger myself, 350 unnecessary calories. I felt gluttonous and fat.

"A psychoanalyst can't help," he said the next morning. "But of course he can," I answered. I myself had no faith in priests or rabbis, I did not believe that we were moving toward a better future for mankind. I did not believe in ideology or in political revolutions. I did not believe in technological wonders, better cars, five colors for nose tissues, the war against multiple sclerosis or the vanquishing of heart disease, in universal or individual meaning. I did not believe in Harry Stack Sullivan, in my country right or wrong, in Martin Buber, the FBI always gets its man, in Joseph McCarthy, the *Enola Gay*, in taxation without representation, in unidentified flying objects, defense through nuclear advantage, capitalism, white supremacy, Trotskyites, Stalinists, Elvis Presley, czarists, Plato, Dick Tracy, Santa Claus, the Katzenjammer Kids, Dr. Christian, the Boston Pops, the guilt or innocence of the Rosenbergs, Milton Berle, Arthur Godfrey, Tonto, Ann Fogarty crinolines, or the innocence or guilt of the German people. But somehow I still believed in psychoanalysis, I believed in Freud.

"A psychiatrist," he said, "will try to adjust me, ruin my talent. I'm an artist, not a maladjusted Babbitt. I know what you want." He turned on me. "A man with a steady job, a split-level ranch house in Scarsdale, you want a station wagon to drive me to the commuter train, you want a barbecue in the back yard. You want a man who takes you shopping on his Saturday afternoons, goes bowling and pays the bills on Sunday. That's what you want to change me into."

"No," I said, wounded as he knew I would be. "I'm not so Philistine. I just want you not to be so driven, not to drink so much, to stay with me more, to have a loving sex life, to be happier. I don't want you to kill yourself."

"All artists kill themselves, one way or the other." He turned away from me.

"Thomas Mann lived a long time," I whispered. "Please, because I ask you. Go see a doctor."

"You'll never find one smart enough for me. I couldn't talk to an idiot."

"There must be at least one," I said.

"Besides, I'll never go to a doctor who doesn't know my work, who hasn't read my novel and who doesn't already know that I am an extraordinary person." I could tell that I had won and that he would go. Relieved, I saw that at least partly he believed that he could change, that the demons that drove him into the streets could be exorcised. He made me promise to make the first visit myself—to check out the intelligence of the doctor and to bring him his novel.

The following weekend, as I dressed to keep my appointment with Dr. Gruenwald, I thought of Jim as the one tragic lemming who sees that the multitude is headed for calamity, who squeals futilely against the patter of running feet. He can't break free of the crowd, but twists and turns, writhes and slips, tries to run backward and fails. He is caught in the lemming current, is destined for the same end as all the others, but suffers as well from sadness and insight all along the way. But walking along the calm Upper East Side, I felt hopeful. Well-dressed people were coming and going from doctors' appointments; heating systems circulated back into the streets the evaporated secrets, the nightmares and disappointments of souls who believed, as I did, that—at least in private lives—things could get better. I imagined Jim, made over, looking at me in bed one evening, his hands tenderly stroking my breasts. I felt aroused. I glanced around guiltily. Could passersby notice the currents that had just passed through my body? It was, of course, too early to anticipate the pleasures we would have when he could truly love me. I hadn't even found the building yet in which revelation, growth, and change awaited. I was twenty-three and married, sort of, and only now had I begun to understand that Jim and I could do in bed the sweaty, personal things other people took as a matter of course. Jim once had lightly said that if I wore black lace panties and high-heeled shoes and painted red lips on my belly button he might be tempted into ordinary plebeian intercourse. "You're a rice pudding," he said. "No mystery about you. A woman should be mysterious. If Sophia Loren is a woman," he had said, "then what do you suppose you are?" I should have bought those panties with lacework flowers with stamens in red satin, or the ones with satin fingers outlined across the crotch, or the bras in shiny white cloth that said, "Suck me here." I had often walked past the stores that sold them, but was too shy to go in. I shouldn't have cared what the salesclerk thought. I tried to prod myself, but it was no use. I just couldn't get through the door. I always pretended I had acute laryngitis and slipped a note to the clerk behind the counter in drug-stores when I wanted Tampax. I was a bird of little courage and I could never pass as a lady of the night. Maybe Dr. Gruenwald would change Jim into a lover of women—this woman—who wore leather sandals and black leotards. Now I wanted that change very much.

Dr. Martin Gruenwald, who had been recommended by one of my Barnard professors, had white hair and a white beard and a Viennese accent. He looked like every-thing I could have hoped for. His office was all in earth colors, browns and yellows, and somewhat shabby. There were books everywhere—medical texts and journals, vol-umes of poetry in German and Italian, books on art his-tory, architecture, and anthropology. Greek vases and small primitive statues of the archaic period stood under glass. I felt as if I were at the vanishing point in a portrait of intellectual civilization—at the center of the search of truth. There was no chinoiserie, nothing turquoise or gold, nothing a decorator had conjured up. I was as joyful and hopeful as any supplicant on his knees before the Pope.

Dr. Gruenwald listened to my story carefully, only occasionally asking a question. I told him everything I knew of Jim's childhood. I told him about the drinking and I told him in not too much detail about his fondness for playing Grand Inquisitor and his avoidance of what, in this office suddenly occurred to me, was biologically normal sex. I told him about Jim's intimate relationship with fame and success. I told him I loved him and wanted to make him whole, contented, and happy, but that I had recognized that I was failing in what appeared to be a Herculean task. I gave him Jim's book and explained that he must read it before the first meeting. "You know," said Dr. Gruenwald, "I think perhaps you could use some help too." I was surprised. "I'm so rational, so balanced, so sane," I explained to him. "I'm certain that all I need is for you to help Jim. Jim is a volcano about to erupt. Compared to Jim, I'm just a small pond with only perhaps a little neurotic algae muddying the waters here and there." It was sweet, chivalrous, I thought, of Dr. Gruenwald to be concerned about me. It was, I understood, a paternal gesture from a caring man. How pleased he would be when Jim came and he saw what intellectual pleasures they would have together. I knew that Dr. Gruenwald could soon boast (psychoanalysts don't boast, of course, they only report at meetings) the most brilliant, interesting patient in town.

Jim went to see Dr. Gruenwald. "He's a boring man," he said after the first visit, "but I've agreed to see him three times a week." Jim and I lay in bed together that night. "I need you," he said suddenly, "you're a part of my work. Whatever I write belongs somewhat to you. Don't ever leave me," he said, rubbing his face against mine, half-child, half-Afghan hound, wet-mouthed and sad-eyed. "Hold me tightly," he said. "I need you to keep me from flying apart." And I held him in my arms through the Late Show's offering of Betty Grable. After the movie we made plans for our old age. Jim would be celebrity-in-residence in Positano or Nice or Geneva and we would walk about the garden of our villa, entertaining guests from the States, opening fine bottles of wine, serving apples and cheese on tables under the mountains and near the sea, whispering secrets to each other in the shorthand of friends whose stories are one. "It won't be like this forever," he said, holding my hand. "I'll find my way as soon as I'm a classic, an Olympian of the American literary scene. I promise you," he said. "I'll do everything to make you happy ever after. That's what I want to do," he said, and his brown eyes veiled over with what I recognized as the fungus of guilt. "It's all right," I said. "I love you the way you are," and it was true. "I don't deserve you," he said, and his hands began their anxious flutter, like tenement laundry flapping in the wind. I looked again at his eyes, mud brown, like the skin of an Indian slave. I felt cold. "It's all right," I said, catching his arms. "Everything will be all right." His hands broke out of mine and the long aristocratic fingers burst into motion and he was sealed off in his own thoughts. I pulled the cover tight about my body and made myself think of the pleasures to come.

The $450 was good for only several weeks with Dr. Gruenwald. I was about to go to my mother and ask her to pay the bills. I had already pawned the silver trays, the knives, forks, and spoons, the hot chafing dish, the Spode dessert plates, the detritus of the wedding gifts my mother's friends and relatives had given us. Jim's binges ran $100 or so—way beyond my income each week, and the deficit was made up by not paying bills, by selling whatever little gifts came my way. Several times, after a particularly lush lunch or dinner, I pocketed the tips my mother left for the waiters. Early one morning, waiting for Jim, watching through the window for the taxi that would bring him home, I had an inspiration. Like other school-children, I had pasted war stamps in little books. I was helping to fight the Nazis, helping our boys abroad, though I was only a little girl, marked, though I didn't know it, for the ovens if we lost. I would go through our building collecting tinfoil from cigarette wrappers, roll it in balls, and carry it to school. For this I would get stamps; for birthdays I would get war bonds, in my name. I still owned $3,000 worth of redeemable Series E bonds. "But really, dear," said my mother, "why cash them now?" "I think," I said, "it's time to do some investing of my own in the stock market." My mother thought this a wonderful sign of maturity. At last my attention was turn-ing to reality, to accumulation, to a recognition that a full bank account—its comings and fillings and goings—was vital to the health and survival of the organism. She ar-ranged for the vault's heavy doors to be opened and my war bonds to be returned to me. At last I could pay for as much analysis as Jim might need. On my way home from the bank, I bought him a cashmere sweater. Then imme-diately I sent one large check for the remainder to Dr. Gruenwald. I knew if Jim found the money in our bank account it would disappear before the following dawn in a pool hustle, a poker game, an expensive trip to the prosti-tutes. In my wisdom I gave nearly $3,000 to Dr. Gruen-wald for future care and past debt. My spirits were as light as those of a traveler to Lourdes.

Months passed with no particular change in the rhythm of our lives. I went to the office every day, answering the phone with clipped, impersonal cheer. I filed Blue Cross forms. I stuffed letters into addressed envelopes. I used a stamp machine to spare the tender edge of my tongue. The head nurse complained about my clothes. "A high-tone girl like you," she said, "should look more classy. Your shoes are always scuffed, your stockings have runs, and your dresses, my God." She shook her head. "What do you do with your paycheck?" "You wouldn't understand," I said. "Improve," she ordered, and I tried. She was a nice person, and the other nurse, the technician, and the junior doctor had also become my friends. They knew, more or less, and did not approve of where my paycheck went.

Sometimes Isaac-Irwin left the yeshiva he was now attending and came downtown to have lunch with me. His payess were long, his hips soft and bulbous like mounds of mashed potatoes, and his face was always half shaven. I didn't want him to meet me in the office or even on the street. One time I found a candlelit hamburger place. We sat down in a booth and I blew out the candle. He ordered a cheese sandwich. Even this represented a concession on his part, as the dishes were of course not kosher. "Marjorie," he said, "Rabbi Ben Ezra in the twelfth century said that if a soul is unhappy during life, after death it attaches itself to its old bedposts and furniture, its dishes and books, and its tears rot everything away—the mattress, the iron, the floor. That's why everything decomposes, falls apart, disintegrates. It's the tears of the unhappy dead." I thought of them gathered like barnacles on a boat bottom. The souls of the unhappy dead—everyone back to paleolithic man and his paleolithic wife. Or did it apply only to Jewish souls? "I wish I could be one of the happy souls," he said, "who cause no disintegration after death but lie peacefully in the grave." "This is not a sane conversation for this century," I said. "Oh, it doesn't matter about the century," he answered me. "The Rabbi of Schall told his followers that time is an illusion, history is the study of fools and politics the work of infidels." Then he said, "I wish you would look at me. You always look away or above my head." He wanted me to love him, to salvage some trace of family affection. "Why, Isaac-Irwin, are you so impressed by God?" I challenged him. "You take his rules seriously. You think God is really interested in what you eat and which words you mumble and how you shuffle back and forth to prayer. How can you, after all that's happened?" He wheezed just a little. Lunching with me always brought back a touch of his asthma. "And you," he said, "why do you believe in art and the artist as if they were the center of the universe?" I tried to explain to him that Gide wrote his best book about the writing of a book, that Joyce wrote a great book about epiphanies, about the discovery of his vocation as an artist, that all of twentieth-century thought was about the salvation of self through creation, that the artist was the only man whose product did not exploit or clutter up the ground. It was the last refuge for individual effort, for some means of staving off the emptiness of an amoral, absurd world spinning for no comprehensible reason. "You sound to me," said my brother, wiping the mustard from his kinky beard, "like a religious fanatic. Come with me to shul, just once." I couldn't say no.

He took me by subway to Williamsburg in Brooklyn the night of Simchas Torah. In the subway he took my hand in his soft, pudgy fingers, grateful that I had come. It seemed as if we were Hansel and Gretel lost together in the woods. I knew, of course, that we were lost in different woods and that more than one witch was loose in this world. The subway rattled and screeched. Next to us an old man breathed whiskey into the air while continually smoothing his wrinkled jacket. "Isaac-Irwin," I shouted above the sound. "Do you remember when we used to play Captain Marvel?" We had a few games that we played. Briefly, one summer in Larchmont, our interests and capacities had brought us together, while Gretchen knitted mittens on the porch, preparing for the cold winter to come. He insisted on being Captain Marvel while I had to be the evil, mad Sivana, who was always trying to damage America's factories or farms or just to steal a fortune. He loved to hear me laugh like Sivana, mean and nasty: "Heh, heh, heh," I would chuckle while my foul schemes were perking. My brother, alias Billy Batson, needed only to say the magic word "Shazam" to be transformed into Captain Marvel, who could fly, deflect bullets, and smash through anything, and always thwarted Sivana in the nick of time. Once Isaac-Irwin was chasing me through the house. "Heh, heh, heh," I laughed, and ran down into the basement. The rule was that I would allow myself to be caught, so that good, as expected, could triumph over evil. Down the basement steps I ran, past my father's golf clubs, past the completely equipped woodworking bench that no one had the time to use, and then up the steps past the mop and pail used by Hilda, the hired maid, on Thursdays. Suddenly I clicked off the light, slammed the door shut, and turned the key in the lock. Up the steps came Captain Marvel. He banged on the door, but the door wouldn't open. "Let me out," he screamed. I remained silent. "Shazam, shazam, shazam," he shouted and pounded his little fists on the door. He began to whimper, "Please, shazam. Let me out, Marjorie. I have to go to the bathroom. I'll let you be Captain Marvel." I was quiet. Soon I heard him weeping on the steps. "Shazam," he sobbed at the indifferent door.

I went up to my room and took a Nancy Drew mystery from the bookcase and curled up in the pink chair by my dressing table with its white organdy ruffled skirt. I read and read through the long afternoon. When eventually Gretchen found him and everyone was accusing me, I looked innocent and said, "I thought he was outside playing. I didn't know he was in the basement." Nobody believed me. "Shazam," I whispered to him several days later and saw the tears well up in his eyes.

"I'm sorry," I said to him now on the subway, "about Captain Marvel, you know." He turned paler than his ordinary pasty white. "I don't mind," he said, "you had reasons." I was glad I had come with him on this pilgrimage to Brooklyn. When we arrived at the Williamsburg stop, stepping over the candy wrappers, pushing our way through the heavy mint smell of gum and sweat, I caught hold of his hand. Now he was the guide—this was his country and I was the one who appeared odd. In the streets there were crowds of bearded men in black coats and hats, dancing and singing Hasidic chants beneath the grillwork of fire escapes. The rhythm was a little like that of an Indian rain dance. It was also innocent and joyous like a children's game, though underneath I heard a whine, just the not-so-faint whisper of a complaint. God was the magician who murdered at will, whose laws must be studied and interpreted and restudied. The rewards were as wonderful as those of any compulsion—the right to repeat, to begin again, to start all over. The shabby houses, the crowded streets of Brooklyn, like the ghettos of Europe, seemed prison-like. Clanking trash cans rolled over in the gutter as lines of singing Hasidic Jews wove around the parked cars. Pale little boys with circles under their eyes and black hats too big for them slipping over their ears skipped along with their fathers and brothers.

"We have been chosen," they seemed to say, as they scampered about their elders' legs. When they grew up, many of them would be diamond merchants on weekdays and holy men on the Sabbath. I smelled pickles and newly baked bread, Lysol and soap, body sweat and babies in diapers that needed changing.

I leaned against a lamppost, dizzy from the swirl of bodies. I thought of a small town in New England with neat village squares and a single white steeple, clean and reasonable, orderly and pure. I thought of riding on the blue sea in my friend Tootsie's father's boat. The sky and the water echoed each other while Tootsie's father drank martinis from a thermos. I thought of having my first rye-and-ginger at Tootsie's yacht club. Everything there was yellow and pink—hair and skin, blouses and pants, all gold and salmon-colored. I had been dazzled. My college roommate had been married beneath the single steeple of a Congregational church. The clean pews and the six purple hydrangeas that stood in simple lines beneath the minister's lectern had made me want to cry. The black hats swirled past. "There are some mysteries," shouted my brother, "of the cabala that I just can't tell you." "Why?" I asked. "Because." He shrugged. The odd shrug of his, so atavistic, so like the shrug of a man whose grandfathers had never left the confines of Lithuania. "You are a woman. You can go upstairs," he said, "and sit with the women." At last we made our way to the synagogue. It looked like the other brownstones with fire escapes dangling down the front. "Can't I go with you?" I said. "You cannot sit near the Torah, or near the rabbi; he's very famous, you know. It's not allowed." My brother looked at me sadly. "I wish you would try to understand," he said. "Everything has an order, a place. Men and women go differently to God. It's good. Please believe me, it's good." "You wouldn't think it was so good," I shouted, unable to hear my own words over the din in the street, which was reinforced by the siren of a police car a few blocks away, "if you had to go upstairs. If they hung a curtain in front of your face." "I'm going in," said my brother, "to hear the rabbi. If you won't go upstairs, wait here for me. Don't move. You'll get lost." I hugged the building wall and watched. I couldn't see the subway entrance. I couldn't remember what street it was on. Everyone else knew the rhythms, the songs. Old women nodded, shaking their shawls over thin shoulders. I alone was rigid. "God's voice can't come to you if you stand so straight," a man shouted at me as he floated by. My mind was prim and proper—logic and reason, order and irony were my sandbags against the flood tides of madness and grief. These whirling Hasidim were using ancient rituals of mystical self-hypnosis, permitting themselves to jump into mud baths of unreason where I refused, was too fearful to go. Religiosity frightened me beyond anything else. Though, looking back on it now, I cannot understand why the madness in my bedroom was more acceptable than the religious madness on the streets of Brooklyn. I did not believe, with these innocents on the street, that falling I would fall into God's merciful hands. I believed that, given an opportunity, God would crush whatever remaining Jews he found clinging to his fingertips. God was nothing more than the mirror of human rage and creativity, a mirror cracked and splintered, bad luck raining down on us all. Fear was the sperm, need was the ovum in which God had been conceived. I didn't understand then that behind a Gentile lunatic was not a safe place to hide. Suddenly I felt a familiar weight in my pelvis, as if a heavy stone had been rolled under my pubic mound, then warm wetness on my thighs. What a place, what a moment to get the curse! If I believed in divine coincidences, this would be one of them. I looked around for a bathroom. The candy store across the street was closed, so was the grocery store and the butcher shop with Hebrew letters in the window—all closed for the holiday. Could I go into one of the dilapidated houses and ring a bell? I couldn't do that. I was wearing only a sweater over my dress. I might stain through and the thought made my face sting with a shame so deep in anticipation I might as well have done it in fact. The only place that was open was the synagogue. I pushed past the throng on the steps which seemed to be moving neither forward nor backward but swaying and swooning in some patient, repetitive way. "A bathroom, please, a bathroom," I said over and over in the little vestibule. "Upstairs, upstairs," I kept being told. How do you say bathroom in Yiddish? in Hebrew? in German? I'd even forgotten the German I once knew. "No, no," I yelled. "I want a bathroom. *Damen. Damen.*" I finally had found a word. At last an old man with a red beard and bushy orange eyebrows understood. "Downstairs," he directed me. *"Damen, Damen,"* he said, and I gratefully saw in his eyes a comprehension of bodily urgency. Way down in the cellar of the old house there was a sign on a little door. Inside, a bare light bulb swung on a chain above a green toilet. The ceiling shook from the stamping of feet above and there was a rustling behind the dusty boiler. Rats in the temple. I looked down at the dark blood gathering in heavy drops at the vaginal opening. As each drop splashed into the bowl below, the water streaked pink like a sunset, then darkened further into a deep maroon, sustenance for a baby that wasn't there. Dark red like my mother's lipstick and fingernails, like Eve's apple, dangerous but delicious and fascinating. I looked around for toilet paper, but there was none. Damn them all, I thought. What if I just walk calmly upstairs onto the first floor, past the men sitting on cheap folding chairs arranged around the rabbi. What if I go quickly past them before they can stop me and there where the white satin covers the ark, where the Torah is waiting— what if I climb into the ark and sit on the Torah and bleed and bleed and bleed away, letting my blood seep into the sacred pages, soil away, blot out the letters back to front, left to right, marking the rhythms of the year? What if I sit on the Torah like a great mother hen on her darling eggs? But I bleed and I bleed and the other women behind the curtains upstairs hear the commotion and dare to peek. Then they come, all the unclean ones, click click clicking downstairs, and sit with me. And the white satin of the ark turns to red. "Murderers," the men scream and the rabbi faints in his chair. "No one has been murdered," we women answer, and the blood begins to form a puddle around the chair legs, and the men are running this way and that trying to decide what to do, and the blood tide rises as we squat on the wooden podium. Up it goes, over the trouser legs up to the hips and the fainted rabbi's beard floats in the thick bloody syrup and soon there are black hats bobbing in the blood. "Open the doors, open the doors," they shout, but the men can't get the doors open and the yarmulkes and white satin prayer shawls are floating like children's toys in a bathtub and everyone is screaming and the ark fills with blood and I spread my legs, take a bath in it. We women scream, "It's cleaner than you think. It goes deep into the pores and brings out all impurities." The Torah, the sacred scroll, floats out into the ocean of blood, tilts end over end, sinks in the blood, like a ship going down at sea.

Actually, I found some Kleenex in my pocketbook and, temporarily saved from disgrace, pushed my way back into the street to wait for Isaac-Irwin. "Don't you see," he said during the subway ride back to Manhattan, "how much vitality there is? Can't you understand why I need it?" "Yes," I said, "I understand. I just can't join you." He looked at me through his thick glasses, his eyes as usual red-rimmed and with granules from his allergy clinging to the lashes. "I wish you would," he said. "I want to save you." I loved him for that. "It's too late," I said.

When Jim began with Dr. Gruenwald I developed a new set of habits: following women with babies in carriages down the street, staring at toddlers pulling wagons and infants dropping plastic rings on the cement. If Jim were to move toward sanity, if he were pushed over the line toward banality—the event he so dreads and I, saboteur that I may have become, am secretly expecting—then we could have a family and I could take care of a child. I could do it all myself. No Gretchens, no kitchen help. I could, like a pioneer woman, raise my kind and create myself, my face, my body, my mind in the daily work, the saving and the planting, the rooting and the weeding and the harvesting, connecting myself to the process of living and dying. The science of reproduction, with its ova and tubes, uterus and placenta, seemed as alien to me as an asteroid. Yet I dimly felt that biology, my self in touch with my biology, was the answer to the sadness that more and more frequently was flooding my consciousness. Despite the brilliance of Jim's work, I was less absorbed in it than I had been, and sometimes in the early dawn, when it seemed that Jim might never stagger back and I was alone and had too much time to think, I thought I was changing into just what I most dreaded, another woman whose cold eyes would reflect too much sophistication and truth. Disappointments turned women into ugly gnomes; I was shrinking a little with each passing week. If religion reduces itself to the staying power of humanity, then a baby is the highest act of worship. Beyond all else I wanted to be a part of some ceremony, some drama of my own. And so I followed young mothers on Saturdays to the grocery store and stood at the edge of the playground peering in, watching the bags of crackers appear and disappear, the dirty bottles and cracked nipples, the bikes, the balls, the motion of arms and legs. Standing outside, peering in through the iron gates, I saw that the morning passed in rituals of "Look at me," "Let me go," "Hold me tight," "Keep me," "Free me," "Love me," "Hate me," "Leave me alone," "Come and get me," and I saw that childless, excluded from that ritual, I was trivial, unnecessary. I thought a lot about conception, about carrying a baby when Jim would be better, more able to love us both. Sometimes I felt ashamed of wanting a baby. Wasn't it enough to care for Jim? Did I indeed want an ordinary life of Girl Scouts and piano lessons and card games and car pools and breakfast cereals piled into shiny Formica cabinets? Jim wanted to gamble at Monte Carlo, to sip tequila in Cuernavaca, to watch the Mardi Gras. "Someday," he once said, "I want to test myself in the desert and ride in the hot sun with Berber princes." I wanted all that too. I wanted to ride across great plains and climb the steps of Tibetan monasteries and discover pottery shards in the Red Sea. But I also wanted to carry with me, wherever I went, a baby on my back or hip. In the bathtub I began staring at my belly, rubbing it carefully with soap. Was it there underneath, all the equipment needed? Was I filled with eggs, burgeoning and breaking like bubbles in a fish tank? Sometimes my muscles ached and my head pounded as I rocked myself to sleep. I needed this baby just as Jim needed fame. I began to understand better the desolation he experienced when he felt he might not get what he so urgently required.

SEVEN MONTHS after Jim began going to Dr. Gruenwald, I came home from work one day to find him lying on the bed with a bottle of brandy cradled in his arms. "I've done it," he said. "I told the good doctor *guten Abend, auf Wiedersehen, mein lieber,* go find yourself another creative guinea pig to test your theories of star-crossed Oedipal development. It's a goddamn cheat. I know more philosophy, more Freud, more Jung, more Ferenczi, Klein, and Horney than that old fool will ever get around to remembering." It was probably true. He had read all the literature, including the internecine quarrels of the famous and the less famous, nibbling at the intellectual corpses of the giants. He read in the morning and at night, taking notes. He badly wanted to hold on to his version of sanity, and his method of participating in his analysis was to learn. I loved him for that and willingly, happily, made trips to the library during my lunch hour, carrying books back and forth for him. "*Gute Nacht. Ich sage nein, nein, Dr. Gruenwald.* I don't want your second-rate mind meddling in my unconscious."

"But, Jim," I said, "I thought something was happening." I had thought—and the rush of what I had thought overwhelmed me—of a cured Jim, a gentle Jim in bed with me, hands and tongue and penis touching me where I hadn't been touched in years. "It's your fault," Jim said to me. "You lied to me. You coerced me into seeing him, as if he were a supermortal instead of a flea eating off the bitch of that pseudo-science, the faith healer's art. At least palm reading, tea leaves, and scientology are cheaper." Jim

181

was pale. His eyes held only a dead light like the hallways of a cheap hotel. "What happened?" I asked. "He thinks I admire him—unconsciously, that is—that I'm afraid of getting close. What bull. I don't like that leech crawling around my inner skin, sucking blood, probably planning to write a scientific paper about the creative mind. Don't you see," Jim took my hand, tilted his head to one side, and gave me a half smile—Huckleberry Finn trapped in the body of a Hapsburg. "Don't you see," he said, "I want to stay on the edge where I can feel the breeze made by the dice, the chance of it, everything or nothing, the palace or the dungeon, the *Orient Express*, not the subway to Bay Ridge; the wines of Stendhal and Flaubert, not the egg creams of insurance salesmen or English instructors in sleazy apartments on Riverside Drive. I'm either a genius or a raving maniac, but I'm not going to be a case history, a sinner against a system riddled with inaccuracies, adjusted by a science as advanced as bloodletting, as logical as astrology. Don't worry," he said. "I'll get the new book finished and then we'll have money and we'll go to Morocco and who knows what we'll find." He kissed me gently on the eyes, he put his long arms around me. "I need you," he said. "I need you not to be afraid." As always I was happy to be close to him.

But I didn't want to go to Morocco. I wanted to lie in bed with a baby, smelling and touching, rubbing and rocking. Of course the manuscript on Jim's desk was the sacred object of our lives, and it was growing, not because of Dr. Gruenwald, but because for Jim the work was his most holy effort and his salvation. As long as he worked I knew he'd be all right, Dr. Gruenwald or no Dr. Gruenwald. Later, lying alone on the bed after Jim had dressed and gone out for the evening, I felt empty and tearful. I realized how much hope I had placed in Dr. Gruenwald.

The war-bond money had been used up, wasted. All right, I thought, I had gambled and lost. A good sport doesn't complain when the results are unpleasant.

A week later I sat in Dr. Gruenwald's waiting room. I wanted to know from him what had gone wrong. At work that morning I had arranged the hospitalization of a young woman, about my age, just diagnosed as having multiple sclerosis. The brutality of what she had experienced and would experience shamed me. How did I dare feel such an inner chill when nothing remotely comparable had happened to me? Dr. Gruenwald seemed glad to see me.

"Mrs. Morrison, I'm delighted you've come."

"What happened?" I asked.

"Well," he explained, in his soft, German-accented English, "the ego of such a man as your husband is perhaps somewhat fragile for analysis. He has after all so many real and instant gratifications. It's hard to induce a storm to study its own origins, you understand."

"But what," I said, "were you doing all these months?"

"Trying," he said, and smiled gently. "But with you," he added, "I'm certain the progress would be steadier."

"I need my money back," I said suddenly, surprising myself with such an unexpected demand.

"Oh, that's impossible," said Dr. Gruenwald, calmly, professionally, sympathetically. "I'm a doctor and not a merchant. You have paid me for my time and I have spent it with your husband. Unfortunately, he was not a willing patient. It was indeed an interesting experience and I deeply regret we did not enter a successful therapeutic alliance. He preferred to be my teacher." Dr. Gruenwald smiled at me, asking for my understanding of his failure. "Analysis," he said, "is a technique, not a miracle."

"But I think I should have my money back. Please give me a check." I stood up. Dr. Gruenwald looked at me, quite startled. "Sit down and we'll talk about it. Do you enjoy your work? Do you have many friends outside of your husband?" "No," I said, "I want my money back now." "I understand," said Dr. Gruenwald, "that you're upset. It must be very trying to be in such a marriage. I would like to help you understand the causes of your choices. Perhaps there are other choices you can make, other paths you can take." His voice was very soft and soothing, his eyes direct and honest. I almost gave in to the urge that was snowballing within to please him, make him smile at me, to tell him how much the job bored me but how I enjoyed my friends, how easy it was to share a sandwich at lunch, to talk about everything or almost everything. My friends knew enough to ask each morning how many pages had been written the previous day. Instead, I reached over to the nearest bookshelf and snatched up three small, old-bronze, valuable-looking statues of rams with curled horns. "Now, look," said the doctor, jumping to his feet. "You really can't do that. Those are valuable pieces from the archaic period. I got them in Greece—with great difficulty. Please just put them down carefully." The beads of sweat that had broken out on his forehead gave me courage. "No, I'm leaving with them," I said, quickly going out the double door of his office and down the vestibule to the elevator. I had pushed the button by the time he caught up to me. "Don't try to take them from me," I said. "I'll drop them." "Theft is a crime," he said very quietly. "I'm sure you don't want to be arrested, in addition to all the other troubles that are causing you to act out your anger, anger at your father, perhaps? Was he an art collector too?" "No," I said, "and, Dr. Gruenwald, if you call the police it will be in all the papers. Would that improve your reputation or not?" The elevator door opened. I stepped in and saw him stand immobile and astonished as the door closed in front of him. As I rode down, clutching the little statues, my heart was pounding with a mixture of exultation and fear. When I walked out of the building lobby, I was already calm enough to say "Nice day" to the doorman. My grandfather had started as a little boy of nine with a pushcart and some shirts. Had he stolen his first shirts? Here I was with three works of art—they could be the beginning of my own gallery, the end of the bondage of a job.

I got to the corner and was suddenly embarrassed, ashamed, and frightened. I was a thief. He might be calling the police right now. I wasn't sure just how afraid of publicity he would be. Not only were the statues valuable, they must also represent something for Dr. Gruenwald: a perfection of the spirit, a solidity of form in contrast to the uglinesses of the human personality. In the midst of fields of infantile rages, hostilities, ambivalences, perversions, fixations, distorted and arrested developments, psychosomatically created chemicals boring holes into human tissue, an array of souls that like the primitive tribes in the bush reinforce the ideal of classical civilized rational proportions, Dr. Gruenwald must have looked at his rams for support for his conviction that beauty was also a human attribute, and form and grace as enduring as the perpetual parade of misery. I turned around and went back into the building. "Forget something, miss?" asked the doorman. "Yes," I said. At Dr. Gruenwald's door I waited for the elevator to go on its way and then I knelt down and arranged the rams on the doormat. First I placed them in a straight line, but then I rearranged them in a casual triangle, as if they were grazing on the straw. Suddenly the door opened and there above me stood the doctor. "I thought it was the next patient," he said stiffly. "It's all right," he said, "you don't have to go down on your knees to me. I understand." He saw the rams and picked them up, cradling them as if I had left a foundling on his step. "Don't stay on your knees," he said. "The floor is dirty." I pulled myself up. I rang the elevator bell. "I'm really sorry. I don't know why I did that," I mumbled. "I've never before. I don't ordinarily, hardly ever, steal." "It's all right," said Dr. Gruenwald. "I hope you get what you want." "I know Jim's new book will be a success," I said, happy that he did not despise me. "I meant," he said, "I hope you get what *you* want." All the way back to the office I repeated his words. I said them to myself with the Viennese accent and without. I translated them into German and I typed them on the office typewriter. After a while I had said them so often they lost their meaning, became gibberish, and I forgot them entirely.

ONE NIGHT not long afterward I woke from a nightmare. I had been standing by the bathroom door holding a towel for Jim, who was lying in the tub splashing water on his thin chest, with his hands like an old lady about to take a dip in a lake. With one foot he reached over and pulled the chain of the white rubber plug. Suddenly there was a huge sound of suction and the water rushed instantly down the drain. Startled, Jim pulled himself up and tried to raise his torso out of the tub, but the force from the drain was pulling him toward it. Jim's long, thin foot went down into the drain. "My God," he screamed. "Marjorie, help!" His face showed panic and pain. I was frozen with fear. His calf disappeared in the drain, which seemed to widen just enough to accommodate the width of his leg. "Help me," he screamed, clawing at the smooth pink porcelain of the tub. He grabbed the soap dish, but it came off in his hand. The force continued to pull more of him down. Now the chrome of the drain came over his penis and his testicles, pushing them tightly together between his thighs. I leaned over and grabbed his arm. "Jesus, Jesus," he screamed. The force was too powerful. He was pulled away from my grip and soon only his head was above the drain. "Shazam," he shouted desperately. For a moment or two his blond silky hair remained floating above the drain, and then he was gone. I was left holding the towel, tears pouring down my face. The drain contracted back to normal size. I woke. He was asleep next to me in the silk monogrammed pajamas my mother had given him.

The next day was a Sunday. Jim slept most of the day, but in the early evening, as he often did, he became frightened and anxious. "What if nobody thinks the new book is any good?" he said. "Marjorie, you're the one who thinks I have genius. Maybe it's stupidity that keeps this illusion alive in your decaying brain. Why do you have to be such an angel? You're driving me crazy with your martyrdom. You make me feel guilty all the time. It's your fault I need to drink. I'm not as good as you think I am." "Yes, you are," I said, as I had said a thousand times before. It was hardly the moment to tell him I wanted a baby. But suddenly, perversely, I told him just that.

"A baby?" he said incredulously. "A child? You must be out of your mind. Why would I want that? Who with any intelligence wants this globe to keep spinning?" He thought I was teasing. Then he realized I was serious. "For Christ's sake," he said, "isn't it enough for you just to take care of me? It was enough for my mother, enough for my grandmother. What's the matter with you? Anyway, you certainly shouldn't have a child. You never wanted to be an ordinary Scarsdale woman. You want to be a part of a larger, more glamorous world." "But I want a baby," I said softly. I was risking his disapproval, his withdrawal, losing him. But I did hold some good cards in this game, his various needs for me and my services. It wasn't just that he owed it to me. I knew he, like a deaf man listening to music, wanted to love me, make me happy too. I made his breakfast and dinner, listened as he read me his work in progress and discussed it with him, sat at the edge of the bathtub and absorbed his rages at other writers. He liked the apartment he and my mother's decorator had designed. He was by now totally attached to the idea of my presence in his life. He couldn't, I hoped, say no to me when at last I chose to demand something for myself. "Are you serious, Marjorie?" he asked.

"I must have a baby. You owe me that." "Why? What for?" He went in the bathroom and closed the door, giving me time to prepare my answer. But I didn't have an answer he would be able to understand. I didn't think I had an irresistible maternal instinct, or that I would achieve immortality through genetic extension. I had no religious conviction of any sort. When he emerged from the bathroom I said only, "Trust me. It's the right thing to do." He looked at me with the expression of a chicken eyeing a hawk. "I'm not sure I can do it," he said mildly. "Of course you can," I said. "All right," he said resignedly, "we'll try."

He was generous and fair and decent after all, or at least was not ready to lose me. I would have my baby and I would make it up to him somehow, see that he wasn't inconvenienced or his work disturbed. My mother would certainly pay for everything. I would minimize his embarrassment about the pregnancy and the infant. He would not have to prepare formulas or walk around with spit-up orange juice dripping down his back. He had his needs too.

The night I chose for our first try he was out on one of his habitual drunken prowls. But I woke him just before dawn. Lying beside me on the bed, his thin, bony body looked frail. His limp penis rested on his wrinkled balls, the organs looking like the face of a clown. Incredible that they should hold such promise. I lay quietly, watching him play with himself. His pink eyes, streaks of blood crisscrossing the pupils, veiled over as he retreated into inner fantasy. At last his penis was erect. It reminded me of the stuffed grape leaf we had eaten at an Armenian restaurant with his literary agent several nights before. I was afraid that it might collapse or that, as they always had before, his fantasies would carry him all the way without me. At last he rose over me and entered me for the first time. We had been living together for years. It was a strange feeling. I fought back the beginnings of pleasure because I feared that it would threaten the most important thing in my life—my connection with Jim. He came in less than a minute, immediately pulled away from me, and lay sweating on his side of the bed. "You see," he finally said, "I can do it any time I want. I just don't find it one of the world's better offerings." "I understand," I said. I kissed him and wiped him dry. "Thank you, thank you," I whispered in his ear. I had chosen, as best I could, the right time of the month. I might not have many more opportunities. I lay back, imagining the swimming sperm, thin and angular like Jim, pushing their way up in the dark in a process of creation which we shared with crocodiles and elephants. No, I wouldn't wax religious, never, Isaac-Irwin would do that. I would try to resist poetic meanderings on the godhead of life residing in the womb, etc., but as I lay there, I knew that although invisible, un-felt, there were motions within me of extraordinary won-der. If Genet could make a cathedral of the anus, why could I not do the same of the womb, whose porous veined tissues would make any stained-glass window look inferior, a callow imitation of the holy place.

I was lucky. It took only that night and one other. I started to throw up on my way to work. Jim got some money from the paperback sale of his book, and from ar-ticles. I quit my job, ignoring his increasing fears that suc-cess would desert him. As I expected, my mother offered to pay all the doctor and hospital expenses. She took me to lunch just before one of her high-stakes canasta games. "I'll win the baby's entire layette this afternoon," she said. She had the fortune-teller come to our table, a black-eyed old woman with bags under her chin and pink lipstick shaped like an invitation. "There's a tall handsome man in your future," she said to me. I laughed. My future and my past were going to be the same.

I was happy to leave my job. I would miss my friends there, but I was glad to repossess my own time, to be able to wander the streets in a delicious freedom which seemed after two and a half years like the headiest of delights. I wondered about the forty years some women put into their jobs—the head nurse, for example, who went on a Caribbean cruise for her two-week vacation each year, re-turning always with nothing but brochures describing next year's trip.

The baby grew inside me, and I spent more and more of my newfound freedom fighting the nausea that signaled hormonal happenings. Could I be allergic to the new being, its fingerless hands clenched over unseeing eyes? Sometimes I lay on my bed while Jim was sleeping into the late morning and I cupped my hands over my round belly and tried to imagine what I couldn't see. I had bought every book on the subject I could find, and week by week looked at pictures of fetuses the age of mine. I was an encyclopedia of information on normal gynecology, and yet sometimes I felt cold terror. I imagined horrors: the baby would grow enormous and its head would push into my lungs and stop my breathing. All the blood in my body would be sucked into the dormant infant and I would, like an exposed Egyptian mummy, crumble into dust. The baby would die within me and the release mechanisms fail, and the baby's body would decompose and putrefaction would spread through my blood and I would, like a gangrene victim, grow stiff, foam at the mouth, choke for breath, and die.

At other times I thought of how I would hold the baby, the new soft skin against my breast. My nipples would be the center of the baby's life, and my arms folding around the infant would fold around myself, holding the two of us together. Never would I allow a Gretchen to touch my child. Never would other hands wash or clean or cut the fingernails of my child. Never would I allow my baby to cry out in the middle of the night and see a stranger appear at the bedside. Never would I, like my mother, go to parties or shopping, never would I leave the child to reach out its arms for the reassuring touch that had disappeared. Never would my child wait outside my door for me to finish a nap, a phone conversation, a card game. I would undo, I would redo my childhood. I would do for my child what had never been done for me. It seemed so simple a way to achieve purification, to make one's way steadily over the debris of the past. I was for the most part confident of the future. These first kicks seemed timid, so light I wasn't certain expectation had not created them, but then, as the weeks passed and they grew stronger, even visible as the mounting flesh of the stomach shook and shifted from the movements within, I grew more confident. As the baby kicked I welcomed this tremor that told me it wasn't a false pregnancy. It was not an illusion. The baby was still only a collection of raw tissue, little knees pulled up, helpless to stop the forces that were causing it to grow, propelling it and the bloody tissue it survived on into the world. I and I alone would, with the power of a feeling so great I sometimes felt crushed and exhausted by it—this love I was readying would make a universe.

Now I waited with diminished attention for Jim to return at night. The sales reports on his book were good. He began to gamble more and more. He wanted proof that fortune was on his side. We were still being invited to all sorts of houses where the people's names were public property. Jim more and more wanted me to stay home. The new shape of my body, which I admired each day in the mirror, for the first time in my life appreciating my form, seemed to embarrass him. He talked more and more of the tall, thin, straight-haired blonde women he met each evening. "They are stupider than you but more beautiful." I laughed it off. Once he said, "I think you're changing. You're going to be one of those women with a cartful of groceries, curlers in your hair, and squalling brats urinating in the supermarket aisles. What became of the girl who loved Thomas Mann and would have walked barefoot over the Alps to meet him? I think you're like a spider," he said. "You've had your use of me and now you're ready to roll me up in cotton spit and dispose of me at leisure." That brought me back from my navel-staring. I reassured him over and over—as he read me pages from the new book he was so terrified would fail—that I still felt total commitment to his life and his work. Like a monk in an isolated monastery, I was still unable to imagine not performing my duties: I continued to tend the holy grounds and daily dust the blank eyes of the holy statue. Hard as it is to understand now, so many years later, my devotions made sense out of an otherwise senseless day.

As I weighed myself each day, tracking ounce by ounce the increased weight in my belly, I tried to isolate an image that would direct my life: the Virgin Mary of the paintings, with her infant looking like a little man decorously wrapped in glorious cloths half falling off the stiff limbs? An Indian squaw with her baby on her back, glaring out at the blank eye of a white man's camera? An Appalachian mother I had read about in a novel, carrying her diphtheria-ridden child to town to a doctor, having to stop at the side of the road and with her knife cut a hole in the child's throat, insert a reed, and suck out the mucus that was stifling it? The French woman on a bed in a country clinic, the baby's head crowning, the grandmother holding the hand of her daughter in labor, and outside, the great-grandmother in black laced boots fetching water from the pump? A suburban woman in her grocery-filled station wagon, children's faces pressed to the windows? Was I hoping to find myself by participating in the biological process of human reproduction or was I merely fulfilling a nasty little need for drama, a desire that attention would be paid to me?

My mother was, in fact, paying attention. She bought me maternity dresses. She phoned every day to find out how I was feeling. She cautioned me not to exert myself and offered cleaning maids and cooks. But I was determined not to have my child in her manner, to have it, if not quite like the peasants in the fields, as a welcome and natural process, without a regiment of experts. Gretchen had taken me, a more or less normal, healthy child, to dozens of doctors—allergists, dermatologists, ear, nose, and throat men, orthopedists. She and my mother had moved gingerly through the germ-filled world, picked their way through it as through a mine field. I would have my baby and raise it without the devils of hypochondria. I knew I would have to take care of both the baby and Jim. Only a strong person could do that, but most of the time I thought I would be up to the double task.

I was healthy and young and there was no reason for anything to go wrong. Naturally I worried sometimes whether the baby would have a cleft palate. I worried, though not excessively, about retardation, torn heart valves, and missing limbs. But I refused to allow my euphoria to be punctured. Unlike any other experience I had known, my pregnancy was imbued with an indisputable moral goodness, a guilt-free joyousness. I wore my maternity bathing suit to the beach when we visited Jim's editor in Amagansett. Jim said that I looked like a flying saucer, that there was no relation between me and the long-legged girls who bent easily, as I couldn't, to pick up from the sand shells and shiny stones. He said I looked like a jellyfish in the water. I didn't mind what he said, but I was embarrassed when he went off down the beach with a long-haired girl who had admired *After Ludwig* enormously. He was pretending virility, playing a charade for his editor and the others on the beach. No one knew quite what to say to me. "Wouldn't you like to go back to the house and lie down?" my hostess suggested. It seemed a good way to save the day, so I went. Jim couldn't help what he was doing. It humiliated him that people assumed he was a happy father-to-be with a dumpy wife, frizzy-haired and shyly smiling. His sense of style required a sensational-looking woman, but his nighttime fears required me. No one else would listen as he spoke them, take care of him when his hands shook from too much

Scotch. I would always take care of him, and so I was safe and didn't really need or deserve those pitying looks on the beach.

My mother had bought us a new co-op apartment with an extra room. Jim loved the new place, which had a wonderful address, on Fifth Avenue. I had wanted to live on Riverside Drive with professors and other writers, not far from old ladies with shopping bags and Puerto Rican children opening fire hydrants in the summer in the real world. But Jim seemed to need the style of the new apartment. It worked like an additional bumper on a car, cushioning the impact of his fear of failure, which continued to grow rather than diminish with success. I began to understand that fame and reputation, and then the need for them, were like some underwater plant that fed off passing fish; with each catch devoured and digested, it would grow new leaves, larger buds, and need even more of a food supply. It never rested, it continuously expanded, and the quantity of fish needed to hold off starvation increased daily. Jim was working on his new book, but it was coming slowly. Too many drunken nights followed by too many days spent in nausea, headaches, waving of hands in front of the face, two-hour baths, and a new habit of watching the afternoon movie on TV.

We were running out of money, but that was all right because my mother was now subsidizing us. Knowing that Jim had expensive tastes, she wanted to be sure he was comfortable while working on the new book. "Son of Ludwig," we affectionately called it. The prose was as cool and elegant as before, but even though, or because, he was writing the story of his own parents and grandparents, it lacked energy. While he read it to me, my mind would wander to methods of natural childbirth, to inner debates about whether I would have my son circumcised or not. If pogroms came again (and history indicated they might), I thought it better for this son of a Jewish mother to carry his flap, a small piece of skin to hide his identity under. Why was I not concentrating, not listening well? At first, I thought it was my fault. The pregnancy was, as Jim had said, making me stupider each day. But then I decided it wasn't that. Something was wrong with what he was writing and for the first time in a long time I said so. "It doesn't quite work," I said one rainy night and Jim froze into a statue. I explained, "I didn't care about the characters, the writing is too distant, too cold, too clinical." "Not like Dr. Spock," he sneered, "or Grantly Dick-Read." "That's not it," I said quietly. "All right," he roared, "if that's the way you feel," and he jumped up, taking pages of yellow handwritten manuscript with him, many months' work. "Into the incinerator, out the window," he screamed. "I'm nothing but a brash kid, Blades Jim from Bay Ridge." Before I could stop him he had opened the window and thrown the manuscript out. I rushed to the window and saw the sheets float down in the rain. Some came to rest on the canopy, others reached the middle of the avenue. Cars ran over pages. A passerby huddling into himself, head down against the cold winter wind and rain, reached out to catch a page, but it eluded him. The trees in Central Park were bending in the wind. I leaned out the window, my large round belly stretched taut, and felt a terrible grief. "I'm going down," I said as he stood there at the window waving his arms in front of his eyes, no longer seeing me at all. I rang the elevator bell. "You need a rain-coat, Mrs. Morrison," said the elevator man. The doorman was probably having a mid-winter nip in the basement, and I had to push open the heavy front door by myself. Outside, it was cold. I found some of the blurred pages in puddles that reflected the red and green of the traffic lights. Jim's neat inked handwriting was fatally smeared by the rain. Many other pages had blown farther away, some in the street where the cars rushed by. Carrying a few soggy sheets, I went back upstairs. Jim was turning my pocketbook inside out looking for cash. "I have to go," he said. "I have to get out. If I can't write I'll put a pillow over your child's head," he screamed at me. "If I can't write another book, then I'll take my pool cue and shove it up your ass till there's nothing left of your bowels." Like an addict threatened with enforced withdrawal, the thought of months without public recognition made him wild with anxiety. I would have to put his faith back together after the fury was spent. "You're doing it," he screamed. "You're making me write. I could be happy in the streets, in the bars, in the poolrooms, but it's your ambitions that are driving me crazy," and without his winter coat but with all the money in the house and with a small silver bell, for summoning the servants (one of the few remaining wedding presents), he disappeared into the wet, cold night. I settled down in front of the television, to find some movies to forget myself in while I waited patiently for his return. As I look back it's hard to understand why I was so eager to have him return, bleary and soused, his energies gone. What is puzzling now was never questioned then. Once Alice is down in the rabbit hole, there are no sensible questions.

In the beginning of December, when I was coming to full term, he began to write again. He had been out every night for weeks, coming back with stories I didn't know whether or not to believe—stories about $150 prostitutes who allowed him to smear his feces on their breasts. To put his feces into their mouths. I wondered if I could do it, taste the poisonous taboo wastes of the body, knowing that the act would relieve his inner pain. Then, finally, the flying, useless sperm would bring him immediate calm. I thought perhaps I would. The compassion I felt for him mingled with horror: at the center of his mind I saw a madness beyond my healing powers. But even though I could effect no change, I would be absolutely loyal. He was, in fact, the part of me that tilted at windmills, that fought for the golden prize, that would not settle for a lifetime of predictability. As long as I was connected to him I would not sink into the grave without accomplishment—without distinction. He was a comet I was riding. I dimly began to think that my love for him might be nothing more than my own ambition.

In mid-December it snowed heavily. Traffic was barely moving; school was out and children were pulling sleds down the streets. My mother called, frantic that I would not make it to the hospital in time, that the baby would be born in a snowdrift and like Russian peasants we would die of the cold. The hospital was less than a mile away, but my mother hired a chauffeured limousine, with snow tires, to wait in front of our building twenty-four hours a day. The baby had "dropped." It could be born at any moment. I was constantly excited—the heartburn, the slowness of breath, the heavy feeling in my legs, and the low back pain all seemed like good signs. I was ready for my metamorphosis. I would emerge from the delivery room a new person, and the infant, whose face and body I now desperately longed to see, would rest against me and our unity would be my salvation.

One morning I told Jim that his portable Olivetti typewriter was broken. The night before, while typing his day's work (with a carbon which I hid in a drawer in order to prevent another loss), the ribbon had snarled. Now it was clear that there was something seriously wrong with the typewriter, another gift to him from my mother.

"Take it to be fixed," Jim said. "I can't work today if I know you won't be able to type tonight. I'll go to the movies this afternoon if you don't take the typewriter to the repair shop," he threatened me. I thought of the chauffeur waiting downstairs. I could get him to drive me. I put on my boots and my coat, which I couldn't button now. I took the typewriter and cradled it in my arms, but when I saw the chauffeur reading a newspaper and drinking his coffee in the lobby I decided not to bother him. This was, after all, not the emergency for which he had been hired.

I began carrying the typewriter the twelve blocks to the repair shop. After a block or so I realized the typewriter was too heavy. I was out of breath and my arms and back ached. But the baby kicked reassuringly. I thought of the snow in Munich, of our falling in the ruined, bombed building. Beneath my gloves my fingers were chilled and I began to feel the pain of cold in my toes and ankles, which were rounded, swollen with fluid, puffed by the hormonal shocks my body was receiving. I put the typewriter down on a parked car, careful to clear away the snow so the machine would not get wet. I looked for a taxi but no cars at all were moving. The buses had stopped. The city was like a village—something out of a Broadway musical— where people walked about smiling at strangers; a glow, a good feeling of community, had come with the extraordinary whiteness of the snow. A man brushed past me, his cheeks and nose red from cold. "Help me," I wanted to say, but I was too shy. I picked up the typewriter and carried it another block. There was no need to stop for the lights that continued uselessly to turn red and green over the snow-covered world. Some children came by pulling a sled. I could put the typewriter on their sled, I thought. I could pay them to pull it for me to the shop. But they were so busy with the intense argument they were having about whose turn it was to pull and whose turn to ride that they didn't hear me calling to them, or maybe they thought I was just another one of the city's mad people, gesturing and talking to herself. Suddenly I felt a strange wetness beyond my control seeping inside my stretched-out maternity slacks. Had a small hand or foot pierced some crucial tissue wall? Then I remembered what I had been reviewing over and over again each night when the pages were neatly stacked and the carbon carefully hidden away—the beginning of labor, the breaking of the sac. I did a strange and thoughtless thing. I left the typewriter in the snow, its gray case peeking out between two drifts like a country rock on an ordinary hill. I hurried back the way I had come.

Jim said, "I suppose you want me to go to the hospital with you. I've got to do that pacing-the-floor thing like all the idiots. That's what's expected, isn't it?" I called my mother and she said she'd meet us at the hospital. "It won't look right, will it," he said, "if I don't come?" "I don't care," I said. "I don't want you to feel uncomfortable." He came, and he and my mother played canasta downstairs. (My father was off at his club and did not arrive till the next day.) My mother had managed to teach Jim to play canasta the summer before. They always played for high stakes, but she had to absorb his debts to her as part of her maternal kindness, while she always paid him in shiny bills and was genuinely pleased when he won. Winning, she felt, was a good character sign. "You left the typewriter in the street?" she said to me as I was being wheeled away to another floor. "Why were you carrying the typewriter? How could you just leave a valuable piece of property like that?" I saw in her eyes that look of betrayal. I had once again ignored the material universe for some whim or another. "I'm sorry," I said as the elevator doors closed behind me. I wanted her with me, not angry at this most important moment. "Do you wish your husband to stay with you in the labor room?" someone asked. "No," he said, "I'll wait." And so I was alone in a white sanitary cell. "Ring this bell," someone said, "if you feel a change in the pains."

Alone, I looked out the window and could see Central Park covered with snow and new snow quietly falling. The hospital gown over my large belly was white and I began to feel as if I were in a crib, deserted by adults. I was afraid of dying. The busy staff rushed by in the hall. Someone came and gave me an enema and shaved, harshly, swiftly, my pubic hair. I was ashamed and ashamed of being ashamed. I was glad when another person came into the room. "I'd like my mother to come," I told the nurse. "Not possible," she said. "Just take it easy," and she left me alone again. I breathed deeply during the pains. I had forgotten about the baby and was thinking only of my own survival. Every now and then, when I thought no one would come again, someone with a stethoscope opened the heavy door and listened to the baby's heart. Then I would remember what it was all about and smile at the someone, who would say, "Just fine," and go away. It got darker outside and the lamplight shone on the clean snow. The pains came closer together and I was frightened the baby would come and no one in the hospital hear my bell, hear my scream, and we would both die unattended. But someone came in and turned on the light, so I wasn't lying in the dark. "Good girl," a voice said. "Everything is fine." But the voice disappeared out the door. Time had become lost in the dimension of space, an hour, five hours. It no longer made any difference. Someone came in and gave me an injection and the pains dimmed and the room seemed to float. I felt as if

I were a fish in a small bowl being carried from place to place and the waters rose around me like tidal waves. The baby and I together under the sea. We had only each other and the snow kept falling. Suddenly there was a pressure, a great and familiar pressure. I had to move my bowels and the pressure was intense and painful, cutting the soft edge of the drug's euphoria. I sat up. I tried to pull down the steel bars someone had pulled up hours ago. I had to get to the bathroom. Even in birth, I would not lose the controls of a human being, controls of a bitter childhood. I started to climb over the bars. I rang the bell. I rang and I rang and suddenly they were all about me. Thick-tongued, I tried to tell them, "I have to go, I have to go to the bathroom. Help me, please, someone, help me get to the bathroom," but they ignored me. The doctor came. I recognized him. "The baby's coming. It's the final stage," he said. "Don't push till we get to the delivery room," and then I floated with handmaidens at my side. Queen of the winter's night, center of the world, Eve of all Eves, wheeled into the elevator, attendants at my head and feet, into the delivery room, and there, amid the whiffs of gas and injections, I fell backward into the navel of the universe, merging, splitting, riding the golden horse of Phaëthon, pulling the sun out of reach of human contemplation, occasionally interrupted by a sharp tearing pain, a final extraordinary push. The walls of Jericho came tumbling down. There was bustling in the room. "Is the baby all right?" I asked, pulling myself into focus. I kept slipping in and out. "I can't see the snow any more," I said. "It's a girl," someone said.

Through the haze of drugs, I knew Jim would be disappointed. I didn't care. My mother, too, would be disappointed, my father diffident. I didn't care. The girl baby would be mine for the raising, and she would be more

loved, prouder, more brilliant than any male. I would protect her, make territorial circles around her. "She's fine,"
said the nurse when she brought her to me. All the nightmares—of monsters, of limbless cripples, brainless vegetables, lipless, earless, blind, deaf, the cosmic jokes on the
daring of the rational human being to reproduce—were
gone. I forgot the dreams of chicken heads squawking on
dog bodies, I forgot months of attention to the kicks that
signaled life was still there. I forgot it all. Now I lay in the
drug haze thinking in the cool blue light of reason of how I
would surround my baby with the miracles of language
and form. She would grow to make the world again with
her speech. I looked at her. I saw thinly spread the fuzzy
beginnings of Jim's soft blond hair, a perfect face. She was
a half-breed, an interfaith mutt (stronger, healthier than a
purebred). As the last of the placenta oozed its way out
and I lay light on the table, it seemed as if I could fly over
the rooftops of the city, over the canyons of Wall Street
and the cold ice cubes of the Upper East Side and drop
flowers over the snow-filled streets.

My daughter would never be touched by the paid hands
of a nurse—no bottles, no baths, no kisses but mine. I
would revise my history, love my baby as I wished I had
been loved. For once, as I drifted on euphoric clouds, I
did not search for meaning, for relevance, for permanence,
for explanation or definition. I floated with the moment, in
and of itself, as if there were no reckoning or judgment or
other waiting pleasures, as if mornings after and recriminations did not accumulate on the soul; as if I had found a
way—simply by giving birth to this little girl whose legs
flushed pink when she cried and whose nose was still
pushed in and swollen from the passage of birth—to redeem, atone, resurrect myself; as if I didn't have to turn
bitter and shrunken; as if I had avoided the decay of hope

that turned the smartest people I knew into dingy versions of their earlier selves. I didn't care for the moment whether or not Jim's book brought increased fame. Through fear and pain I had come to understand that squaw, Eskimo, cavewoman, pioneer, from Samoa to Shaker Heights, from Egypt to St. Tropez, *Gemeinschaft*, *Gesellschaft*—where the sun hardly ever rose and where it never set—we were all alike. Damn to all the rest. Damn to husbands and doctors and nurses whose mouths went up and down. I celebrated with myself a holy celebration, right at the navel of the universe—the infant that came from me.

"Well," said Jim when he came in to see me, "I have an heir. Someone to lecture on my work after I die, I guess."

"Are you happy?" I asked, demanding a reflection of my mood.

"I really think," he said, "the announcements from Tiffany your mother has picked are bourgeois beyond acceptability."

"They're just for her friends," I explained. "It doesn't matter."

"I don't know why," said Jim, standing at the window looking out at the white snow that covered Central Park, "why it is I feel like an impostor, like a clown or a buffoon. I really want to go home."

"It's all right," I said soothingly. "You'll get used to the idea of having a daughter. You'll see, you'll love the baby, and that strangeness will fade when you've been with her more."

"I doubt it, Marjorie," he said. "If only you'd believe me sometimes. If you'd only let my way of seeing things alone. If you'd only hear me. It seems to me as if doors are closing all around me. I'm being herded into a Dagwood Bumstead future where I don't belong. I'm an artist, not a man who goes to the zoo: 'See the camel, see the duck, it goes quack, quack.' Marjorie," he said, the cigarette falling from his long cigarette holder, taking off the dark glasses he always wore at night indoors to create the effect of a master mobster, a supergambler, a bad-boy mathematician, one of Walter Pater's crowd who has turned to bank robbery. "Marjorie, I'm going to be immortal, but not because some boring, burping body stole my genes." Nevertheless, he was interested enough to push for a classical name for the baby, Persephone or Clytemnestra. I wanted a New England, Puritan name—Faith. He left. I felt the stitches burning between my legs. I was hungry. I wanted a chocolate milkshake or a lollipop. I wanted child's food, reward food for an ordeal at the dentist or a shot at the doctor's. I wanted to see my baby again.

My mother came the next morning. She watched the baby through the window of the nursery. My mother was happy. "She's beautiful," she said, "but I hope no one else sees her for a while."

"Why?" I asked.

"Because," said my mother, "everyone knows that too much admiration for a baby brings on a curse. Something terrible will happen if people compliment her."

"You don't really believe that." I looked at her carefully. Her hair was freshly dyed strawberry blond, her eyelids were puffy and mascara-streaked, but underneath the anxious habits of expression there were gratitude and a new hope. She laughed, embarrassed. "My aunt used to say that. It's just an old-country fear, but you never know"— she shrugged—"which of those superstitions might be true." I held Faith-of-the-swollen-nose in my arms. I was still awkward with her, my breasts ached from the engorgement, milk nodes swollen and hard. It hurt to shift my body even a little. "No one will curse my baby," I said. Leaning over, I wanted to draw a lead sheet over both of us, blocking out the X-rays of hate that, invisible and powerful, were trying to attack us. If only I had a fallout shelter where we could hide together, nursing and sleeping, touching and smiling, looking in each other's eyes till the dangers were gone. For Jim, my mother had brought a Patek Philippe watch with his name engraved on the back.

AT FIRST I was frantic when the baby cried and I couldn't instantly soothe her. I punished myself with terrors of inadequacy that made me once stab the palm of my hand with a diaper pin in a sudden gesture of self-contempt. My hands were clumsy, my arms seemed to bend stiffly. Only my breasts knew what to do, dependably filling and refilling, milk leaking onto clothes and running sticky under the armpits and over my soft belly, which would never be anyone's pride. My mother kept offering to hire a nurse, a Gretchen, a Schinke, or an Ilse, but I refused and refused, though sometimes I felt I was making a mistake. I did need rest, I did need help. I really was afraid that I could not take care of Faith, that perhaps I was a non-maternal person. She was a burden, an anxiety that never ceased. I could do nothing without listening, half listening for her cry, her waking sounds, always abrupt and angry as if sleep had only stirred up energy for new discontents, demands I might not be able to meet. But soon she began to smile when she saw me coming; she was growing amid the boxes of presents my mother brought each day and the laundry that I could hardly remember to do and the smell of the regurgitated orange juice that had become my personal perfume. Through those labors came the metamorphosis. I was pushing the carriage along the street one day while Faith was talking to herself in that secret language of babies that idiots and animals are supposed to understand and I felt strangely wistful because I knew I would never be the same again, my true colors had been baked in, like on a pot coming out of the kiln. I had edges and a shape and nothing was the same as before. If building a bridge could make an engineer discover his power, so making Faith had put steel in me, rustproof, warp-proof steel.

Sometimes in the afternoon Isaac-Irwin would come sit with me in the park. He was studying eight, nine hours a day, analyzing the texts on the texts on the original texts on the words of God. "Faith is not a Jewish name. It is not even translatable into Hebrew," he said one afternoon as she was just beginning to crawl in the dirt, picking up the cigarette butts and giving them to me. "Faith Morrison is a name," I said, "that protects from quota systems and gas chambers. It's a disguise for survival, protective coloration." The other women in the East Side playground had clearly been startled by the grotesque rabbinical figure playing with the little girl. "Stay with me all afternoon," I asked him. "I can't," he said. "I have to study in the library." I was truly sorry. I wanted to talk to an adult. I would even talk about God if I had to. I was beginning to like him better. He was a purist, an idealist, a romantic, a lost child, but what, after all, was I?

"I am not going out on the street with you," Jim said one sunny morning months later. "What if somebody saw me pushing a stroller? You go push your baby around. You like that kind of thing," and he rolled over back into his broken sleep. I had not yet succeeded in breaking through his indifference to Faith. He would not look at her as she crawled over the bed sheets pulling on the blankets, trying to catch his eye for a smile. He complained about the smell of her diapers, insisting it made him sick, interfered with his work. He despised the signs of babyhood that I had strewn through the house: the little chair with plastic beads, the rubber teething toys, the playpen with sponge blocks. The more pink plastic filled the apartment, the more comfortable I was. I knew I was undermining the decorator's best intentions with Magic Marker scribble on the front wall and a diaper pail by the Louis XIV chair.

The money from the paperback sale of Jim's first book ran out. The new one was moving slowly toward completion. My mother agreed to support us till the book was done. I was asking on behalf of her grandchild now. Moreover, she continued to be pleased with Jim. She talked about his work as though the credit for recognizing his genius were hers alone. In the empty hours of her long afternoons, on days when there was no canasta game, she would come to visit. Faith would pull at her grandmother's earrings and gold necklaces, bang together the chunky bracelets, and try on the topaz and emerald rings. After a few minutes my mother, lighting her cigarette, would say, "How do you do it all day? Aren't you bored? Wouldn't you like to go out a while?" The strange thing was, I was not bored. I was hypnotized by the rhythm of my days. It was absurd, I knew, and yet splashing water on Faith, playing peekaboo in the tub, chasing her red and blue plastic tugboats, it seemed as if I no longer worried about meaning. I just lived it in something akin to peace.

Sometimes now I fell asleep with Faith, clinging to her smell of powder and freshly washed baby pajamas, and didn't wake till Jim came home. Now his disheveled hair, his hands waving frantically, his pink eyes, slanted and frightened, seemed an interruption, a breaking apart, a rising from a pleasant dream landscape into the tension of the preliminary stages of a nightmare. When he came home I would put Faith in her crib and drag myself back to the bedroom, where dutifully I performed the rites that made him fall quickly into a deep sleep. "Urinate on me," he screamed one night. "Right on my face," he yelled, ecstatic with his new idea. He needed to make changes in the scenario—as if his fantasies ran on batteries that eventually burned out. "Pretend you've got electrodes attached to your cunt and asshole and nipples, and now, when I press the switch, scream as if you've never had pain like this before." I screamed and his sperm flew. The baby woke up crying. When I came back from comforting her, Jim was asleep. He was going further and further into Rimbaud's jungle. All semblance and hope of reasonable loving had long since been abandoned. I no longer daydreamed about the intimacies we would share when greater success came for him. I was only waiting for what would happen next, like someone treading water while waiting either for rescue or for a shark.

Sometimes now I lay back in our bed, impulses, erotic waves rocking me gently as if his kind of sexuality were contagious, my hand moving slowly on my once dormant genitals, as if I had taken a giant leap forward in the purgatory of my love and was more like him, more inside his self, more his disciple. Images passed through my mind . . . I saw him naked, lying on his stomach, lashed to a narrow table as in a doctor's examining room. A swarm of women in black leotards, firm-breasted, long-legged, milled around, poking at his ribs, squeezing his testicles, inspecting him, coldly appraising the merchandise. At last one of them picked up an enema bag the size of a large cow's udder and held it high while another woman calmly wound the thick hose around his neck and, pulling it over his back, inserted the elephant's trunk nozzle into his clenched, panicked anus. Gradually she released the metal clip. Sweat poured off him. He screamed. "Stop! Stop it, please," he begged. "Help me!" But the woman coolly continued to hold high the bag until it was empty. The nozzle remained in him and tears ran over his fine Roman nose. She loosened the straps, turned him over on his back so that the nozzle was forced deeper into his inner pathways, and then she refastened him to the table. Another woman began with a small tweezers carefully to remove, depilate, the thin hairs that, moist and limp, decorated his pubic area. Each tweeze heightened my pleasure, speeding my fingers till at last these pictures, which had come unbidden, were washed away in an orgasmic torrent. I was frightened by my anger, which I now knew could take erotic form. I thought perhaps I was going crazy. Madness is where love and hate, eros and destruction, mingle and distort each other. Was it happening to me?

MONTHS LATER, after Faith had learned to walk and begun to talk, she woke in the middle of the night gasping for breath. Shaking and perspiring, her eyes with the glazed look of an animal, each breath rasping against her larynx, scraping and pulling its way out, unable to cry or scream so involved was she in the sheer necessary matter of breathing. Instantly I knew what it was. My brother's asthma, dormant in me, had passed through the genetic screens and descended on my daughter. Never again could I imagine her running free on basketball courts, strongly pulling a horse to a stop, or climbing the peak of a mountain. Now would begin the invalidism that would turn her inward, to a life under steam tents, away from the sunshine, the seashore, and all free-floating pollens. Had I already damaged her psyche, created a fungus growth in her lungs by my very touch, had I transmitted an addiction to pain, did neurosis flow from my fingertips when I bathed her? Were we all caught, generation after generation, in a twisted bind where even breathing is not so natural a child can take it for granted? What did it mean that my child, untouched by any nurse, heaved with the illness of the overprotected, the warped, and the infantile, the demanding and the terrorizing, my brother's illness, which kept cats and dogs, curtains and chocolate, at a distance? Always, with each distress, each failed friendship, each challenge to his strength or independence, he had returned limping to his bed and gasped, each time afraid again that air would not flow and his heart stop. This sickness had no right to my daughter. As I held her in the bathroom, letting the steam of the hot shower wash over both of us, I liked her less in the same measure as I liked myself less. The imperfections in us both were only beginning to show. What had hours before been pure and untainted now shared in the hobgoblin-filled air of my home, polluted, stained by the very person whose pride she was. I reasoned with myself, scolded myself for expecting too much. I sat by her bed listening to the heavy sounds of air forcing its way in and out, watching her in the shadows turning and twisting as if there was a side or position she could find that would relieve the tensions in her chest. Tomorrow I would buy a vaporizer to moisten the air—a hot-house flower needs special treatment. Her nightmares would be sharp and real, and there was no way cosmetically to cover the bruises I would give her and she would give me—I must already have given her. I wasn't strong enough to have a strong child. It wasn't Jim's fault. He never looked at her. Once I asked him to carry her in to me in the living room and he had banged the baby's head on the doorknob. White and shaken, he had apologized to me. "I just can't," he said. "I'm not the paternal type." He hadn't lied to me, he hadn't hurt the baby by his lack of interest. Only the mother, I thought, counted in these early years of childhood. For now, the responsibility was all mine. And later he would change, though my conviction on this point grew hollower with each passing day. I couldn't keep him working as much any more. He seemed to wait for the evening like some kind of night ferret. He dozed and dreamed through the day, and the new manuscript, little more than half done, seemed to weigh on him hardly at all. He gambled in high-stakes crap games, losing our candelabras, the $500 bond my uncle Louis had given us for Faith, his silver cigarette holder, the Patek Philippe watch. I had always lived with my mother's fondness for Mah-Jongg, backgammon, canasta, and playing the stockmarket, and so I had accepted Jim's love for risk, for danger. I even loved that part of him. Like a reincarnation of his riverboat-gambler granddaddy, he was tilting at capitalist windmills, fighting the industrial complex by sneaking around at night throwing dice on cold floors, mocking everything with the grace of a plantation owner drunk in the local jail.

When we were invited to cocktail or dinner parties I would get a babysitter and dress up to go with him. "God," he would say as we stood at the elevator, "you don't look like you belong with me." He was right. I would watch him talking with women who found him, as I had, totally brilliant and filled with a suggestive charm. They were spellbound: like lions in the circus, they would circle him, each showing off her own most particular promises and virtues.

I would talk to my dinner partners about Faith, about the asthma that forced me to phone the babysitter two or three times during the evening. I had no way of projecting across the clatter of plates and the talk of politics and art who I was or why I was there. I ached with jealousy, even though I knew he wasn't going to be unfaithful in any literal sense. At last we would say good night and he would call a cab for me and head off by himself in another direction. At night, while the rest of us slept, he was fiercely awake.

One afternoon I was playing with Faith in her room. She was banging on a xylophone and sometimes on the floor. "Keep the kid quiet," Jim called from our bedroom, which also served as his study. I went into the bedroom and found him lying naked, face down on the bed, with a pencil flashlight—bought so I could make my way into the baby's room without turning on any lights—embedded deep in his rectum. "What are you doing?" I asked. A half-empty bottle of Scotch stood on the floor. "I'm looking," he said, "for an honest man." I might have laughed, but his face was contorted in an odd mixture of pain and wonder. "Get away!" he suddenly screamed, but obeying an impulse I could neither understand nor control, I went right to his side. I leaned over to see if the light was shining through his pale skin or if the darkness of his bowel tunnel had absorbed all of it. The switch was on, but his buttocks were not illuminated. I wondered if there was light in his rectum. Was it like the well-known tree that falls in the forest when no one is there—did light depend on a receiving eye to exist? I leaned closer. Without planning it, surprised myself, I suddenly slammed my hand down on the base of the flashlight, pushing it deeper into him. Jim screamed. Faith came to the door. "What's the matter with Daddy?" she said. "Nothing," I answered, quickly ushering her out the door. I dressed her and we went out. No wonder she has asthma, I thought, trying to hide my tears from the elevator man and the doorman.

I could no longer tolerate Jim's tales of crap games lost and whores humiliated. But his second novel was now going well, and it became the main basis of my continuing love for him. I was close to the heat of creation. I had been the first to believe in him. I had given him breakfast at lunchtime and hamburgers at dawn. My love had given him the strength to write, and so the product was in some sense mine. I looked at the manuscript on his desk with some of the sense of possession and worth of the immigrant mother watching her son receive his degree in dentistry or accounting. But the novel was far from finished and my demands that he work each day, my anxious peering into his study, increasingly irritated him. He had every right to be irritated, but I just couldn't help myself. (I nagged and hated myself for it.)

My mother began to badger me. "How much longer am I supposed to support you?" I was ashamed. Faith developed a stutter. Why, when I was trying so hard to take good care of her? I was ashamed of that too, as if everyone would know that I was not really a good mother. At nursery school I was questioned carefully about her toilet training. They were polite and professional, but it was clear that they found me suspect. "Are you perhaps being overprotective?" "Why is she so anxious when you leave the room, Mrs. Morrison?" "Where is Mr. Morrison? Why didn't he come to this conference?" They were judging me and I couldn't blame them for whatever conclusions they drew. Faith continued to wheeze through every season. The steam in her room seemed to protect us both from the chill of our household.

I was coming to realize—so belatedly!—that I was a fake wife, virtually chaste, a nun whose satisfaction lay in sweeping the chapel and dusting the pews. I even began to be disgusted with myself and to think seriously of leaving

Jim. But he beat me to it. On Faith's third Christmas Jim did not come home. I waited till two the following afternoon and then I called Amanda. I thought maybe he had gotten so drunk he had returned to his childhood home. She hadn't seen or heard from him. I opened the presents for Faith under the tree I had decorated the night before, hoping that my mood would not affect her wonder at the musical bear and the small rocking horse. At six in the evening I began to phone the bars he frequented. I was afraid of his fury at my tracking him, but I was more afraid that he'd been in a fight or gotten sick or the alcohol had caused some kind of temporary amnesia. In all our years together he had always come back—bruised, drunk, vomiting, calling for his mother, telling tales of prostitutes left tied by ropes on beds in cheap hotels, he'd always come home. I was afraid that the bounds of his sanity, the sandbag line along his flooding Mississippi, had given way and that he had been carted off to Bellevue, where he would now be calling for me: "Marjorie, please help me." I called there and other hospitals. Perhaps an automobile had hurtled into him as he had loped diagonally across some street. I called the poolrooms. Maybe he hadn't been able to pay off his losses and been hit or shot or kidnapped. I could scarcely keep myself from flinging open the window and shouting down at an empty Fifth Avenue: "Wherever you are, come back." I waited another twenty-four hours. With Faith in my arms, I held on to the smell of her as if she were the mother and I the child. I finally called my mother. "It's the baby," she said. "He's avoiding you because of the baby." And after she said that, she called a private detective she had once used to follow my father. The information he had brought was accurate but ignored. As the hours passed I began to feel more and more dread. My mother was right, I had allowed the ties between us to loosen as I turned my physical attention to Faith. I realized that for the last month or so he had not bothered to read me his day's work. I thought he knew I was too tired in the evening to concentrate well, but maybe he had lost the habit of needing me, while, despite everything, I had not entirely lost my need of him. The detective could not find his trail. He'd been last seen in a well-known bar with a tall young woman. "See," said my mother, "you've let yourself go, you're dumpy and your clothes are drab." I was so obsessed with jealousy that I was frozen like a prehistoric animal in an ice block. I was numb with cold and there was a twitch, a tic on my eyelids, where little muscles went into involuntary spasms. I was afraid to go out of the house in case he came home. I wanted him to know that I had been waiting. It was possible that he was testing me. He needed signs of love. He wanted me to worry about his safety in the night. While Faith slept I sat and read all of his manuscript. It seemed so brilliant and I felt so dwarfed by his ability with words that I kissed the pages, then gathered them neatly and laid them on the desk next to the typewriter. I sat at the desk for hours, feeling close to him.

A week and a half went by. I knew that if he was all right, sooner or later he would return home, at least for the sake of his manuscript. It was not Faith who had sent him away. Although he had not wanted a baby at all and considered the project entirely mine from the beginning, he was fascinated by the similarity of their faces, his and Faith's. Her features were certainly his. "It's a good thing," he said one day, "the baby has my looks and your brains," and I had laughed because I knew I was supposed to. "Let the baby spend next summer with a nurse at your mother's. She'll be delighted and give us a present— maybe a trip to Paris or Rome, a little junket to the Riviera. Blades Jim breaks the bank at Monte Carlo and punches the croupier in the mouth for saying 'Yankee, go home.' " No, he had not left because of the baby.

Even for me, patient, abnormally used to waiting, it had been a very long wait. Then one evening in mid-January, while I was vainly trying to read, the door opened. Only Jim had another key. When I rushed into the hall, there he was. With him was a tall woman whom we had met at a party many months before. "Marjorie," he said, "this is Alissa. She's from Palm Beach." He winked at me. "And you know what that means." He went on quickly, as though he was making a rehearsed speech. "She feels she'd really like to take care of me for a while and I've decided to move in with her. I don't want to hurt you. It took me a long time to be able to tell you, but I've had enough of you and your mother and, you know, I know you'll understand. A writer has to grow, he has to live life to the fullest. I need excitement and glamour, and I know you don't want to stifle me." Of course, I didn't. "Alissa has her Jaguar parked downstairs and we'll just get a few things together." I looked at Alissa. She was perfectly chiseled, like a *Vogue* model. She didn't seem uncomfortable at all, not guilty or embarrassed by her "other woman" role. I gave Alissa a suitcase—the one my mother had given me for the European trip five years before. She went into the bedroom to pack Jim's clothes. I fixed him a drink. "Do you have sex with her?" I asked calmly. "Really," he said, "you have a base mind. No, nosy, Alissa is interested in art. She's a collector. She works in a museum. She's not as smart as you are, though," he added. I was enormously grateful to him for saying that. He packed his manuscript in a new black leather briefcase that Alissa must have given him. He took the typewriter, one my mother had bought to replace the one I had left in the snow the day Faith was born. In a half hour, they were ready to go. "There were lots of goods times for you to remember," he said, "weren't there?"

THAT WAS all some fifteen years ago. The fog will be gone by tomorrow, and we'll walk again along the dunes looking for treasure—driftwood, perfect shells, forgotten toys, or unbroken sunglasses. It's August, our vacation time, and the beach plums are beginning to turn deep purple. The blackberries my husband picks each morning to make into jam are hanging full and heavy on their canes. Our two boys, Nick and Max, aged nine and seven, are off fishing with the first sunrise. Faith has a job as a babysitter in the mornings. In the afternoons she plays tennis with friends. She still has asthma symptoms now and then but seems to be holding on as well as anyone else. The boys ride their bikes out to the Brandt Point lighthouse and cast lines off the rocks into the harbor waters. They bring home for lunch little pike and small porgies. My husband is a pediatrician. In August Bert is tired—so many calls at night, routine measurings and weighings, vaccinations, so many new mothers to encourage and support, and always a quota of real tragedies: accidents, poisonings, carcinomas.

The boys are packing the car with wood and charcoal and marshmallows because tonight we go on a family picnic with friends and their children. The sandwiches have to be made and Bert will help me with them when he finishes untangling his casting rod. He has a deep tan now, like the surf fisherman he pretends to be each evening. He's trying to catch a bluefish from the shore, and although he spends hours at it, in all the years we've been coming here he always returns, telling me how beautiful it was out on the beach with a few friends, the gulls, and the dusk. "I don't mind," he says, "that the fish are always at some other spot." At the picnic we'll make a bonfire and the adults will sing, old songs from a war the children haven't even studied yet: "Johnny Got a Zero," "Saturday Night Is the Loneliest Night of the Week," "The Last Time I Saw Paris." These children of lawyers and doctors with middle-age paunches and long memories will look at us a little puzzled by our foolish giggles and the peculiar seriousness with which we sing. Later we'll send out litter teams. The small children will already be asleep in arms and blankets and the men will throw sand on the fire and carry buckets of water from the ocean to put out the last burning coals. Faith and a friend sit a little apart from the rest of us. "In a few years," Bert says, "she'll come closer." He's proud of her. They clearly belong to each other. Last time we had a picnic, we all hated to leave even after the fire was out, though it was cold on the beach and the pounding of the ocean was not friendly and the stars seemed far away. We noticed the sand slugs, the tiny insects that shine a luminescent, iridescent violet purple in the night. Each about a quarter inch long, they jumped among the sand grains like ghosts of bugs killed during the day. Everyone, adults and children, started trying to catch them, hold them cupped inside a hand. Strange primeval creatures without a brain, they outwitted us at every turn, till laughing, a little high from wine and sun and fire, melted chocolate and sticky marshmallows, we said good-bye and each family rode back to its own house. The boys had fallen asleep in the car and Faith, Bert, and I unloaded the picnic boxes ourselves, shaking out sandy towels, washing off jars of ketchup and mustard. Later, in bed, we lay naked as we always do, summer or winter, wrapped around each other. There was not much to say. After a while we made love on the sheets, grains of sand sticking to all our crevices. We licked and sucked and stroked and fondled. It was a sandy, salty love screw, and when it was over we slept.

In the morning, while Bert was making pancakes for breakfast and I cut flowers in the garden, I thought of the years I had wasted with Jim. Even now, some mornings I wake up listless, bored, as if I were waiting for the electricity generated by his flirtation with fame, his courtship of immortality. His pretenses, his delusions, his hatreds, and his madness made each day a cliff-hanger. Jim distracted me from myself. He filled me with expectations of dreadful and wonderful things. He filled certain voids in myself that remain now and forever voids. Nothing burns and purifies like a first love—there's too much reason and caution in what follows. The ultimate questions of meaning, of purpose rarely arise now, but when they do, I have no place to hide from the answers that echo through empty rooms and then slide off into appalling space.

Sometimes I hardly see why I should, how I can get out of bed in the morning. Yet I always manage, after a while, to start up.

I've read all of Jim's novels. I've seen pictures of him on the society pages with his third, most fashionable, now ex-, wife. The reviews of his books have not all been good. Some have questioned his intellect, calling it cold, mathematical, without empathy. There are other writers whose books are more widely read, and though his own work is far from ignored, I know what gall another's success brings. Maybe that's why he's always gambling. I heard he'd lost his shirt at Las Vegas and then again was in trouble in Monte Carlo. He may have proved that he is the world's best at losing the most and I know how important being best is to him. At any rate, he's married well, if frequently. Perhaps he gets alimony. He always said he would die young, but he's already missed that. He may yet be a wise old man sitting in a rocker in his villa outside Florence, pinching the cheeks of young admirers, recounting great sexual exploits that Ph.D. candidates will record as literary history.

My brother had to shave a little cleaner in order to get a congregation. His flock is fond of golf and tennis and he himself has learned to water-ski with board members and large contributors to the building fund. He hasn't married yet, but there are many divorced women whose sons he has taught Hebrew who still are hoping and constantly invite him to dinner. His relationship with God seems to be tamer, more comfortable. Sometimes I wonder if it's there at all. He has adjusted well enough, I suppose, and we have more in common than we ever had before.

Last night Bert went out. Fishing. The boys were down at the docks watching the big yachts come in from Key

West and Nova Scotia. Faith was at a beach party in the dunes. Bert had gone out so many nights in his rubber overalls that the sea always managed to splash over, with new lures, and some new wisdom on how to land his fish, from a local guru, and so often he had returned, a sheepish grin, a report of the spectacular sunset on the waving beach grass and a shrug of resignation. Last night there was a loud knocking on the front door, and when I opened it, there he stood, with two huge bluefish, one swinging from each hand, and the light of victory in his eyes. I screamed my appreciation. Anyone can catch a bluefish from a boat, one has only to go out and look for the oil slicks where they are feeding and cast a line. But to cast into the surf, standing on the shore with the foam coming back over your boots and into your eyes, that's another matter. Surf-casting for blues is a special sport. You need to be patient, to reel in an empty line night after night and hurl it back out, farther, hopeful each time of feeling a tug, a pull. There he was with two magnificent fish, his day-old beard glistening with dried salt and his gray curly hair stiff and wild from the spray. "It may never happen again," he said. We took old newspapers and spread them on the kitchen floor and he scraped the scales and gutted the fish, peacefully concentrating on his work. I made a big salad and he lit the charcoal fire and we called up friends and broke out a bottle of good wine and we had lemon and dill on our fresh fish; the boys stayed up with us all night, Faith and her friends played records upstairs, and at dawn we all went out to watch the sun rise over the empty beaches.

THE FOG will roll back out to the center of the sea and disappear. The shell of my story and Jim's rests on this beach, washed nearly clean, buffed to a shine by waves. Any passing gull is welcome to pick it up, drop it on the rocks, and poke around in the smashed bits for matter worth chewing on. I'm done with it.